MICHAEL VEY
STORM OF LIGHTNING

BOOK FIVE OF SEVEN

MICHAEL VEY
STORM OF LIGHTNING

BOOK FIVE OF SEVEN

RICHARD PAUL EVANS

MERCURY INK

SIMON PULSE

NEW YORK   LONDON   TORONTO   SYDNEY   NEW DELHI

SIMON PULSE / MERCURY INK
An imprint of Simon & Schuster Children's Publishing Division
1230 Avenue of the Americas, New York, NY 10020
First Simon Pulse/Mercury Ink paperback edition May 2016
Text copyright © 2015 by Richard Paul Evans
Cover illustration copyright © 2015 by Owen Richardson
All rights reserved, including the right of reproduction in whole or in part in any form.
Simon Pulse and colophon are registered trademarks of Simon & Schuster, Inc.
Mercury Ink is a trademark of Mercury Radio Arts, Inc.
For information about special discounts for bulk purchases, please contact
Simon & Schuster Special Sales at 1-866-506-1949 or business@simonandschuster.com.
The Simon & Schuster Speakers Bureau can bring authors to your live event. For more
information or to book an event contact the Simon & Schuster Speakers Bureau at
1-866-248-3049 or visit our website at www.simonspeakers.com.
Cover designed by Jessica Handelman
Interior designed by Mike Rosamilia
The text of this book was set in Berling LT Std.
Manufactured in the United States of America
6 8 10 9 7
Library of Congress Control Number 2015947032
ISBN 978-1-4814-4410-1 (hc)
ISBN 978-1-4814-4411-8 (pbk)
ISBN 978-1-4814-4412-5 (eBook)

To Kevin Balfe

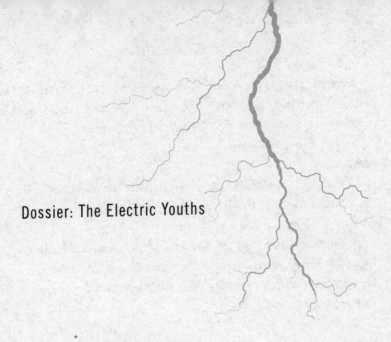

Dossier: The Electric Youths

Michael Vey
Power: Ability to shock people through direct contact or conduction. Can also absorb other electric children's powers.

Michael is the most powerful of all the electric children and leader of the Electroclan. He is steadily increasing in power, which may be connected to his Tourette's syndrome.

Ostin Liss
Power: A Nonel—not electric.

Ostin is very intelligent, with an IQ of 155, which puts him at the same level as the average Nobel Prize winner. He is one of the original three members of the Electroclan and Michael's best friend.

Taylor Ridley
Power: Ability to temporarily scramble the electric synapses in the brain, causing confusion. She can also read people's minds, but only when touching them.

Taylor is one of the original three members of the Electroclan. She and Michael discovered each other's powers at Meridian High School, which they were both attending. She is Michael's girlfriend.

Abigail

Power: Ability to temporarily stop pain by electrically stimulating certain parts of the brain. She must be touching the person to do so.

Along with Ian and McKenna, Abigail was held captive by the Elgen for many years because she refused to follow Hatch. She joined the Electroclan after escaping from the Elgen Academy's prison known as Purgatory.

Bryan

Power: The ability to create highly focused electricity that allows him to cut through objects, especially metal.

Bryan is one of Hatch's Glows. He spends most of his time playing video games and annoying Kylee.

Grace

Power: Grace is a "human flash drive," able to transfer and store large amounts of electronic data.

Grace was living with the Elgen but joined the Electroclan when they defeated Hatch at the Elgen Academy. She has been working and living with the resistance but has not been on any missions with the Electroclan.

Ian

Power: Ability to see using electrolocation, which is the same way sharks and eels see through muddy or murky water.

Along with McKenna and Abigail, Ian was held captive by the Elgen for many years because he refused to follow Hatch. He joined the Electroclan after escaping from the Elgen Academy's prison known as Purgatory.

Jack

Power: A Nonel—not electric.

Jack spends a lot of time in the gym and is very strong. He is also excellent with cars. Originally one of Michael's bullies, he joined the Electroclan after being bribed to help Michael rescue his mother from Dr. Hatch.

Kylee

Power: Born with the ability to create electromagnetic power, she is basically a human magnet.

One of Hatch's Glows, she spends most of her time shopping, along with her best (and only) friend, Tara.

McKenna

Power: Ability to create light and heat. She can heat herself to more than three thousand Kelvins.

Along with Ian and Abigail, McKenna was held captive by the Elgen for many years because she refused to follow Hatch. She joined the Electroclan after escaping from the Elgen Academy's prison known as Purgatory.

Nichelle

Power: Nichelle acts as an electrical ground and can both detect and drain the powers of the other electric children. She can also, on a weaker level than Tessa, enhance the other children's powers.

Nichelle was Hatch's enforcer over the rest of the electric children until he abandoned her during the battle at the Elgen Academy. Although everyone was nervous about it, the Electroclan recruited her to join them on their mission to save Jade Dragon. She has become a loyal Electroclan member.

Quentin

Power: Ability to create isolated electromagnetic pulses, which lets him take out all electrical devices within twenty yards.

Quentin is smart and the leader of Hatch's Glows. He is regarded by the Elgen as second-in-command, just below Hatch.

Tanner

Power: Ability to interfere with the electrical navigation systems of aircraft and cause them to malfunction and crash. His powers are so advanced that he can do this from the ground.

After years of mistreatment by the Elgen, Tanner was rescued by the Electroclan from the Peruvian Starxource plant and has been staying with the resistance so he has a chance to recover. He carries deep emotional pain from the crimes Dr. Hatch forced him to commit.

Tara

Power: Tara's abilities are similar to her twin sister, Taylor's, in that she can disrupt normal electronic brain functions. Through years of training and refining her powers, Tara has learned to focus on specific parts of the brain in order to create emotions such as fear or joy.

Working with the Elgen scientists, she has learned how to create mental illusions, which, among other things, allows her to make people appear as someone or something else.

Tara is one of Hatch's Glows. She and Taylor were adopted by different families after they were born, and Tara has lived with Hatch and the Elgen since she was six years old.

Tessa

Power: Tessa's abilities are the opposite of Nichelle's—she is able to enhance the powers of the other electric children.

Tessa escaped from the Elgen at the Starxource plant in Peru and lived in the Amazon jungle for six months with an indigenous tribe called the Amacarra. She joined the Electroclan after the tribe rescued Michael from the Elgen and brought them together.

Torstyn

Power: One of the more ruthless and lethal of the electric children, Torstyn can create microwaves.

Torstyn is one of Hatch's glows and was instrumental to the Elgen in building the original Starxource plants. Although they were initially enemies, Torstyn is now loyal to Quentin and acts as his bodyguard.

Wade

Power: A Nonel—not electric.

Wade was Jack's best friend and joined the Electroclan at the same time he did. He died in Peru when the Electroclan was surprised by an Elgen guard.

Zeus

Power: Ability to "throw" electricity from his body.

Zeus was kidnapped by the Elgen as a young child and lived for many years as one of Hatch's Glows. He joined the Electroclan when they escaped from the Elgen Academy. His real name is Leonard Frank Smith.

PROLOGUE

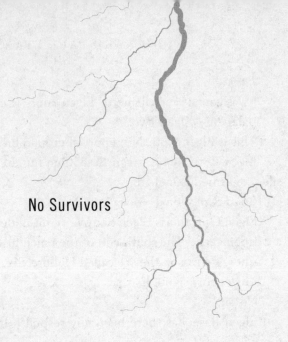

No Survivors

**Elgen radio communications during
attack on Timepiece Ranch**

"This is Elgen One. All helicopters prepare to commence Mexican Lightning Storm."

"Elgen One, this is Elgen Twelve. Be advised there are power lines along the south ridge of the compound. All copters stay clear."

"Copy, Elgen Twelve. Elgen Base, target is in range of missiles. All helos ready to launch Hellfire missiles on command."

"Roger, Elgen One. Lethal force is authorized."

"There's motion on the ground, Elgen One. Enemy helicopter is powering up. Enemy helicopter is powering up."

"Elgen Six, take out enemy helicopter. All helos let missiles fly."

"Hellfire missiles away."

[Massive explosions]

"That's a beautiful sight, *amigos*."

"Burn, baby. Burn."

"How do you say 'fire' in Spanish?"

"Fuego."

"I was gonna say 'habanero,' Elgen Four." [Laughter]

"'Jalapeño,' Elgen Two."

"This is Elgen Nine. No report of ground fire."

"Elgen One, this is Elgen Base. One hundred and fifty-four missiles confirmed launched."

[Loud explosions]

"Elgen One, this is Elgen Six. We've hit underground fuel tanks or a weapon cache. The south end of the ranch just rose twenty feet."

"There's a reason they're called Hellfire, Six."

"Any enemy sighted?"

"No, sir."

"Elgen Base, has there been any response from the Mexican air force?"

"Negatory, Elgen One. Skies are clear."

"All helos commence strafing area with fifty caliber."

[Sound of sustained machine-gun fire]

"What are those explosions along the road, One?"

"They appear to be enemy land mines."

"There must be hundreds. The place is jumping."

"Mexican jumping beans, Elgen Nine."

"Elgen One, this is Elgen Three. We are directly above target. All primary targets are destroyed. All secondary targets are destroyed."

"Roger that, Elgen Three."

"Wait, there's motion at two o'clock."

"Elgen Two, RPG at two o'clock! RPG at two o'clock! Firing."

"This is Elgen Two. . . ." [Static]

[Pause]

"Elgen Two is hit. Elgen Two is hit."

[Pause]

"Elgen One, Elgen Two is down."

"Fire on RPG, Three."

"Missile launched."

[Explosion]

"Target is neutralized."

"Elgen Two, do you copy? Elgen Two, do you copy?"

"Elgen One to Elgen Three, what is status of Elgen Two?"

"There's too much smoke to confirm, Elgen One."

"Elgen Two, Elgen Two, do you copy? Repeat, Elgen Two, do you copy?"

"This is Elgen Four. We're dropping down to check on Two."

[Female voice. Automated warning] "Altitude low."

[Sound of explosion]

"Four, pull out. There's unexploded ordnance."

"I think that was just a land mine."

"Too much blast for a land mine, Four."

"Maybe another fuel tank."

". . . Or a weapons arsenal."

"Good of them to provide the ordnance."

"Elgen Three, any response from Elgen Two?"

"Still no response, One."

"Elgen Two, Elgen Two, do you copy?"

"Elgen One, we have a visual. Elgen Two is in flames. There are no signs of survivors."

"Roger that, Elgen Four. Let's seal the site. All helos clear ground, Nine and Eleven fire napalm."

"What about Elgen Two?"

"There are no survivors on Elgen Two. Fire napalm on my command." [Pause] "Fire."

"Elgen Nine. Napalm released."

[Explosion]

"Elgen Eleven. Napalm released."

"Nothing like the smell of napalm in the morning. . . ."

"That is what hell looks like, gentlemen. Let's get out of here before the Mexican air force arrives."

"What's that, a biplane?" [Laughter]

"All helos back to Elgen Base. Elgen Eleven, record damage, then return with fleet."

"Copy, One."

"This is Elgen One reporting to base. Mission accomplished. Target is neutralized. There are no enemy survivors. Repeat, there are no enemy survivors."

PART ONE

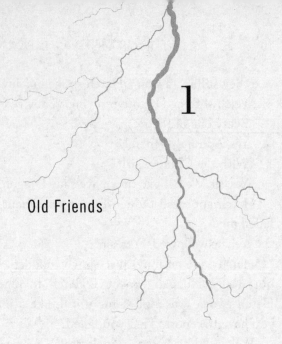

1

Old Friends

It was nearly midnight, and Elite Global Guard Welch stood at attention, his back to the door of Admiral-General Hatch's office. "Sir, we've destroyed the terrorists' home base. The resistance's ranch has been annihilated."

Hatch nodded but continued reading his book. "What have you done with the prisoners?"

"There were no prisoners taken. There were no survivors."

Hatch looked up from his book. "No survivors?"

"We killed every last one of them. After our barrage of missiles, we dropped napalm. I've reviewed the footage. The compound looked like Dresden after World War II. I can provide the video for you if you wish."

Hatch was quiet for a moment. "No, I'll take your word for it." He set down his book, stood, and walked to the side of the room, avoiding eye contact with Welch. "What is the status of the Electroclan?

Are they still in Taiwan?" Hatch spoke in a low, threatening voice.

Welch stiffened before replying. "They've escaped, sir."

"Every one of them?"

"Yes, Admiral-General."

"With the Chinese girl?"

"Yes, sir. We believe they have Jade Dragon."

Hatch appeared thoughtful for a moment, then said softly, "You failed me."

Welch swallowed. "Yes, sir."

Hatch said nothing, just slowly nodded. Welch looked at him quizzically. He had expected Hatch to rage, to explode. Instead Hatch's voice was almost mournful, like a jilted lover's. "Is that all you have to report? That you failed?"

Welch did his best to remain stoic. "Yes, sir."

Hatch stared at the ground for a moment, then said, "Okay. You've given me your report."

Okay? Welch was as baffled as he was nervous. He wondered if Hatch were drunk. He had never seen him behave so calmly in the face of failure.

"What is the word on Schema?" Hatch asked. "Has he been captured yet?"

"No, sir. He's vanished."

"Vanished?"

"Even before you left Switzerland. One of our men had him for a while, but he disappeared."

Hatch's brow furrowed. "Who disappeared? Schema or our man?"

"Both, sir."

Again, Hatch seemed unmoved. "It doesn't matter. Schema's inconsequential." He poured himself a drink from a crystal decanter, then downed a shot and poured another. "Would you care for a drink, EGG Welch?"

"Yes, sir. Thank you, sir," Welch said, his confusion growing. He had expected Hatch's fury. Not a drink.

Hatch poured another shot glass of the caramel-colored liquor and handed it to Welch. "To old times," he said. "And old friends."

"To old friends," Welch repeated.

He drank and quickly put the glass down as Hatch slowly sipped his, looking deep in thought.

"We've been together a long time," Hatch said. "So much has changed since the beginning. The world has changed."

"We have changed, sir. We have grown powerful."

"So we have." After a moment Hatch said, "We've acquired two new ships to replace the *Watt*: the *Edison*, a battle cruiser from Russia, and the *Franklin*, a Mistral-class amphibious assault ship from France. They are already manned and on their way to Tuvalu, as are the *Ohm*, the *Tesla*, and the *Joule*. They left port six days ago.

"This evening, the *Faraday* and the *Volta* will set sail for Tuvalu. I am flying with EGGs Despain and Bosen to Jakarta to inspect the *Edison*. Then we will fly to Tuvalu for the opening ceremonies of our Funafuti, Tuvalu, Starxource plant. We already have a force of four hundred guards stationed on the island.

"While I am hosting the Tuvaluan dignitaries, the fleet will rendezvous twelve miles from the main island and commence Operation Home Base. If things go as planned—and I expect that they will—we'll overthrow the island and establish our base. We are going to finish what Vey delayed when he blew up the *Ampere*."

"You don't need me to escort you to Jakarta, sir?" Welch asked.

"No," Hatch said bluntly. "I have a different assignment for you."

Welch nodded. "And how may I serve my admiral-general?"

Hatch pressed a button on his desk. "As an example." Four guards stepped into Hatch's office. "Mr. Politis," Hatch said calmly. "EGG Welch is officially relieved of his title and command. Strip him of his weapon and insignias and arrest him."

"Yes, sir."

Welch paled. "Sir . . ."

Two men took Welch by the arms, removed his sidearm, and handcuffed him. Politis took a knife from his utility belt and cut the EGG and Elgen insignias from Welch's shoulder and breast. "Now what, sir?" Politis asked.

"Take him to the brig. When we reach the Tuvalu plant, he will be put into the rat bowl."

Welch shuddered as the realization of Hatch's pronouncement spread over him.

"Yes, sir," Politis said.

"My General," Welch said.

"Yes," Hatch said. "I am still your general. You took a vow to serve me until your death, which is precisely what I am requiring of you now—your death. And in fulfilling this duty, your colleagues will understand that I expect my orders to be carried out, and failure is not an option." He nodded at Politis.

"Move it," Politis barked, pulling Welch from the room.

When everyone was gone, Hatch downed the rest of his drink, then poured another. "To old friends."

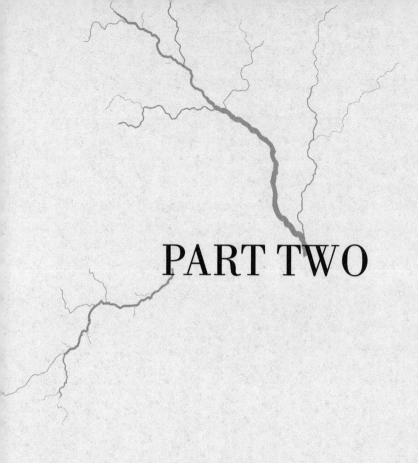

PART TWO

Sparking

My name is Michael Vey. Right now I'm sitting in a private jet, staring at my hand. It's shaking. And it's sparking, which, if you don't know anything about me, might sound a little weird. If you know who I am, then you know I'm electric. Even though the lights are off in the plane, the sparks arcing between my fingers are bright enough to illuminate the plane's fuselage, like strobe lights at a dance club or something. I can't stop it any more than I can stop the twitching from my Tourette's syndrome.

Other than my electricity, it's quiet on the plane. Nichelle got airsick and threw up a couple of hours ago. Earlier, my girlfriend, Taylor, tried to put her arm around me but gave up after I shocked her three times.

I've been getting more electric for some time, but I don't think that's why I'm generating so much electricity right now. I think it's because my electricity is exacerbated by emotion. And at the

moment I have so much emotion, I can barely breathe. It doesn't help that I've slept fewer than four hours in the past two days. Everything in my world is raging.

The Electroclan and I are on a flight back to the United States from Taiwan. We just rescued a young Chinese girl named Jade Dragon from the Elgen. We were at a safe house in Taiwan when we learned that Timepiece Ranch, the headquarters of the resistance, had been destroyed by Elgen forces. The last communication we received from the voice is that there were no survivors.

For me this is personal. My mother was at the ranch. I was only eight when my father died. I remember feeling like my world had died with him. The only person who got me through it was my mother. Now she's gone too. I'm an orphan.

Ostin's parents were also at the ranch. Ostin's never lost anyone close to him, not even a goldfish. He's not taking it well, not that he should. None of us are. McKenna, his girlfriend, has stayed close to him. Even Abigail tried to take away his pain, until he made her stop. He said he felt like he was betraying his parents by not suffering. I keep telling him that we don't really know what happened yet, but I'm lying. It's not like the voice would be wrong about something like this. My mother, Ostin's parents, the resistance, are all gone. The Elgen have killed them all.

Our pilots told us that Taylor's mother had flown back to Idaho before the attack. That's good news for now but, I suspect, not for long. The Elgen do not forgive. It's only a matter of time before the Elgen hunt her down as well.

My emotions are revolving like a great wheel, spinning between denial, hope, despair, and rage—the strongest of which is rage. I want to burn Hatch and the Elgen into ashes. If I could turn myself into a massive bolt of lightning and destroy them all, I would. Even if it took me with them.

That's where I am. That's what I'm thinking. That's why I'm sparking so much. I don't know what we'll find back in America. All I know for sure is that the next twenty-four hours will forever change the course of my life.

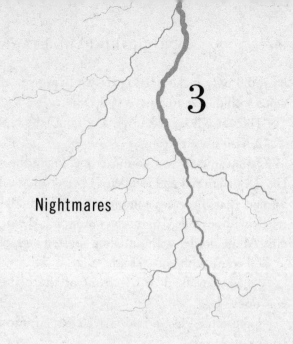

3

Nightmares

"What are you thinking?" Taylor asked softly.

"Why don't you just read my mind?" I said.

"I'd rather you tell me what you want to tell me."

I turned and looked at her. "Remember our conversation on the rooftop in Taiwan? How I said we were going to retire?"

She nodded sadly. "Yes."

"I can't believe how much has changed in just a few days. We'll never retire. There will never be peace."

"There could be," she said. "We can still hope."

"*Hope* won't bring my mother back. It won't bring anyone back."

"We don't know for sure if she's . . ." She couldn't say the word. "Maybe she escaped. Maybe she had already left before they attacked."

I took a deep breath and bowed my head. I was afraid to hope.

It would only make hearing the truth worse. "If that were true, the voice would have told us," I said.

"The voice doesn't know everything," she replied.

"It hasn't been wrong yet."

Ostin came up next to me, crouching in the aisle next to my seat. His eyes were red and swollen. "I've got to ask the pilot something," he said. "I don't understand how the Elgen could have attacked the ranch without the U.S. military stopping them. They couldn't have crossed the border without being spotted on radar."

"I'll come with you," I said.

We both walked to the front of the plane. The cockpit door was open.

"Excuse me," Ostin said as we stepped into the small cockpit. "I have a question."

The captain, Scott, quickly turned back. "Whoa, Michael, you need to step back. You're affecting the instrumentation." He turned to his copilot, Boyd. "You take the controls, we're going to step out."

Boyd nodded. "Got it."

We backed out of the cockpit, and Scott followed. He asked Ostin, "What's your question, son?"

"How could the Elgen have attacked a target inside America? Why didn't the U.S. military stop them?"

"The ranch isn't in America," Scott said. "It's in Mexico. The Elgen launched a surprise attack by air through the Gulf of California. They never entered U.S. airspace."

"We were in Mexico?" I asked.

"We were in a remote part of Sonora."

"Mexico," Ostin said. "That's why they were left alone . . ."

"They weren't left alone," I said.

". . . by the government," Ostin said. "How much longer until we land?"

"About four hours. So get some rest. We have some intense days ahead."

"How do we know if the ranch's landing strip is safe?" Ostin asked.

"We don't," Scott said. "We don't even know if the Elgen are still at the ranch. So we're going to land in Douglas, Arizona, on the U.S. side of the border, then drive down. So get some rest."

Ostin and I went back to our seats. I don't know why I was so eager to go to the ranch. I guess we don't really accept that someone is dead until we see them. Maybe that's why we have funerals.

I reclined my seat, lay back, and closed my eyes. I suppose my exhaustion was finally greater than my anxiety, because I fell asleep. I woke as we were descending. I looked over at Taylor. She was looking at me.

"How long have I been asleep?"

"About three hours. You were making a lot of noise. Did you have more nightmares?"

"Yes," I said. "More nightmares. You didn't look into my mind?"

"No. Your nightmares scare me too much."

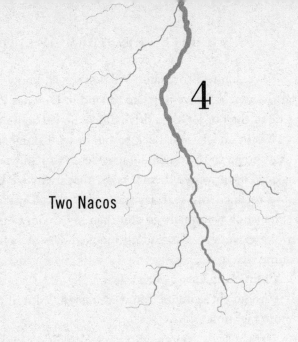

4

Two Nacos

Our plane touched down at the Bisbee-Douglas International Airport a little after five p.m., Arizona time. The wheels screeched on contact with the baked, dusty runway, as if they were in pain.

Even though the airport's proximity to Mexico made it an international airport, the title seemed a bit grandiose for such a tiny, run-down airstrip. In fact, it didn't even look functional.

The airport had just two narrow asphalt runways surrounded by desert and lined with fifty-gallon metal drums, painted white with thick red stripes around their middles. Weeds grew up through the cracks in the runway's tarmac. Around the airfield was an eight-foot-high weathered wire fence that, in places, was covered with tumble-weeds and flanked by short, sunbaked palms.

About a hundred yards from the runway were three arched-roof airplane hangars paneled with corrugated tin. They had rusted metal

doors and hardware. There were no glass windows, just portals covered by metal grates.

On top of the closest hangar was a pole that extended up into the air with a wind sock and an instrument (Ostin called it an anemometer) to measure wind speed, though it didn't look like anyone was around to receive its information. The place looked like it had been built a hundred years ago, back when planes only had propellers.

"Where are we?" Taylor asked.

"Bisbee-Douglas International Airport," Ostin said.

"It looks deserted."

"It ain't Los Angeles," Ostin said.

"It's not even Boise," I said.

The plane came to a stop, then circled back, slowly taxiing toward the hangars. Above the first hangar door, affixed to the corrugated tin siding, was a faded orange logo that read:

APACHE AIRLINES

There was a tribal symbol next to the name.

"That's ironic," Ostin said.

"What's ironic?" I asked.

"It was near Douglas, Arizona, that Geronimo, the last Apache chieftain, surrendered and ended the Indian resistance in the United States."

"Maybe this is where our resistance ends too," Tessa said.

Everyone looked at her.

"You're supposed to enhance our power," McKenna said, "not diminish it."

"Just sayin'."

"No," Jack said. "This is where our resistance begins."

Partially obscured behind one of the hangars was a faded, aluminum-sided trailer home with a rusted, older-model Yamaha motorcycle parked out front. As our plane powered down, Scott emerged from

the cockpit. He opened the door, and a stairway protruded from the plane. "All right," he said. "Everyone off. We have a van in the hangar. I need to get the key; then we'll load up."

Taylor and I were the last to get off the plane. There was a light breeze, and the Arizona air was warm and dry. I stepped down onto the runway, then looked around at the rugged desert landscape that surrounded us. There were cacti and tangled trees with yellow and white blossoms. The air smelled fragrant, like some kind of exotic flower.

"Mexican plums," Ostin said as if reading my mind.

"How do you know all this crap?" Tessa said.

"I read a lot," he said. Then, with an uncharacteristic edge added, "Can you read?"

Tessa stared him down. "I can't shock you, but I can still punch you out."

"Try it," McKenna said.

"Your girlfriend is protecting you?" Tessa laughed. "How pathetic is that?"

Ostin looked even more pained than he already was. "I didn't ask for her help." He looked at McKenna. "I didn't ask for your help."

McKenna frowned. "I'm sorry. It just made me mad."

"Stop it," I said, looking at Tessa. "There's enough pain without you adding to it."

She wilted beneath my gaze. "Sorry."

As I turned away, Taylor gently touched my back.

"Don't read my mind," I said.

"I'm not trying to. But you're too electric right now. It's like you're shouting out your thoughts."

"Lucky you," I said.

"I'm sorry. I wish I could help."

The sky was streaked with orange and yellow as the sun began its descent on the western horizon. Under different circumstances I would have been moved by its beauty, but inside I felt too ugly to appreciate it.

"Nothing out here," Ian said. "This place is quiet."

"Is there anyone in the trailer?" Scott asked.

"An old woman," Ian said. "She's watching TV."

"Good," Scott said. "Good."

Scott walked off to the trailer while Boyd handed us our bags. As Scott approached, the trailer door was opened by an elderly Mexican woman. They spoke for a few minutes. The woman left for a moment, then returned and handed him something.

Scott took out his wallet, handed her some bills, and walked over to the hangar. He unlocked and unchained the doors, threw them wide open, then disappeared inside. A few minutes later he drove out in an unwashed, navy-blue van that I think was similar in make to the one that had picked us up on our first visit to the ranch.

He pulled up next to us, killed the car, and got out. "We need to pull the plane into the hangar; then we'll go. Do you all have your bags?"

"Yes," I said, looking around.

"Go ahead and put them in back. Jack, after everyone gets their bags in, would you mind moving the van? I need to help Boyd store the plane. It's going to take a little while to lock everything up."

"No problem," Jack said, climbing into the driver's seat.

I was surprised that Jack could move like he did. He was still nursing eleven broken ribs from the Elgen beating him. He hadn't complained once. He's the toughest person I've ever met.

Boyd raced the plane's engine as Scott walked in front of the plane to guide it into the hangar.

We finished putting our bags into the back of the van. When we all got in, Jack turned on the radio. It was set to a Mexican talk radio station, and he pushed buttons until some music came on. Then he drove us over to the side of the hangar while Scott and Boyd maneuvered the plane inside.

It took the pilots nearly an hour to get the plane secured. We had gotten bored, so we got back out of the van, looking for something to keep ourselves occupied. For a while, Zeus shot grasshoppers off the metal fence with electric bolts while the rest of us just watched.

"There's one," Taylor said, pointing at a large green insect climbing a nearby post.

I made an electric ball and lazily threw it. I missed the grasshopper

but caught the weeds in front of it on fire, and we all had to run over and stomp on the flames to put them out. Finally Scott and Boyd emerged from the hangar. They locked the large steel doors, then walked over to the van.

"Sorry that took so long," Scott said. "Is everyone here?"

"Yes."

He looked at the patch of burned weeds. "What happened?"

"We were just having a little fun," Jack said.

"All right," he said. "Everyone get in."

"Where are we going?" Taylor asked.

"We're headed to Bisbee, then down into Naco, where we'll cross the border."

"How long will that take?" I asked.

"It's less than an hour from here."

"Why can't we just cross the border right here?" Ostin asked.

"We could, but it's not as safe. Security is much tighter here. And the town on the other side of the border, Agua Prieta, has undercover DEA agents looking for drug smugglers. No one cares about Naco. Less chance of problems that way."

"How far is it from Naco to the ranch?"

"About two hours. But we won't be going tonight. It's too late."

"Why is it too late?" I asked impatiently.

Scott looked at me with a stern gaze. "The dirt roads to the ranch are dangerous to drive anytime, but especially at night. And if there are still Elgen around, they'll see our headlights long before we get there. Hardly anyone goes out that way but us, so if they're there, they'll be waiting for us.

"There are also drug cartels operating out of some of those areas. If they mistake us for *Federales*, we're in trouble. Trust me, it's best we wait until tomorrow. For now we'll cross the border into Naco, Mexico, then leave early in the morning."

"What time will we leave for the ranch?" Tessa asked.

"I think the best time is just before dawn."

"Just like George Washington attacking Trenton at sunrise," Ostin said, nodding. "Surprise them while they're still in bed."

"We're not *attacking* anyone," Scott said. "If the Elgen are there, we pull back."

"How do we get across the border without passports?" Ian asked.

"It's not hard getting into Mexico," Tessa said. "It's coming back that's the problem."

"They'll still stop us," Scott said. "People smuggle guns into Mexico. But we've got passports for you. We had them made while you were in Taiwan, just in case we needed to fly somewhere else. Now let's go. We can talk more on the way. I'll drive."

Jack handed him the keys, and Scott climbed into the driver's seat. "Michael, sit up here with me."

"All right." I walked around to the front and got in.

Everyone got into the van except for Boyd. "Good luck," he said to us. "And be careful. I'll see you in a few days."

"You're not coming with us?" I asked.

"No. Someone needs to stay with the plane."

"*Vámonos,*" Scott said.

I saluted Boyd as we drove off. We took highway 80 northwest to Bisbee, then turned south toward Mexico. The road down from Bisbee led us into a great, sloping plain with the Sierra Madre of Mexico rising ahead of us in the distance.

I soon discovered that there are two Nacos—Naco, Arizona, and Naco, Mexico, the two small towns divided by a twenty-foot-wide gravel road surrounded on both sides by a ten-foot metal fence lined with razor wire. I couldn't tell if the fence was rusted or had just been painted to look that way. There was an uninhabited border control truck about fifty feet from the crossing.

The town looked deserted, and we didn't see anyone until we reached the border crossing, which was pretty quiet as well. It was a single-lane crossing, and a female Mexican immigration officer with a badge and a khaki uniform sat on a folding chair near the stop sign, smoking a cigarette and looking bored. As Scott had told us, this wasn't a popular crossing. From what I could see, neither of the towns was very large, which I guessed was one of the reasons we'd chosen to cross here.

As we approached the gate, a red light came on, signaling us to stop. The immigration officer stood and walked up to our van. She said with a heavy accent, "May I see your vehicle registration, please? And your passport and credit card."

Scott must have been familiar with the routine, as he already had all the items ready. The officer shone her flashlight back through the van.

"You have many youths," she said to Scott.

"Yes, I do. They're friends."

"What is the purpose of your visit to Mexico?"

"We're here on vacation. I'm chaperoning."

"Just a moment, please."

The officer went into the building. A moment later she returned. "Are you carrying any guns or drugs?"

"No, ma'am."

She looked back at us again, then said, "There is a twenty-seven-dollar fee." Scott counted out some bills and handed them to her. She handed him a clipboard with a form. "Sign here, please."

Scott signed the paper and handed back the clipboard. The officer tore off the top sheet and handed it back to Scott. "Please keep this paper with your vehicle. How long will you be in Mexico?"

"Only a few days," Scott said.

"Okay. You may go."

Scott put the van in gear, and we drove over some weird, shiny metal balls that were imbedded in the asphalt, across the border.

"We're in Mexico," Jack said.

"Mexico," Tessa sighed. "Makes me want a burrito."

5

A Small Village Forgotten by God

The Mexican town of Naco looked rustic—like the movie set of an old Western. The main street was lined with stucco-covered buildings: taquerias, ice cream shops, and, most noticeably, a *farmacia*, which was one of the largest buildings in the town. There were also a lot of skinny stray dogs running around in packs.

A couple of blocks from the border we passed the Cruz Roja—the Mexican Red Cross—which Scott told us had been set up there to help illegal immigrants who were caught and deported from the United States.

"Every year the border patrol catches more than three hundred thousand illegal immigrants attempting to enter the U.S.," Scott said. "They return many of them here. Most go back to their homes, but not all of them."

After we passed what looked like a taco stand, Ostin asked, "Is anyone hungry besides me?"

"I think we're all hungry," I said.

"I was serious about the burrito," Tessa said. "Think we could find some decent Mexican food?"

McKenna looked at her. "Are you kidding?"

"What? I just don't want any more Chinese food. Especially swamp eel."

"There's a restaurant across the street from the hotel," Scott said. "But let's check in first. Michael, open the glove box."

I reached down and opened it. Inside was a thick bundle of brightly colored bills. "Go ahead and take those. That's a thousand pesos. In case any of you want to buy something."

"Whoa," Jack said, leaning forward. "*Mucho dinero.*"

"Don't get too excited," Scott said. "It's only worth about sixty U.S. dollars."

A few minutes later, we reached the Naco Hotel. Scott parked the van near the front doors, and we all went inside. The hotel clerk was an older Mexican man with salt-and-pepper hair and a gray mustache.

"I need six rooms," Scott said. "Do you have that many?"

"*Sí, señor.* For how many nights?"

"Just for tonight," he said.

The man looked at the screen of an aged computer. "That will be 7,286 pesos." He brought out a calculator and typed in some numbers. "That's four hundred and sixty American dollars. Will that be on a credit card?"

"No, I'll pay with cash," Scott said, taking out his wallet. "You take dollars?"

"*Sí, señor.*"

Scott laid out five one-hundred-dollar bills.

"I only have change in pesos," the clerk said.

"That's all right," Scott said. "We can always use pesos."

The man figured out the change on his calculator and gave it to Scott. Then he unhooked six brass keys from the wall behind him and set them on the counter.

Scott turned back to us. "We're going to sleep two in a room, so buddy up."

Ostin looked over at me, and I nodded.

"Is the taqueria across the street still open?" Scott asked the man.

"For all of you to eat?"

"Yes."

"*Sí.* I will call the owner and he will open. He is my *amigo.*"

Scott said to us, "Everyone grab a key and put your things in your rooms; then we'll meet across the street at that restaurant."

As I took our key, Taylor touched my arm. "What floor are you guys on?"

"Three."

"We're on the main floor. We'll wait for you."

The hotel had an elevator, but it was tiny, so Ostin and I just took the stairs. We were in room 327, a small, rectangular room with one window and two beds covered with sun-bleached chocolate-brown bedspreads.

"I'll take that one," Ostin said, throwing his bag onto the bed closest to the door. "If you don't care."

"I don't. Let's go eat."

We locked our door, then went downstairs, where Taylor and McKenna were waiting for us. The four of us crossed the wide street to Miguel's Taqueria.

The restaurant was old, but fairly clean. Three tables were already set with utensils, tortillas, hot salsa, and iced bottles of pineapple and strawberry Mexican soda pop. Everyone was eating flour tortillas and tortilla chips with guacamole and bean dip. Taylor, McKenna, Ostin, and I sat down at the table with Scott. There was a black lava rock bowl in the center of the table piled high with fresh guacamole. Scott pushed a woven basket of tortillas toward us.

"These are fresh. They just cooked them for us."

"I love homemade tortillas," Ostin said. He rolled up a tortilla, dipped it into the guacamole, then took a big bite. "That's better Mexican than Idaho has."

"You think?" Zeus said sarcastically. "Maybe it's because *we're in* Mexico?"

"Idaho has excellent Mexican food," Ostin said. "We have lots of Mexicans living there."

"Everyone, look over your menus," Scott said. "Lillia will be back in a minute to take our orders."

"Who?" Taylor asked.

"The owner's wife," Abigail said.

The menu was printed in both Spanish and English, though the English translations were pretty funny. There was pig-spit. (I assume they meant pig roasted on a spit.) Roasted rabbi. (Rabbit?) And Jack's favorite, "The water served here was passed by the owner." No comment.

I was really hungry and ordered a combo plate with two shredded beef tacos, a chile relleno, and a side serving of rice and refried beans.

Taylor ordered the same but with only one taco. Less than twenty minutes later Lillia brought out our meals. While we were eating, Scott said, "Naco's really an interesting town."

"By 'interesting' do you mean 'lame' or 'ghetto'?" Tessa said.

Scott grinned. "Maybe not as interesting as it used to be, but it has history. Its nickname was, '*Un pueblo chico, olvidado de Dios.*'"

"A small village forgotten by God," Ostin translated.

"That about sums it up," Tessa said.

"Naco is where the longest sustained battle of the Mexican Revolution took place. Any old building here still has bullet holes. The hotel we're staying at used to advertise that it has thirty-inch-thick mud walls that are bulletproof."

"That's how to advertise a resort," Tessa said. "'You probably won't be killed until you go outside.'"

"For entertainment, U.S. citizens used to line the border to watch the fighting. The Mexicans were careful not to shoot over the border, because they didn't want America getting involved in the war."

"Now, there's a wholesome family activity," Tessa said. "Let's go down to the border and watch them kill each other."

"Speaking of bullets," I said, "let's talk about tomorrow."

Scott groaned a little. "*As I said*, there're not going to be any bullets or fighting. If we see any sign of the Elgen, we turn back."

"Yeah, I heard you," I said.

Taylor looked at me with a worried expression. She knew I wanted to fight.

Scott continued. "I asked the hotel clerk if he'd seen any Americans wearing black or purple uniforms. He said he hadn't, but he did tell me that there had been some explosions down south, then some smoke for several days. He thought that either the Mexican Army was conducting war games or there was a raid on a drug cartel. Of course he didn't know anything about the ranch."

"Did you ask if he saw any other Americans?" I asked.

"I asked if your mother or Ostin's parents had stayed at the hotel. He didn't remember them, and he couldn't find their names on the guest register."

"If they came this way, I doubt they'd use their real names," Taylor said.

"No, they wouldn't," Scott said. "And to escape the Elgen, they might have gone west or even south."

The idea of my mother fleeing for her life made me start ticking. Taylor put her hand on my arm to calm me.

"What time are we leaving in the morning?" McKenna asked.

"The ranch is a two-hour drive from here, so I think we should leave around four. We'll be coming in from the east on an old mining road that will give us some cover. With Ian's help, we should be able to see them before they see us."

"*If* they're still there," Ostin said. "I'm betting they're not."

"We can hope," Scott said.

We finished our dinners, with some churros and an order of flan for dessert. Scott spoke to us again before we left the restaurant.

"Remember, we're leaving at four, so get some rest and be in the lobby ready to go no later than five minutes to the hour."

"Do we need our luggage?" Abigail asked.

"No. If all goes well, we'll be back tomorrow night, then head back the next morning. So get some rest."

Everyone walked back to the hotel. Taylor and I were the last to leave the taqueria, and she took my hand as we walked outside. It was dark except for a nearly full moon that lit the sky.

"You didn't eat very much," I said.

"My stomach hurts."

"Maybe you should see a doctor or something."

"It's probably just stress." She looked at me. "You're the one I'm worried about."

I didn't say anything. It felt like my brain and heart were tied up together in knots. We walked slowly, taking in the cool night air. Neither of us spoke for a while. A brindled dog ran toward us, growling. I began sparking, but Taylor just reached out her hand, and he suddenly stopped, then wandered away.

"It's cool how you can do that to animals."

"They're a little harder than humans," she said. "I think it's because they act more on instinct than thought. Thoughts are easier to control. At least for me."

I didn't reply. These days I didn't feel like I had any control over my own thoughts, let alone someone else's. After a few minutes Taylor said, "What are you thinking?"

"I was just thinking that it's hard to believe that's the same moon we were looking at in Taiwan just a few days ago."

"Same moon, different world." She sighed. "Just imagine what she's seen."

"The moon is the earth's witness," I said.

She smiled sadly. "That's poetic."

For a moment we were both silent. Then I said, "You were right. There is no going back."

"There never was," she said. After a moment she leaned into me and we kissed. Suddenly I felt a current of electricity flowing through our mouths, and Taylor leaned back. "Wow. Your kisses are electric."

"That's what all the girls say," I said.

She grinned. "You already told me that I'm the only girl you've ever kissed."

"It's true."

"That's still hard for me to believe," she said.

"I think my Tourette's scared them."

"Or maybe you just thought it did."

"Maybe," I said.

We kissed again. Then Taylor said, "Tomorrow starts early. We'd better get some sleep."

We turned and walked back to the hotel. When we entered the lobby, Ostin, McKenna, and Nichelle were sitting on vinyl couches near the front door playing cards.

"You guys want in?" McKenna asked. "We're playing hearts."

"No, thanks," I said. "We're going to bed."

"You guys should too," Taylor said. "Tomorrow could be crazy."

"We'll just play one more hand," McKenna said.

Taylor asked, "Would you like me to stay with you for a while, or do you want to be alone?"

I shook my head. "I don't want to be alone."

"I don't want to leave you alone," she said.

We headed upstairs to my room. I unlocked the door, and we went in. I lay back on my bed, and Taylor lay down next to me. "I'm so worried about you," she said again. "Can I hold you?"

I nodded. "I'll try not to shock you this time."

She put her arms around me. "Don't be afraid. Remember what your mother always said, 'Things have a way of working out.'"

Hearing this made me angry. "My mother's dead. So things didn't really *work out*."

"You don't know that, Michael," she said quietly. "At least not yet." Neither of us said anything for a while. Then Taylor said, "If it's true about your mother, what will you do?"

"If Hatch killed my mother, I'm going to hunt him down."

Taylor thought for a moment, then said, "Whatever you want."

"I didn't mean you."

She raised herself up on one elbow. "What are you saying?"

"I'm just saying you don't need to come with me."

"Is that what you want?"

"None of this is what I want. I'd just rather not see you die because of me."

"Maybe I'd rather die than never see you again."

"Why?"

"You're asking why? After all we've been through, you still don't know I love you?"

"I'm sorry," I said. "I'm just upset."

"I know. Let's not talk, okay?"

She pulled me into her again, and for the next ten minutes we just lay together in silence. Taylor had just fallen asleep when someone knocked. I carefully undraped her arms from around me, then got up and opened the door. It was Ostin.

"Sorry, you have the key." He stepped inside. "Taylor's here."

"Yeah," I said.

"Where's McKenna?" Taylor asked sleepily.

"She went back to your room. She was tired."

"Do you want me to leave?" Taylor asked.

"No, you're good," Ostin said.

I lay back on the bed, and this time I held her. In just a few minutes, Taylor fell asleep again. After a half hour or so, I looked over at Ostin. His eyes were wide open. "I can't sleep," I whispered.

"Me neither. Let's see if we can get something on TV."

"Taylor's sleeping," I said.

"I'll keep the volume low."

The television was ancient—the kind with an antenna on top. Not surprisingly, the picture came in fuzzy. Ostin adjusted the antennas, which made the picture a little better, but not by much. Then he flipped through about a dozen channels, most of which were in Spanish. He finally stopped on a show called *Gilligan's Island*. It was an American show, but Spanish had been dubbed in over their voices. I had seen the show in English—I had watched it on reruns—but it was funnier in Spanish.

After it, there were other old American shows, one called *Hogan's Heroes*, the next called *The Wild Wild West*.

By the time the third show came on, Ostin was asleep. I looked at

my watch. It was half past twelve. We would be meeting downstairs in just three and a half hours.

I carefully let Taylor go, then got up and turned off the television. It was strange that turning on the TV hadn't woken Taylor, but turning it off did. As I was about to leave the room, Taylor said, "Michael?"

I turned back. "Yeah."

"Is it time to get up?"

"No. It's only twelve thirty."

"Where are you going?"

"Out for a walk. I can't sleep."

She rubbed her eyes. "Do you want me to come with you?"

"No. Get some sleep."

"Okay." She rolled back over. I grabbed the room key, stepped out into the dimly lit hallway, and then walked downstairs to the lobby. There was now a young Mexican woman at the front desk. I nodded as I walked past.

"*Buenas noches,*" she said.

"Yeah, *buenas noches,*" I replied, which is about all I remembered from eighth-grade Spanish.

I walked out into the warm night air. The small town was asleep, and the only sound was that of crickets and the occasional howl of a dog or coyote. I looked around, then walked out to the main road and back toward the U.S. border.

Even though there were no streetlamps, the moon was bright enough to see where I was going. Normally I would have been worried that someone might notice my glow, but I didn't care about that right now. The truth was, I didn't care much about anything. My mind was too preoccupied by other emotions. In six hours I'd know the truth about my mother. I was already in so much pain that I couldn't even imagine how the truth would affect me. What if I found her body? I didn't know if I could live with that.

I walked about three blocks from the hotel, turning at a road sign that read CALLE HILDAGO near some kind of weird monument in the

center of the road—a stucco and concrete slab adorned with the plaster bust of a man wearing a bow tie. Several old pickup trucks were parked up against the curb, and as I walked around them, I saw a group of young Mexican men. A gang. They immediately started walking toward me.

"*Güero!*" one of them shouted.

I counted seven guys, all a little older than me. Three of them carried bottles of beer, and two of them were probably drunk, as they were wobbling a little. Three of them wore white tank tops, and one wore a T-shirt that read:

> I got caught trying to cross
> the border, and all I got was
> this lousy T-shirt

Three had no shirts at all, exposing myriad gang tattoos that covered their arms and backs. The one who seemed to be the leader, the tallest of the group, said, "*¿Qué estás haciendo en nuestra ciudad?*"

The man next to him with a bottle said, "*Está caminando en nuestra calle.*"

I looked back and forth between them. "I don't speak Spanish."

I didn't know whether they understood me or not, but they all laughed. The tall man nodded. "No worry, *gringo*. I speak English. Bad news for you. We will take your money. And your watch."

"I'm not giving you anything," I said. "Just leave me alone." I turned away from them.

"*¿Qué dijo?*"

"*Dijo déjame en paz.*"

As I was walking away from them, an empty beer bottle hit me on the side of my head. Fortunately, it wasn't a direct hit, or it probably would have knocked me out. Instead, it caught me in the back of my jaw, cutting the skin beneath my ear. I spun around. It took every ounce of willpower I had not to fry them all to ashes. "Who threw that?" I shouted.

They looked at one another, coolly, smiling. Then the shortest of

them motioned to himself with both hands. *"Lo hice yo, güero. Ven por mí."*

I didn't know what he said, but he wore a big, stupid grin. Then I noticed that he was blinking wildly, imitating my facial tics. I wanted to melt his face.

"You have five seconds to run away," I said. I thought about what Spanish I knew and said, *"Cinco secondi vámonos!"*

They all burst out laughing. Then two of the guys pulled out switchblades. The one closest to me said, *"Vamos a cortar ese güero."*

"My friends do not like you, *gringo*," the tall one said. "They want to cut you." The gang fanned out, forming a near circle around me. ". . . And then we take your money."

The small guy with the knife was now behind me, walking toward me.

"Times up," I said. I spun around and pulsed, blasting the little dude so hard that his feet left the ground. He slammed into an adobe wall, and plaster fell around him as he crumpled to the ground, unconscious.

"Bet that hurt," I said. Then, as I turned back around, something bizarre happened to me—something that had never happened before. Electricity completely encompassed me in a brilliant, bluish-green light. It was almost as if I had become one of my lightning balls, and the sound of electricity sizzled like a hundred frying pans of bacon. I looked down at my arms and couldn't see my flesh, only the brilliant glow of electricity. When I looked back up, the gang was just staring at me like I was a ghost. Actually, I was something much stranger.

I spread out my arms and pulsed. The force blew out from me in a shock wave more than fifty feet in diameter. When I looked around, all the gang members were lying on their backs. Most of them weren't moving. The tall guy was still conscious, staring at me in fear. As I started toward him, he pulled out a gun.

"Diablo," he said, pointing his gun at me.

I shook my head as I walked toward him. "You really don't want to do that," I said. "It will just make me angrier." My eyes

narrowed as I raised my hand in front of me. "And I am already really, really angry."

I was so electric that I could actually see waves of electro-magnetism blurring the air in front of me. The guy fired six times, and the bullets flew around me, ricocheting against cars and build-ings. One of the bullets hit one of his buddies. When he had used all his bullets, I said, "I warned you." I blasted him so hard, his clothes caught on fire.

Then I looked around. All of the gang members were still uncon-scious, or pretending to be, except for one—the guy with the border-crossing T-shirt. He had gotten to his feet and now raised a knife at me, though he seemed to be having trouble holding it steady.

"If that's your plan, *amigo*, you're gonna need a bigger knife," I said. He looked so pathetic, I shook my head. "Didn't anyone ever tell you never bring a knife to a lightning fight?" I walked toward him. "Let me show you something." I produced a lightning ball about the size of a volleyball. *"Mucho* interesting, *sí?"*

He just stared in fear. *"No, señor."*

"Now I'm '*señor*,'" I said. "But I made it especially for you. Catch." I lobbed it to him. He weakly raised his hands to block it. It exploded on contact with his flesh, knocking him out with the force.

I walked to his side and pushed him over with my foot. "You think you can go around threatening innocent people? Maybe you'll think twice next time." I reached down and picked up the guy's knife, folded it back, and put it into my pocket as a souvenir, then started back to the hotel. Only then did I really feel the sting of my gash. Blood was trickling down my jaw and had soaked my collar.

As I walked into the lobby, I put my hand over my cut to cover it from the woman who was still at the front desk. She was staring at me.

"Buenas noches," I said.

"Buenas noches," she repeated with a frightened expression.

I ran back upstairs. I entered my room as quietly as I could, but Taylor still woke.

"Michael?"

"Go back to sleep," I said.

She watched me as I walked to the bathroom. I turned on the bathroom light, then soaked a towel with cold water and put it against my face.

"Michael, what happened?"

"It's nothing."

Then Ostin woke. "Is it time to go?"

"It's time to go back to *sleep*," I said.

"What's up?" Ostin asked. "Besides us."

Taylor got up and walked toward me. "Michael, what happened?" she asked again.

"Some loser threw a beer bottle at me."

She looked at me with a peculiar gaze. "I meant to your arms."

I looked down. "What the . . ." There was a strange reddish fern-leaf-like pattern on my arms.

"Holy moly," Ostin said. "Those are Lichtenberg figures."

"They're what?" Taylor asked.

I tried to wipe the marks off with my towel, but they appeared to be permanent. Like tattoos. "What is it?"

"They're called Lichtenberg figures or lightning trees. They appear with extremely high voltages. I've seen pictures of scars like that on lightning strike victims."

"Will they come off?" Taylor asked.

"No," Ostin said. "They're scars. Michael, did you just have a super-big surge?"

"Yes. When the gang attacked me. It was like I had become an electric ball."

"Gang?" Taylor said. "What gang?"

Ostin walked over to examine my markings. "Wow. They look kind of cool."

"Do they hurt?" Taylor asked.

"No. I didn't even feel it happen."

After a moment Taylor said, "Well, I'm sure your jaw hurts. It's swelling up. We need to get some ice on it. Ostin, there's an ice machine at the end of the hall. Would you fill up that bucket?"

"On it." Ostin grabbed the ice bucket from the dresser and left

the room, while Taylor soaked a washcloth in cold water from the sink. I just stared at my arms. Was this really permanent?

When Ostin returned, Taylor dumped some of the ice onto the towel and rolled it up. As she held the cloth to my face, she suddenly closed her eyes and grimaced. "Oh, my . . ." She was watching the replay of my attack. She looked into my eyes. "Did any of them die?"

"I don't know," I said.

"You know they're going to tell others," Ostin said.

"I don't care," I said.

He frowned. "You will when they come after us."

"I pity anyone who comes after us," I said angrily. "I'll take down this whole country if I have to."

"Michael," Taylor said. "You need to calm down. You're really upset."

"I wonder why," I said sardonically. "Maybe because I was just attacked by a gang that was planning to stab me to death."

"You have every reason to be upset for that, but that's not why you're upset." She looked me in the eyes. "They didn't kill your mother."

"I don't care."

"You need to care. You need to stay in control." She pulled back the blood-soaked cloth to examine my wound. "It's not that deep. Ostin, go down to the front desk and see if you can find a bandage."

"You got it." He walked back out.

Taylor rinsed the blood from the washcloth, put more ice in it, and held it against my jaw. I just kept looking at my arms.

Ostin returned a few minutes later with a box of off-brand Band-Aids. "This is all they had."

"It will take a few of them," Taylor said. She dabbed the cloth around my wound again, then applied three different bandages. Then she got a fresh washcloth and soaked it in water, wrapped it around more ice, and gave it to me. "Keep this on your face. Now you better get some sleep. We have to leave in two hours." She kissed me on my other cheek. "I'm going back to my room. Get some rest."

"Thank you," I said. After she left, I took the switchblade out of my pocket and tossed it on the floor. I turned out the lights and got back into bed, holding the cloth against my cheek.

"Are you okay?" Ostin asked.

"No."

"Yeah, me neither," he said. "Good night."

"Night."

It seemed like just a few seconds after I'd shut my eyes that I woke to the room's phone ringing. The wet, bloodstained washcloth was lying on the other side of the bed, soaking and staining the sheets.

Ostin grabbed the phone. "All right," he said groggily. He hung up. "It's Scott. He says to meet downstairs in fifteen minutes."

We all arrived at the van about the same time. Scott was holding open a large pink box of Mexican pastries—where he'd found an open bakery at four in the morning was beyond me. As I walked toward him, he stared at my bandaged jaw. "What happened?"

"Some guys tried to mug him," Taylor said, walking up behind me. "They hit him with a bottle."

Scott looked at me nervously. "What did you do to them?"

"Invited them up for churros," I said angrily. "What do you think I did to them?"

"Mexican barbecue," Zeus said. "Wish I had been there."

"Me too," Jack said. "I would have loved to help out."

"Trust me, he didn't need any help," Taylor said.

Jack grinned. "Still would have been fun to watch."

Suddenly Abigail gasped. "Michael, what happened to your arms?"

Everyone looked at me.

"They're lightning burns," Ostin said.

"Lichtenberg figures," Zeus said.

"How did you know that?" Ostin asked. I'm sure he was disappointed that someone besides him knew what they were called.

"Because I've given them to people," Zeus said. "It's like my calling card."

"What people?" Taylor asked.

Zeus frowned. "GPs—Hatch's guinea pigs—mostly."

"Sorry I asked," Taylor said.

"It's my past," Zeus said. "It is what it is."

"I don't get it," Jack said, still staring at my arm. "What are they?"

"They're scars made by the diffusion of electricity through his skin," Ostin said. "Lichtenberg figures were discovered in 1777 by a German scientist named Georg Christoph Lichtenberg. He built a machine to generate high-voltage static electricity, then recorded the resulting patterns it made by sprinkling powder onto a nonconducting surface. Afterward, he pressed blank sheets of paper onto these patterns. It's how he discovered the basic principle of xerography and today's laser printers."

"You asked," Tessa said to Jack.

"Do they hurt?" Abigail asked.

"No. I didn't even feel it happen."

"It looks cool," Nichelle said. "Really cool. Maybe I'll tattoo myself like that when we get back to civilization."

"It's like a battle marking," Jack said. "Like the way Maori warriors tattooed themselves before going to war. I think I'll do it too."

Everyone kept staring at me until I finally said, "All right, quit looking at me. Let's go."

"You heard him," Scott said. "Everyone into the van. Grab a pastry if you want one."

I passed on the food. We all piled into the vehicle. Taylor, McKenna, Ostin, and I crowded into the backseat. I must have been ticking a lot, because Taylor put her hand on my face. "Michael, you can lie against me if you want. You need sleep."

I lay my head on Taylor's shoulder, and she ran her fingers through my hair until I fell asleep. I didn't wake until about two hours later when we pulled off the freeway onto a dirt road.

"Where are we?" I asked, lifting my head.

"Still Mexico," Ostin said.

"We're about a half hour from the ranch," Taylor said.

"Ian, keep your eyes open," Scott said. "Let me know if you see anyone. And keep your eyes open for land mines."

"I can blow them," I said. "If I have to."

"We don't want to blow them," Scott said. "If the Elgen are still around, they'll hear it."

"Why do you think they're still around?" Jack asked. "That's like robbing a bank and then hanging around until the police arrive."

"It only makes sense if your real target isn't the bank but the police," Ostin said.

"Exactly," Scott said. "You know better than anyone that Hatch doesn't give up easily. You escaped the Elgen in Taiwan, so they might assume you'll be returning to the ranch. They may be waiting. The Elgen love traps."

"The Elgen love traps like spiders love webs," Ostin said.

For the first time I understood exactly why Scott had been so cautious. He was right. There was a very good chance we were walking into a trap. But trap or not, if I saw them, I was going to fight.

PART THREE

6

The Kidnapper

Boise police headquarters
Boise, Idaho

Chief Davis stuck his head into the break room where Taylor's father, Officer Charles Ridley, was eating his lunch from a brown paper sack—his usual pastrami-and-mustard sandwich on rye with dill pickles and a bag of potato chips. He was reading the sports page of the *Boise Herald*. The Boise State Broncos were having another unbeaten season, and he was angry that his team still couldn't get any respect from the national press. These days he spent a lot of time reading about sports. It helped him keep his mind off his missing daughter.

"Chuck, could I speak with you for a moment?" Davis asked.

Ridley looked up from the paper. "Sure, boss. What do you need?"

"Come to my office, please."

Ridley chuckled nervously, as the chief was rarely this formal. "I'm not in trouble, am I?"

Davis didn't smile. "Just come with me, please."

Ridley wiped his mouth with a paper napkin, then wadded it up into a ball and tossed it into the corner wastebasket. "No problem."

He followed the chief down the hall to his office. To Ridley's surprise there were two men in suits waiting for them. One was a tall sandy-haired man in a navy blazer. The other was shorter with a shaved head exposing just a shadow of hair stubble. He had an ash-gray pin-striped suit. They were both standing behind Davis's desk, wearing serious expressions.

"Gentlemen, this is Officer Ridley," Davis said.

"Have a seat, Officer," the taller of the two men said. "I'm Officer Cazier, and this is my partner, Officer Ogden."

Ridley looked at the chief, who nodded. Ridley sat down in one of the black vinyl chairs in front of the desk, his eyes nervously darting back and forth between the two men. "What's going on?"

Chief Davis folded his arms at his chest. "Chuck, these officers are from internal affairs."

Ridley's blood pressure rose. "Internal affairs? Have I done something?"

"It's not what *you've* done, Officer. This matter concerns your daughter."

He leaned forward eagerly. "You found Taylor?"

"No, I'm sorry. We haven't. But we have a lead and a possible new suspect in her disappearance."

Ridley's brow furrowed. "A suspect? What do you mean a 'suspect'? She ran away."

"We don't think so," said Ogden. "We have reason to believe that your daughter was abducted."

Ridley felt his chest constrict. "Abducted. By whom?"

The officers looked uncomfortably at each other. Cazier said, "What we're about to tell you is highly confidential."

"Of course," Ridley said impatiently. "Who took my daughter?"

Cazier took a step toward him. "We believe your wife might have something to do with your daughter's disappearance."

Ridley almost laughed. "My wife? Julie?" He shook his head.

"That's ridiculous. She's cried herself to sleep every night since Taylor ran away. You're crazy."

Cazier didn't flinch. "Like we said, we don't believe your daughter ran away. In fact, the evidence is pretty clear that she didn't."

"Evidence!" Ridley said angrily. "I read the text messages from her."

"The text messages you read weren't sent from your daughter's phone, Officer."

Ridley looked at them quizzically. "What?"

"We've been unable to track down the owner of the phone that the messages were sent from, but we know for certain that it wasn't your daughter's."

"Then how did it show my daughter's name on my caller ID?"

"Whoever did this had advanced technological capabilities. They might have even been watching you through *your* phone."

"Does your daughter have friends in Peru?" Cazier asked.

"Peru? What does that—"

"That's where the texts originated."

Ridley was flustered. "I don't know. Maybe she met someone online."

Cazier leaned forward. "Does your wife have any friends in Peru?"

"No."

"Are you certain?"

Ridley exhaled loudly. "I don't know, maybe she has a client there. Her travel agency sends people all over the world. Why?"

"Because your wife has received several phone calls from that same phone in Peru," Cazier said.

"Do you know where your wife is right now?" Ogden asked.

"She's at work."

"Has she been traveling recently?"

"A few weeks ago she went on a business trip to Scottsdale."

"How long has she been back in Idaho?"

"Like I said, about three weeks."

"Was she acting differently when she returned?"

"What do you mean?"

"Did she say or do anything out of the ordinary?"

Ridley rubbed his forehead. The truth was, he had thought she was acting strange. He had even asked her what was going on, but she had just brushed him off. Still, he wasn't about to tell them that. "No, she's just been stressed by work. As usual."

"Do you know why she went to Scottsdale?" Cazier asked.

"She said . . ." He stopped himself. "She had a meeting with a new client."

The officers looked at each other. "Do you know who this client is?"

"Of course not," Ridley erupted. "I don't know any of her clients. Just like she doesn't know who I pulled over today." Ridley leaned forward. "Look, if you're accusing us of kidnapping—"

Chief Davis raised his hand to calm his officer. "Chuck, these men aren't accusing you of anything. They're just trying to help find your daughter."

"Then stop wasting time harassing the victims!"

The two men just looked at Ridley stoically. "Officer, are you sure your wife told you she was going to Scottsdale?"

"Of course I'm sure."

Both of the agents just looked at him.

"Why? Are you saying she didn't go there?"

Ogden shook his head. "Your wife never went to Scottsdale. She was on a private jet that crossed the border into Mexico into an area that's known to be controlled by drug cartels."

"Drug cartels?"

"We've secured flight information that verifies that."

"Why would she do that?"

"That's what we want to know," Cazier said.

Ogden said, "We have reason to believe that your wife was meeting with some suspicious individuals. We don't know if they're trafficking weapons, drugs, or people, but they are under FBI investigation. We have this satellite photo from Homeland Security." He lifted a photograph of the Timepiece Ranch compound. "It appears to be a compound of some type near Nogales, Mexico. They have advanced weaponry and even a helicopter."

Ridley looked at the photograph, then handed it back. "Where are you coming up with this stuff?"

"Three days ago we received a tip from an anonymous source."

"An anonymous tip," Ridley said disparagingly.

"If these people are as dangerous as we believe they are, it's not surprising the leak would choose to remain anonymous," Ogden said.

Cazier nodded. "You should be advised that everything this source has told us so far has been verifiable. Does your wife often take off on business trips?"

"No. This is the first trip like this she's ever been on."

The officers nodded, as if their point had been confirmed. Cazier looked Ridley in the eye. "Your daughter isn't the only missing person report we're working on. There have been four other kids and three adults who have gone missing as well, all of them from this same area and most of them disappearing at the same time as your daughter."

"How did I not know this?" Ridley asked.

"Are you familiar with a youth named Michael Vey?" Ogden asked.

"Vey?" Ridley said. "He was one of Taylor's friends."

"Vey and his mother have both disappeared. The peculiar thing is that when we did background checks on them, we couldn't find anything. They've been living off the grid for more than five years, except for their cell phones. We've traced numerous calls between your wife and daughter and Vey prior to your daughter's disappearance. We're guessing there's a connection."

Ridley shook his head. "We went to see Vey the night Taylor disappeared."

"Who, you and your wife?"

"Yes."

"Where did you go?"

"Vey's apartment."

"Was he there?"

Ridley nodded. "Yeah. We talked to him."

"Do you remember what he said?"

"Not really. I mean, it was a rough night. We asked if he knew

where Taylor was. He said he didn't, so we asked him to let us know if she contacted him. That's the last we heard of him."

"The day your daughter disappeared, was she with him?"

"She was supposed to go to a party with him. . . . I think it was his birthday."

Ogden asked, "Was his mother at the apartment when you visited?"

Ridley thought. "No. She wasn't. It was just the kid."

"We've done some checking around. The last contact anyone had with Vey's mother was the day of your daughter's disappearance. She worked at a grocery store and missed her shift the next day."

Ridley took a deep breath. "Look. I deal with guilty people every day. I have a sixth sense when they're lying and when they're hiding something. My wife isn't guilty. She's been inconsolable since our daughter disappeared."

"I understand," Cazier said. "But we both know that there is more than one reason to be inconsolable."

"What are you saying?"

Again the chief interrupted him. "Chuck, just keep it cool. No one's accusing anyone of anything."

"Except my wife!" Ridley shouted. "They're calling her a kidnapper. Where's the proof?"

"Officer Ridley's right," Cazier said. "The truth is, we don't know what's going on yet. We have a few new leads and a lot of unanswered questions." He took a deep breath. "I hate to bring this up, but you know as well as we do that after all this time, the odds aren't great that your daughter is still alive. But there's still a chance. So you can either cooperate with us and help us find your daughter, or you can fight us. What will it be, Officer?"

Ridley was quiet a moment, then said, "Of course I'll do whatever I can to find my daughter."

"Good. Then you'll understand why you'll have to be suspended from your job for a while."

"What?" Ridley spun toward the chief. "You're letting them suspend me?"

"It was my decision to suspend you, Chuck. For your own safety, as well as the department's. It's best for everyone if you're not around."

Ridley covered his eyes with his hands. "This is nuts."

"We'll keep the department informed of our investigation," Ogden said. "In the meantime, we need to question your wife."

Ridley looked back up. "Are you arresting her?"

"Yes," Ogden said.

Ridley groaned. "Can you keep this out of the news?"

"You know we can't," Ogden said. "But we might be able to delay it a day or so. We wanted to give you some time to contact your other children and let them know. But not until after we have your wife in custody."

"There's no way she's involved in any of this. I don't know what she was doing in Mexico, but I'm sure there's a simple answer."

"Which is why we're questioning her. To give her a chance to explain herself. If you're right, and we hope you are, there's nothing to worry about."

"Please don't arrest her at work," Ridley said. "She doesn't need that kind of embarrassment."

"You know that—"

"Please," Ridley interrupted. "She's not a criminal. I don't know what's going on, but she's as pure as snow."

Davis said, "Gentlemen, we have no reason to believe that Mrs. Ridley is a flight risk. I think we can wait a few hours until she's home."

"All right," Cazier said. "But we'll be staking out her office and following her home. We can't afford to lose her."

"Fair enough," Davis said.

"Thank you," Ridley said.

"One more question," Ogden said. "I realize that this is a difficult question for you, with serious implications, but does your wife use drugs?"

"Of course not."

"Are you certain?"

"I'm a police officer. I think I would notice that. She has trouble swallowing a Tylenol."

The men looked at each other. Then Cazier said, "I think that's all for now. Do you and your wife share cars?"

"No. I drive the patrol car; she has her van."

"Okay. We'll need to have forensics check her van for evidence," Cazier said. "Good day."

Once the men left the office, Ridley just sat in the chair, stunned. Then he buried his face in his hands.

After a moment Chief Davis walked over to him, putting his hand on Ridley's shoulder. "I'm sorry, Chuck. This caught me by surprise too."

"I know Julie. She couldn't be guilty of this." He looked up. "She's never even had a speeding ticket. But why would she lie to me about Scottsdale?"

"I'm sure there's a reasonable explanation," Chief Davis said. "I'm sure everything will turn out just fine."

Ridley just shook his head. "But why would she lie to me?"

PART FOUR

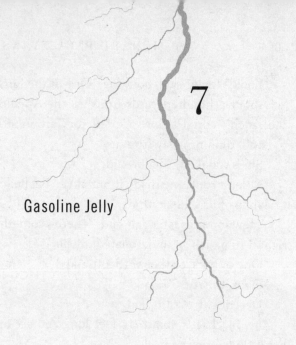

7

Gasoline Jelly

Nogales, Mexico

The sun was rising behind us as our van rattled slowly along the rutted, dusty road. After another twenty minutes the landscape changed from plains to small rolling hills and valleys. The vegetation, mostly saguaro and mesquite, was charred black. In the distance we could see a thin gray column of smoke rising into the sky.

"They used napalm," Ostin said, his voice quivering.

"How can you tell?" I asked.

"You can smell the phosphorous."

"What's napalm?" Nichelle asked.

"It's like gasoline jelly," Ostin said. "The U.S. Army used it for attacking bunkers and machine gun nests in World War II. Then they used it to clear the jungle in Vietnam. Whatever it hits, it sticks to and burns."

Again, my thoughts turned to my mother and the horror she must have experienced. As we neared the ranch, Scott had to slow down even more to avoid the large craters in the road.

"Look," Taylor said, pointing. "One of the horses."

About a hundred yards from us, the Appaloosa we had seen in the ranch's corral before we left for Taiwan stood looking at us. It took off, running away from us.

"She's spooked," Taylor said.

"At least someone made it out alive," Nichelle said.

None of us said anything.

A few minutes later, Ian said, "There's something up ahead, to the right. I think it's an undetonated missile."

"One of ours, or theirs?" Scott asked.

"Does it matter?"

"Describe it," Ostin said.

"It's black. It's about six feet long and six inches in diameter. It has little tail fins on back."

"Do you know what it is?" I asked.

"Sounds like a Hellfire missile," Ostin said. "It's an air-to-surface missile originally designed for antitank attacks, but now it's used for precision strikes. They have a fairly short range, less than five miles, which means the Elgen must have flown in for the attack. Probably in helicopters. That's what the Hellfire was originally designed for."

Scott slowed the van down. "Are we safe passing it?"

"How far is the missile from the road?" Ostin asked.

"About a hundred yards."

"We're safe. Hellfires carry a highly explosive twenty-pound warhead, but they're directional. If it's not flying at us, we're okay. It's highly unlikely it would go off now."

"How many of those missiles can a helicopter carry?" I asked.

"Sixteen," Jack said.

Ostin looked like someone had beaten him to the buzzer on a game show. "How'd you know that?"

"The marines use them to clear the ground before landing," Jack said. "My brother told me."

"They must have had a lot of helicopters to fire that many missiles," Nichelle said. "The ground looks like the moon."

"The missiles made some of these craters," Ostin said. "But most of them are from the ranch's land mines."

"How can you tell?" Taylor asked.

"Hellfire missiles are shot down to penetrate a target. The land mines are designed to explode upward, so the hole they leave in the ground is more shallow."

A mile later we passed two destroyed Hummers. Both of them were scorched, and one was still smoking. It had nearly been blown in two. As we neared the ranch, the devastation grew even worse. Much worse.

"We're getting close," Scott said. "Everyone keep your eyes open." He turned toward Ian. "If you see any movement at all, you tell me."

"I don't see anything," Ian said. "Except ashes and holes."

Scott slowly edged the van to the upper rim of the canyon until we could see the compound below us. Or at least what was left of it. My stomach turned at the sight of what was before us. What had been the great ranch house was now a pile of charred rubble and brick and twisted chicken wire. Everything had been destroyed.

The buildings were all burned down to their concrete foundations, with smoke still rising from the debris. There were overturned cars and trucks, and the resistance's sole helicopter was on its side, its propeller lying twenty yards away from its burned-out fuselage.

The only thing still standing was one of the windmill generators at least three hundred yards away on the opposite mountain—though every one of its blades was damaged.

"I can't believe this is the same place where we stayed three weeks ago," Taylor said softly.

"They must have fired more than a hundred missiles," Ostin said, his voice strained with emotion. "At least."

After a couple of minutes I said, "I want to go down and see."

"No," Scott said. "It's too risky. It would be too easy for them to trap us in the ravine, and there might be more unexploded bombs."

"There is no *them*," I said. "The Elgen are gone. Just like everyone else."

"We can't take that chance."

"Then I'll walk down," I said, reaching for the door handle.

"Michael," Taylor said. "Please don't."

"Wait," Ian said. "We can go. There's no one around. I'll keep a close watch."

"If Michael's going, I'm going too," Jack said.

"Me too," Zeus said.

Scott took a deep breath, then exhaled slowly. "All right. I'll drive down. But we won't stay long." He shook his head. "I have a bad feeling about this."

He shifted the van into drive, and we slowly made our way down into the ravine and the smoking remains of the compound. In a couple of places the road was nearly impassable, and it took some expert driving to navigate the craters and ruts.

As the road leveled out into the valley, any hope I had that there might be survivors was gone. Nothing could have survived the missile attack that had pulverized the compound, or the firestorm that had followed.

"Welcome to hell," Nichelle said.

A sickeningly sweet, acrid smell filled our nostrils. "Yeah, they used napalm," Ostin said softly. "Lots of it."

The first time we'd seen the compound, Ian had told us that the buildings were surrounded by metal electrical cages, which were now visible, as the buildings' wood had all burned away. The resistance had prepared for an EMP attack, but apparently not a conventional attack of bombs and bullets. They had little armament other than an attack helicopter and a few armed vehicles, most of which had, apparently, never even made it out of their garages. They were now nothing more than burned, mangled metal surrounded by the remnants of their housing's concrete foundations.

"They must have been taken totally by surprise," Jack said. "They didn't even get their weaponry out."

"Overkill," Zeus said, shaking his head. "It's overkill."

"It's strange," Ian said.

"What's strange?" I asked, ticking painfully.

He looked back at me. "Why aren't there any remains?"

"Remains?" Taylor said.

"Bodies. Or bones."

"Maybe they took prisoners first," Tessa said. "Then destroyed the place."

"It doesn't look like it," Ostin said. "They were going for complete annihilation."

The van continued slowly forward, snaking between piles of smoldering rubble smoking like funeral pyres. Finally we stopped in front of what had been the main building.

"I want to get out," I said.

Scott shut off the van, and we all climbed out. There really wasn't anything to see but the building's charred concrete foundation and twisted, black metal wire. I stepped over a wagon wheel, as black as ash. I could see the bones of a horse in a clearing. Other than that there was no evidence of life. Or death. It looked like those war pictures from our history books. I had never seen such devastation in real life.

I bent over and vomited. Abigail put her hand on my back and relieved some of my pain, although I'm sure she was hurting too.

"Ian," Ostin said. "Gervaso said there were underground bunkers. Do you see anyone?" Gervaso had been one of the military coordinators at the ranch. And our friend.

"I'm looking," he said. "So far they're empty."

"I don't get it," I said. "If they came in by helicopter, Tanner could have brought them all down. Just like he did in Peru."

"Unless he wasn't here when they came," Jack said.

"Or maybe they surprised them in the night."

"The Elgen are careful," Ostin said. "They would take the possibility of him being here into account. The Hellfires have a five-mile range. They could fly close enough to fire missiles, then come in after the first attack. There were more than a hundred missiles; he couldn't stop all of them."

"Look," Ian said, pointing southward. There was a burned-out helicopter smashed into the ground. "It's one of theirs."

"Maybe Tanner got one of them," I said.

"Or they shot it down," Jack said. "They had RPGs."

We walked over to the helicopter. As we looked in, Taylor gasped, then quickly turned away.

"What is it?" Tessa asked.

"Bones," I said.

There were burned remains of two Elgen guards inside, still buckled into their seats.

I continued wandering past glowing cinders of debris, looking for some evidence of non-Elgen humanity. But everything was ashes. That's how I felt inside. Ashes.

After a few moments I turned and walked back to the van. Everyone else followed. When we were back inside, Taylor said, "Can we go down that dirt road a ways?"

"Why?" Scott asked.

I glanced over at Taylor. Her eyes were red. "Just, please. I need to see something."

"Just do it," I said.

"All right," Scott said reluctantly. "We've already come this far." He slowly pulled the van forward. Fifty yards from the house there was a large crater in the center of the road, and we had to drive up onto the road's shoulder to get to where Taylor wanted to go—the redbrick utility building where we had had our prom dinner.

"This is the place," she said.

Scott stopped the van, and Taylor slid the door open and stepped out. Only I followed her.

The building wasn't completely decimated like the others—probably because it was so far from the main compound—but it was still reduced to a pile of bricks with only one and a half walls still standing. Taylor walked up to where the front door had been, then picked her way through the rubble. She suddenly stopped to bend over and pick something up. She turned to show me. It was one of the silver candleholders from our dinner.

"It's all gone, Michael." She looked at me with tear-filled eyes. "You were right. They've taken everything."

I took her hand. Just then I heard the sound of a helicopter. I looked up but couldn't see it through the clouds.

Scott yelled, "Everyone out of the van! Take cover, fast!"

We all scrambled from the vehicle, everyone running in different directions before lying flat on the ground. For several minutes we waited tensely.

"What kind of chopper is it?" Scott yelled to Ian.

He paused, then said, "Maybe U.S. border control. There aren't any missiles or guns. They don't look like Elgen."

Less than a minute later the sound of the chopper passed and faded. Scott stood up, visibly shaken. "We've been here too long. We've got to get out of here."

"What a chicken," Jack said to me under his breath.

As we were getting back into the van, Ian said, "Wait. I see something."

I turned to him. "What?"

"It's a person. They might still be alive."

"Where?"

"About a half mile that way," he said, pointing. "He crawled the whole way."

"How can you tell?" Taylor asked.

"He left a trail."

"He?" Taylor asked.

Ian shook his head. "Or she. I can't tell from here."

"Are they one of ours?" I asked.

Ian shook his head again. "I don't know. But whoever it is, they're in bad shape."

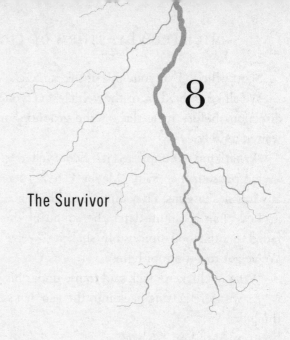

8

The Survivor

Scott drove off road, following the direction Ian pointed, along a rutted path.

"Are they armed?" he asked.

"Only a pistol," Ian said.

"Keep a close eye on him. If he makes for his weapon . . ."

"If he makes for a weapon, I'll divert it," I said. "Just get us close to him."

"A little to the left," Ian said. "About fifty yards ahead."

When I first saw the man, I didn't recognize him as human. He was grotesque-looking. His skin and clothes, what hadn't been burned off, were charred black, and most of his hair was singed off his head. My first thought was, *Gervaso*. If anyone could have survived an attack, it would be Gervaso. But it wasn't him.

"He's Elgen," Ian said.

"How do you know?" I asked.

"His utility belt is standard Elgen. And I can make out part of an Elgen tattoo."

Scott stopped the van about thirty feet from him.

"He looks dead," Tessa said.

"His heart's still beating," Ian said. "And he's breathing. Barely. He has lung damage."

"I'm going to go talk to him," I said, grabbing the door handle.

"What are you going to ask him?" Scott asked.

"I'm going to ask him where everybody is."

"I'll help," Taylor said. "In case he can't speak."

"Abigail, we may need you, too," I said.

The three of us climbed out of the van, followed by Zeus and Jack.

When we were a few feet from the man, he tried to move his hand toward his gun but couldn't. His injuries were so severe, it was difficult to even look at him. I couldn't imagine what pain he must have been in. I would be lying if I said that I wasn't glad to see him suffering. He was Elgen. For all I knew he had personally killed my mother and Ostin's parents.

I squatted down next to him. "You're Elgen."

Only his eyes moved. He looked at me less in fear than in resignation. In his condition he probably welcomed death. I would have. "I'm Michael Vey."

His eyes opened a little bit wider, and he grunted.

"Can you speak?"

"Wa . . ."

"He wants water," Taylor said.

"I'll get him some," Abigail said.

"No water," I said.

Abigail stopped.

"Not until he talks." I leaned closer to the man. His face was covered in dirt. "Were you part of the attack on the ranch?"

He just looked at me.

"Taylor," I said. "I need your help."

She crouched down next to the man. She found a place near the

crown of his head that wasn't burned, and touched him. "Ask again," Taylor said.

"Were you part of the attack on the ranch?"

Taylor glanced up at me. "He was. He was in that helicopter that was shot down."

"Where are all the people who were here? What did you do with their bodies?"

He tried to move his lips but was unable.

"They didn't do anything with the people," Taylor said. "He doesn't think there was anyone here."

"If there was no one here, how did he get shot down?"

Taylor closed her eyes. A moment later she said, "A missile brought down his helicopter. He thinks the missile was fired by remote. The Elgen left him and his crew. He's the only survivor."

I looked into the man's eyes. "Where are our people?"

He suddenly forced open his mouth. "No . . ."

"He never saw anyone else on the ground. No one tried to kill him or save him. Then the Elgen fired . . . I don't know what this is . . . *Na-pom* . . . over the site while he was on the ground."

"Napalm," Jack said. "That stuff Ostin was talking about."

Taylor nodded. "Napalm. That's it." She looked up at me. "He hates the Elgen."

"So do I," I said. "And he's still one of them."

The man grimaced. "No . . ."

"He says he's no Elgen," Taylor said.

I turned to Abigail. "Get him some water. And get Scott."

Abigail ran back to the van. She returned with a bottle of water. Scott was with her.

"Is there a hospital in Naco?" I asked.

"There's the Red Cross clinic in Naco, but he'll need a hospital. There's a good hospital in Bisbee."

"Could we save his life?"

Scott looked at the man. "Maybe. If he can survive the ride."

"He's lasted this long," Zeus said.

"Do you want me to help him?" Abigail asked.

I didn't answer but glanced at Taylor. She nodded. "We're not like them, Michael."

After a moment I turned back to Abigail. "All right. Help him."

Abigail knelt down next to the man and touched him on the shoulder. He gasped out in relief, and his eyes filled with tears. I opened the bottle of water, then put it next to his cracked lips and slowly poured it into his mouth. He drank greedily, choking a little on it.

The man looked up at me, then Abigail. "Thank . . ." It was all he could get out.

"It's okay," she said.

"What are you thinking?" Jack asked me.

"He knows all about the attack. He knows all about the Elgen. The Elgen think he's dead, so if he really hates the Elgen, he won't be afraid to talk. He can help us find them."

"If we can keep him alive," Jack said.

"Then let's keep him alive," I said.

Scott looked at me, then nodded. "All right. Let's get him back to America."

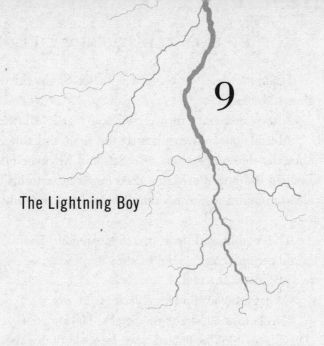

9

The Lightning Boy

I had assumed we would return from the ranch knowing what had happened to my mother and friends, but now I had more questions than answers. I didn't know what to think. No one could have survived an attack of the magnitude that destroyed the ranch. But why hadn't we found any sign of our friends? No bodies, no bones, there was not one shred of evidence that anyone had been there.

And then there was what the guard had said—or thought—about no one being there. *Could they all have gotten away?* For the first time in days, I felt hopeful.

I looked down to see Taylor running her fingers along my arm across my new markings. "I hope it doesn't go away. I think it looks cool."

"I hope it fades a little. I look painted."

"You're pretty painted." She ran her finger along my arm for a little while longer, then said, "Do you really think they're alive?"

I suppose that I was getting used to her reading my mind, as her question didn't surprise me. Half the time I don't think she even knew she was doing it.

"I don't know. There were at least fifty people there. How could there have been no sign of anyone? And what the guard said . . ."

Taylor shook her head. "You're right, it doesn't make sense. But why would the voice tell us there were no survivors?"

"Do you think the voice always tells the truth?"

"I don't know."

"Would you lie to save my life?" I asked.

Taylor didn't hesitate. "Of course."

"Would you lie to save the world?"

"Of course," she repeated.

"Me too," I said. "I think the voice will say whatever he has to to help the cause."

"But why would telling us everyone's dead help the cause?"

I shook my head. "I don't know. Maybe the guard knows something."

"I just hope he makes it to the hospital alive."

We had laid the guard in the back of the van on the floor of the cargo area, and Abigail and Jack sat in back with him. As we approached the Mexican town of Naco, Scott said, "We'll go straight to the Red Cross clinic and get him help. Zeus, Tessa, Jack, and Abigail will stay with him while the rest of us get our bags from the hotel. Will someone collect the room keys?"

"I'll do it," Taylor said.

Everyone handed their keys to Taylor.

"They'll probably need me at the Red Cross to translate," Ostin said.

"You're right," Scott said. "McKenna, you're still with us."

"No worries," she said.

We pulled into the dirt parking lot of the Red Cross building, and Ostin ran inside. A moment later two Mexican men, one of them wearing a blue doctor's smock, came out carrying a cloth stretcher. Jack opened the back doors.

The doctor gasped when he saw the guard. "*¡Qué espantoso!*"

Jack helped the men lift the guard and carry him inside, followed by Zeus, Abigail, Ostin, and Tessa.

Scott climbed back inside the van, and the rest of us drove just a few blocks back to our hotel. When we arrived, Taylor, Nichelle, McKenna, Ian, and I went to the rooms to collect everyone's things. As we carried the luggage out to the van, a young Mexican man standing across the street in front of the hotel suddenly pointed at me and shouted, "*¡El niño relámpago! ¡El niño relámpago!*"

"What's he saying?" Taylor asked.

"*¡Allí está el niño relámpago!*"

"He's calling you 'the lightning boy,'" Scott said, walking up to me. "How would he know that?"

"He might have been one of the gang members who attacked me," I said.

"Might?" Scott said.

"I don't know. It was dark. We weren't posing for selfies."

People began walking out of buildings to see what the man was shouting about.

"I've got this," Taylor said. "Nichelle, can you amplify me?"

"Sure," she said, taking Taylor's hand.

Taylor reached her other hand toward the kid and closed her eyes. He abruptly stopped shouting. Then he and the people around him suddenly looked confused, as if they'd all forgotten why there were standing in the street—which was likely true.

"You're so cool," I said.

"Thank you," Taylor said. "And thanks to Nichelle. I usually can't reboot so many people at once."

"No problem," Nichelle said.

"We've got to get out of here," Scott said. "Who knows how many people this clown's told. Word will spread quickly in a place like this."

Taylor and Nichelle kept the crowd confused as we finished throwing the bags into the back of the van and climbed in. We sped back to the Red Cross.

The small clinic was crowded, and Jack waved us over to where our friends were gathered. The guard was lying on a small cot with an IV going into his arm. A doctor was standing next to him, spraying his wounds with something. The rest of our group was standing a few yards from him, watching.

"What's going on?" I asked Ostin.

"They gave him some pain medicine and some antibiotics," Ostin said.

"They also gave him an IV for his dehydration," Abigail said. "The doctor says they need to take him to a hospital in Sonora."

"No," Scott said. "We need to get out of Mexico. Does the doctor speak English?"

"I speak English," the doctor said, with only a slight accent. "Do you know this man?"

"He was at our ranch in the desert. There was an explosion."

"We heard explosions a few days ago," the doctor said. "Were there others hurt?"

"He's the only one we know of," Scott said. "We'll take him over the border to Bisbee to the Copper Queen hospital."

"Copper Queen is good," the doctor said, nodding. "They're better prepared for burn trauma."

"We'll take him immediately," Scott said.

"What's the hurry?" Ostin whispered.

"Someone recognized Michael," Nichelle said. "They're calling him 'the lightning boy.' By the time we left the hotel, a crowd had gathered."

"I was afraid of that," Ostin said.

The doctor finished wrapping the man's burn with gauze, and then two men carried the guard back out to our van with the IV needle still in his arm, the tube connected to a bag of saline that we hung from one of the van's clothes hooks.

Fortunately, the traffic at the border crossing back into the United States was light, with just three cars ahead of us.

"This could be tricky," Scott said. "Transporting an undocumented burn victim across the border."

"I know a way to get across the border." I turned back to Taylor. "Remember the mind trick you did in Peru at the Starxource plant? Could you do that again?"

"Yes. I'll need someone to translate."

"This guy will speak English," Ostin said. "They're American border guards."

"What if it doesn't work this time?" Abigail asked.

"It will work," Jack said. "If not, Michael, Zeus, and I will take the place down."

"No," Scott said. "No fighting unless they try to arrest us. We can't draw attention to ourselves. This place has massive video surveillance."

"Zeus can take out the video," Jack said.

Zeus nodded. "It's my specialty."

"But we still don't know how many guards are inside. The last thing we need to do is turn this into a war zone."

"Don't worry," I said. "It won't come to that. Taylor will get us through."

"I hope so," Scott said, pulling the van forward. "Because we're here."

We drove past a blue-and-white sign that read:

WELCOME TO THE UNITED STATES
BIENVENIDOS A LOS ESTADOS UNIDOS

In front of the building was a flagpole with an American and an Immigration and Naturalization Service flag. The American border station was two stories high and constructed after traditional adobe architecture, with the butts of logs sticking out of its pale yellow stucco walls.

A long metal fence led up to the station, running parallel with a paved walkway on the east side for pedestrian traffic. There was a stop sign in the middle of the road, with the word "STOP" above the word "*ALTO*."

Scott pulled up to the final checkpoint before the border crossing. The uniformed and armed U.S. border guard was tall and lanky with a serious expression. It took just a few minutes before he waved the car ahead of us through and motioned us forward.

"Get ready," I said to Taylor. "It's showtime."

"I'm ready."

We pulled up to the guard and stopped.

"Good afternoon," Scott said.

The man showed no emotion. "Are you U.S. citizens?"

"Yes, sir."

"Your passports, please."

"Of course." Scott handed the guard our documents.

Suddenly the Elgen soldier groaned out loudly, and the border guard looked inside the van to see where the sound had come from. Ostin grabbed his stomach. "I knew I shouldn't have drunk the water. Can we please hurry? I might blow."

"And now I'm going to hurl," Tessa said. "You're so gross."

The border guard looked at Ostin for a moment, then back at Scott. "There are eleven of you?"

"Yes," he said.

I whispered to Taylor, "Are you ready?"

She slightly nodded. All he had to do was walk around the car to see the Elgen.

The border guard quickly looked our passports over, then, without comment, handed them back. "You're free to go."

He waved at someone inside the building, and the gate rose. I think Scott was so surprised, he didn't move.

"Go ahead," the guard said.

"Yes, sir," Scott said. "Have a good afternoon." We pulled through the border crossing.

After we had passed over the border, Ostin said, "That was, like, easy."

"It was *too* easy," Scott said.

"Maybe someone wants us back in the U.S.," Ostin said.

"That's a scary thought," I said. "Since nobody is supposed to know we're here."

About a half mile from the border, Scott pulled into the parking lot of a small taqueria and put the van in park. He reached over to the glove box and took out a hand radio.

"I'm going to radio Boyd and see if he's seen anything suspicious." He pushed a button on the radio. "Come in, Albatross, come in." There was no response. "Albatross, come in. This is Falcon." Still no response.

"Maybe he's at dinner," Taylor said.

"He should have his radio with him at all times," Scott said. "Come in, Albatross. Over." He checked the radio's settings, then lifted the radio one more time. "Come in, Albatross. Are you there?"

Still nothing.

"This is strange," Scott said, pulling back out into the road. "Everyone, stay alert. Especially you, Ian. Something's not right."

"It never is," Taylor said softly. "It never is."

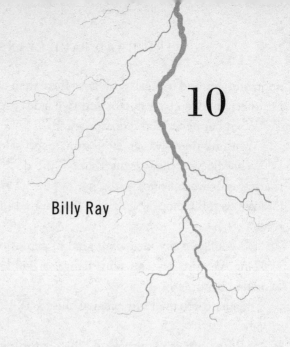

10

Billy Ray

On the way into the town of Bisbee, we passed a massive, terraced, open-pit copper mine several hundred feet deep. The town itself was beautiful, built in the lap of a mountain, with buildings climbing higher and higher up the foothills until the mountain's incline allowed no more.

The town had started to die after the mine closed in the seventies, then hippies found it and made it thrive again. Because it was a copper town, many of the buildings' roofs were covered with copper paneling and shingles. Copper is a powerful conductor of electricity, which may have had something to do with why I felt so different in the city. Stronger. More electric. As if I needed that.

When we reached downtown Bisbee, Scott followed the local road signs to Copper Queen hospital. We pulled up to the ER and parked the van; then Scott ran inside while Jack opened the back

door and he and Abigail got out. Less than a minute later Scott returned followed by a doctor and two aides pushing a metal gurney.

"What happened?" the doctor asked.

"We think there was an explosion," Scott said.

"What do you mean, you 'think'?" the doctor said curtly. "Either there was or wasn't one."

"We weren't there," Scott said. "We found him by the side of the road."

"Do you have any idea what kind of explosion?"

"No. We just saw burning debris around. Maybe a fuel tank exploded or something."

The guard groaned out again as the techs lifted the man onto the gurney.

"So he's not with your group," the doctor said.

"No. We were headed down to a Mexican dude ranch for a weekend church retreat when we found this man about a quarter mile from the main road. He was nearly unconscious. We drove him to Naco, but they weren't equipped to help him."

The doctor examined the guard some more, then said, "Peculiar. I haven't seen burns like that since . . ." He hesitated, then looked up at Scott. "I saw this in Vietnam. They look like napalm burns."

Ostin almost said something, but Scott stopped him. "Like I said, we don't know what happened."

We followed the doctor and techs into the hospital. At the operating room door the doctor turned to Abigail. "Young lady, you'll need to let go of his hand."

The guard gripped her hand tighter. He must have figured out that she was taking away his pain.

"He needs me," Abigail said. "For support."

The doctor hesitated. "All right. You'll have to scrub up, though. And get gloved."

"Can her power work through latex?" Taylor whispered.

I shrugged.

After Abigail and the doctor disappeared into the ER, a nurse led the rest of us out to the waiting room. As we walked down the

hallway, the nurse looked down at my arm. "Excuse me for asking, but were you struck by lightning?"

I wasn't sure how to answer. Finally I said, "How did you know?"

"Lichtenberg figures," she said. "I've only seen them in manuals. That must have been very painful."

"It wasn't too bad," I said.

Her brow rose. "Wasn't too bad? They're electricity burns. They're some of the worst kind."

"I guess I was a little out of it when it happened," I said. I quickly walked away from her and sat down on a couch while Scott, Ian, Zeus, and Tessa went outside to keep watch. Nichelle asked for a pencil from the registration desk, then sat in the corner sketching while Jack, Taylor, Ostin, McKenna, and I sat on the sofa across from her.

"The guard's name is Billy Ray," Taylor said. "He was raised by his grandmother. She's ninety-two and still alive."

"Elgen guards don't have grandmas," Jack said. "They're not born; they're spawned. And they don't have names. Just *Elgen*."

Taylor continued. "He's from Huntsville, Alabama."

"That's so weird that he's from somewhere," McKenna said.

"Everyone's from somewhere," Ostin replied.

"I know, but it still seems weird. It's like thinking about where Colby Cross went to elementary school, you know?"

"Or Hitler," Jack added.

"Where do you think Hatch is from?" Ostin asked.

"Hell," Jack said without hesitation.

"It's not an accident, you know," I said to Taylor.

"What's not an accident?" Taylor asked.

"That he's letting you know about him," I said. "He's doing it for a reason."

"Why?"

"So you would help him live."

"I don't get the connection."

"It's harder to kill people you know. That's why in wars the first thing they do is dehumanize the enemy. They're not people like us; they're gooks or krauts, or infidels or Charlie. After you know they

have a family, that they're somebody's son or grandson . . . it's a different thing."

"He's right," Jack said. "My brother was stationed in Afghanistan at a combat outpost when the Taliban attacked them. A Taliban soldier tried to stab my brother, but my brother turned the knife on the guy.

"While my brother's squad was waiting for reinforcements, my brother had to sit in the room with the dead man for two hours. He took out the guy's wallet. The man had a picture of his wife and a little boy. My brother said even though the guy had tried to kill him, it still made him sad. . . ."

Jack's words trailed off into silence. A few minutes later Scott walked into the waiting room from outside. "Any word on his condition?" he asked.

"No," Taylor said.

"See anything?" I asked.

"No. Neither has Ian. It doesn't appear that we were followed. But that doesn't explain why they let us across the border so easily."

"Maybe we were just lucky," Ostin said.

"Since when have we been lucky?" Taylor replied.

"We're still alive, aren't we?" Nichelle said, suddenly joining the conversation. "I'd say we've been pretty lucky."

Nichelle's optimism surprised me. "Any word from Boyd?" I asked.

"Not yet," Scott said. "I'm going to have to drive back to Douglas to check things out. I'll need some backup."

"So after we find him, then what?" I asked.

Scott sat down next to us. He leaned in, his hands clasped in his lap. "There's a safe house in Albuquerque," he said softly. "Assuming we still have a plane, I think we should fly there and wait to hear from the voice."

"The last safe house wasn't so *safe*," Jack said.

"Nothing's safe anymore. We don't know what information has been leaked, but it's still our best option."

"I want to go back to Idaho and get my parents," Taylor said.

"We will," Scott said. "But I need to get you to safety first, then go get them."

"You should talk to your mother first," I said. "You need to make sure that they're still in Boise."

Ostin said, "If the Elgen have their phone lines traced, they'll track the call back here. Just seeing a call this close to the border, they'll know we're back."

"Then we should make the call just before we leave Arizona," Scott said.

"What about the guard?" McKenna asked. "He's not going to be ready to go by tomorrow."

"We can't all stay here until he's better," Scott said. "It's too risky."

"Abi and I can stay with him," Jack said. "Then we'll meet up with you."

"I don't like breaking us up again," I said. "The last time we did that, we were captured."

"It's better than all of us being captured," Jack said.

"We don't know if what he knows is worth losing any of us," I said.

"Michael's right," Scott said. "We'll all stay in Douglas tonight, then fly out in the morning. We can come back for the guard later." His brow furrowed. "But first I need to find my copilot."

11

Haunted Hotel Gadsden

We left the hospital in Bisbee and drove from Bisbee twenty-three miles back to Douglas to the hotel where we planned to spend the night: the Hotel Gadsden, a tall, historic building that looked as old as the city and was, by far, the largest structure on the aged main street.

"I've heard about this place," Ostin said. "It's on the U.S. National Register of Historic Places. It's been used in a bunch of movies. They say that room 333 is haunted."

Tessa rolled her eyes. "Haunted? Really? I thought you were smart."

"I am," Ostin said. "And yes, I believe in ghosts, spirits, and paranormal beings."

We parked on the street in front of the hotel and walked inside. The hotel's lobby was high ceilinged and surprisingly beautiful, with tall, marble columns extending to the ceiling. Across the wall on the

split stairway leading up to the indoor balcony was a forty-foot-wide Tiffany mural of the Mexican desert.

"I want to stay in room 333," Nichelle said. "I've always wanted to see a ghost."

"There are no such things as ghosts," Tessa said.

"I'm glad you feel that way," Nichelle said. "You can be my room-mate."

We followed Scott up to the check-in counter. "Do you have any vacancies for tonight?" he asked.

"Yes, sir," the clerk said, looking us over. He was a fortysomething blond man with a name tag that read TOM. I noticed that his eyes lingered on the scars on my arm.

"I need six rooms for the night," Scott said. "Double occupancy."

"We can accommodate that. May I see a credit card?"

Scott took out his wallet and showed the man his ID. "We should have an account here."

"Just a moment," he said, looking at his computer. "Of course. It's good to have you back, Mr. Allen. Shall I put all the rooms on the same account?"

"Yes, please."

"I see the last time you were here, you stayed in 110, our Jacuzzi suite. Would you like the same room, or do you have a preference?"

"We'll just be staying in your regular rooms this time," Scott said. "The historic rooms."

"I want room 333," Nichelle said.

Tom looked over at her with a half smile. "So you've heard of our ghost."

Nichelle nodded. "Have you seen a ghost?"

"Once," he said. "In the basement. The power had gone out, so I went down there with a flashlight to check the fuse box. Suddenly the hair on the back of my neck rose, and I had this feeling that I was being watched. Then I saw a cloud in the shape of a man come toward me."

"That's creepy," Taylor said.

"A *cloud* in the shape of a man?" Tessa said. "That's bogus."

"Ah, a skeptic," Tom said. "At least once a week I hear something about a ghost from a guest. Especially from those staying in room 333. Once we had a movie crew stay here while they were filming a documentary on the old West. One of the cameramen said his room's light kept flipping on and off all night; then something threw all of his clothes off their hangers in the closet."

"I'm pretty sure that was an episode of *Scooby-Doo*," Tessa said.

Tom just smiled. "Another time a woman, a college professor, told me that she felt someone get into bed with her. When she rolled over to see who it was, no one was there."

"She was probably just lonely and dreamed it," Tessa said.

"Maybe, but *she* certainly believed it. She had reserved the room for three nights, but she packed up and checked out in the middle of the night. We have an entire binder filled with supernatural accounts recorded by our guests. Most are simple things, lights or televisions turning on and off in the night, or strange sounds coming from the radiator. Especially in room 333."

"All old radiators make strange sounds," Tessa said. "Old buildings make noises."

"You may be right, but after hearing these stories for the last ten years, you begin to think that there must be something going on."

"Logically, I'd come to that conclusion," Ostin said. "Though it's possible that the expectation created by previous ghost stories might create an expectant psychological environment for mob hysteria."

Tom just stared at Ostin.

"He always talks that way," Tessa said. "It's annoying."

"Actually, I was admiring his vocabulary," Tom said, handing out our room keys. "And here is 333 for you," he said, handing the key to Nichelle.

"Thanks," she said.

"Is there a restaurant nearby?" Ostin asked. "I'm starving."

"Yes, sir. We have our famous Saddle and Spur Tavern just behind you to your right."

While we were getting our keys, Scott took out his cell phone to make a call. I glanced over at him. He looked as frightened as if he

had seen a ghost. He hung up his phone, shaking his head. "I can't believe it."

We all turned to him.

"What?" I asked.

"The plane is gone."

"What do you mean *gone*?" Zeus said.

"Boyd flew out the same night we landed."

"Why would he do that?" Tessa asked.

"There's no reason. . . ." He stopped, the look of concern evident on his face. "There's no *good* reason."

"Could he have been working with the Elgen?" Zeus asked.

"I've known him since he was nineteen. He wouldn't leave without us unless"—he closed his eyes—"something bad happened."

Taylor looked at Scott. "What do we do now?"

"I need to go over to the airport and see if anyone knows what's going on," Scott said. "Ian, could you give me a hand?"

"No worries."

"And, Tessa, we could use some amplification powers."

"Yeah, I'm down."

"I'll go too," Zeus said, taking Tessa's hand. "In case we need some firepower."

"We should all go," I said.

"No," Scott said. "I think it's best we not keep all our eggs in one basket. I'll take Ian, Tessa, and Zeus. Michael, I want you to keep everyone else together."

"How long will you be?" I asked.

"It's only twenty minutes from here, so no more than two hours. If you haven't heard from us by then, you'll know something's wrong."

"All right, we'll stay together until we hear from you," I said. "Call our room if you have news."

"Which room will you be in?" Scott asked.

"The haunted one," Nichelle said.

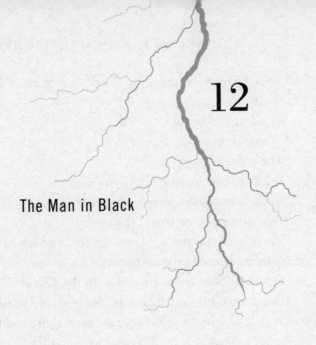

12

The Man in Black

After Scott left with Ian, Zeus, and Tessa, the rest of us followed Ostin over to the hotel restaurant, the Saddle and Spur Tavern. The restaurant appeared to have been newly renovated, and the textured plaster walls were painted pale yellow and decorated with the markings of dozens of different cattle brands. The floor was made from stained, dark wood planks, and against the main wall there was a long bar with chrome-and-black-vinyl barstools. On the opposite side of the room was a brightly lit jukebox.

We pushed two tables together and sat down. Less than a minute later a waitress walked out to us.

"Hi, y'all. I'm Carla. How are you youngsters tonight?"

"Fine, thank you," Taylor said for all of us. I don't know how long it had been since anyone had called me a youngster.

"You must be headed to Mexico on vacation."

"We just got back," Taylor said.

"Oh? What did you see?"

"Carnage," Ostin said.

McKenna gave him a scolding look.

"Mexicans," I said. "Mostly."

The waitress laughed. "I suppose you would."

"So is this place really haunted?" Nichelle asked.

"Sure is, honey."

"Have you seen a ghost?"

"Not the headless phantom you hear everyone talk about, but every now and then the electricity in here will go kind of haywire, blenders turning on, lights turning on and off, lights flickering."

"Sounds like bad electrical wiring," Ostin said.

"I thought you said you believe in ghosts," I said.

"I do. But I'm logical about it."

The woman grinned. "All the electrical was redone last January when we remodeled the dining room. A while back we had a ghost expert come through here. He was from one of those ghost hunter TV shows. He said that ghosts and poltergeists are really just electrical energy, so they're attracted to electricity. Some say they eat electricity."

"Great," I said. "That makes us a banquet."

Taylor playfully punched me on the arm.

"We're definitely going to see some ghosts tonight," Ostin said.

The woman looked at us with a quizzical expression, then said, "So, down to business. What can I get y'all to eat?"

"We all want lemonade," Taylor said.

"Except me," Ostin said. "I'll have a root beer."

"Six lemonades, one root beer."

". . . And throw in a couple of orders of these bacon-wrapped jalapeño poppers," Ostin said.

"All right. I'll get those going; then I'll be back to get the rest of your order." She walked away.

After she was gone, Nichelle said, "If ghosts are electric, I should be able to feel their presence. Maybe even affect them."

"That would be cool," Ostin said. "You could be like the ghost punisher."

"Can we stop talking about ghosts?" Taylor said. "It's creeping me out. And we already have enough to worry about."

"Yeah, like paying for dinner," I said, realizing I only had Taiwanese NT and pesos. "Does anyone have any American dollars?"

"I'm sure we can charge it to the room," Ostin said.

When our waitress returned, we ordered bean-and-cheese burritos, a taco salad, beef tacos, and chicken fried steak. After we finished eating, I said, "We better go up to the room, in case Scott calls."

"I'm going to stop at the front desk and see if they'll let me borrow their ghost binder," Ostin said.

"I want to read that too," Nichelle said.

We charged our meals to the room, then stopped at the front desk. The clerk let Ostin sign out the ghost book, and he took it with him as we went to the third floor, room 333. The room was at the end of a long corridor, lit eerily by green lights.

"Look," Taylor said when we reached the room. The door had been painted dark green, and people had scratched names and messages into the door. Someone had scratched a 666, and someone had crossed it out and scratched the word "JESUS" above it with a cross.

The hotel's "historic rooms" were a sharp contrast to the splendor of the lobby.

"This looks like my old room in Pasadena," Nichelle said, looking around.

"They must not have gotten around to remodeling this part of the hotel," Taylor said.

"They did," Ostin said. "It was just sixty years ago."

"It's just one night," I said. "It still beats camping in the jungle."

While Ostin, Taylor, McKenna, Abigail, Jack, and Nichelle looked over the ghost book, I lay down to take a quick nap. I must have been more tired than I realized, because just a few minutes later I fell asleep. When I woke, Taylor was sitting next to me on the bed.

"How long have I been asleep?" I asked.

"About an hour."

I looked at my watch. "Has Scott called?"

"No."

"How long has it been?" McKenna asked.

"Almost two and a half hours," Ostin said.

"He said two hours at the most," Nichelle said, looking up from the ghost binder.

"They'll call," Taylor said.

"What if he doesn't?" Nichelle asked.

I looked over at Jack, who also looked concerned. I was really blinking. "Well, there's not much we can do this late at night," I said. "We don't even have a car."

"I can hot-wire a car," Jack said.

"And go where?" Taylor asked.

"The closest big city is Tucson," Ostin said. "It's about a hundred miles north of here. We should go there."

I thought for a second, then said, "If we haven't heard from Scott by four a.m., we'll find a car and drive to Tucson. In the meantime we stay together in the same room. And everyone should try to get some sleep. It might be a while before we get the chance again. I'll keep watch."

"I'll keep watch with you," Taylor said. "I'm not that tired." She yawned almost immediately after saying that.

While everyone else slept, Taylor and I sat on the burgundy shag carpet next to the door, listening for sounds from the hallway. It was quiet until a little after one in the morning, when there was a sudden rush of footsteps. At first I thought we were under attack by an Elgen patrol, but as I looked out the peephole, it was just a bunch of college kids who had probably come down to the border for a wild weekend.

About a half hour later Taylor fell asleep. I lay back against the door trying to keep my eyes open. Fortunately I had a lot to think about. And I was ticking a lot, which always makes it harder to sleep. I thought about the ghost, too. If there were such a thing, I wondered if I could shock it. Or scare it. *Do ghosts get scared?*

Around two thirty in the morning the radiator began making a

strange knocking sound in a distinct pattern, almost like someone was tapping out a code on it. I wished that Ostin were awake to decipher it. I was intrigued, but it didn't frighten me. I was more afraid of what I knew existed in the world than something that I couldn't see. *Why hadn't Scott called? What could have happened to them?*

I must have fallen asleep a little after that, because I woke with a start. I was lying with my face next to the door, and I could hear slow, heavy footsteps in the hallway. I heard them go up and down the corridor, finally stopping near us. I quietly stood and looked out the peephole. There was a man dressed in black standing two doors down on the other side of the hallway in front of Ostin's and my room.

I watched him for a moment, then carefully woke Taylor, holding my hand over her mouth to keep her from making a sound. She looked at me with a confused expression. "Someone's out there," I whispered. "Wake Jack."

Taylor crawled over to the bed and gently shook Jack.

"Wha . . ."

She put her hand over his mouth. "Shhh. There's someone outside."

The man tried the door handle again; then he took something out of his pocket, slid it into the door lock, turned the handle, and went inside.

"He picked the lock," I whispered. "He's inside my room."

While Taylor woke everyone else, Jack went into the bathroom. He came out wielding the towel bar like a club in one hand. Everyone else gathered around the door.

"Now he's going into the room across from us," I said.

"My room," Jack said.

"Is he Elgen?" Ostin asked.

"I can't tell. He's wearing all black and a face mask. I think he has a gun."

"You can see a gun?" Jack asked.

"No, he's wearing a vest. But it has a bulge."

"I wish Ian were here," Taylor said.

"I wish they were all here," I said.

"How many are there?" Jack asked.

"Just one," I said. "That I can see. But if he's Elgen, you know he has backup."

"This is like Taiwan all over again," McKenna said.

"Except this time we're only on the fourth floor," Ostin said. He walked over to the window and looked out. "There's a roof about fifteen feet down, then another about the same. We can tie bedsheets together and climb down."

"Good idea," I said.

"What's the plan?" Jack asked.

"When he touches the doorknob, Michael can shock him," Taylor said. "Then we escape."

"Bad idea," Ostin said. "If he has backup, they'll know we're here and storm our room."

I thought for a moment. "He's going into the rooms alone," I said softly. "I say we let him in. If it's just him, we can take him. If he's here with backup, we need to make them think everything's okay until we have time to escape." I turned back. "Ostin, Abi, McKenna, and Nichelle, you guys take the sheets into the bathroom and tie them into a rope.

"When he gets to this room, we'll let him enter. Then, once he's inside, Taylor reboots him, Jack tackles him to the ground, and I'll shock him unconscious. Then I'll lock the door while Jack disarms him and ties him up.

"Then we'll lock him in the bathroom and climb out the window." I looked at Jack. "What do you think?"

"I think it's a good plan," Jack said. "As long as they're not waiting for us outside."

"Can you take him down with your broken ribs?" I asked.

"What ribs?" he replied.

"All right," I said. "Let's do this."

Ostin and the three girls pulled the sheets from the beds, then took them into the bathroom to make a rope while I looked out the door's peephole. Jack crouched down behind Taylor.

"You should put some pillows down so when he hits the floor, it's not so loud," Taylor said.

Jack frowned. "You're right."

"What, you don't like that?"

"I was just looking forward to body slamming an Elgen guard onto the floor," Jack said.

Taylor put her hand on my back so she could read my mind and see what I was seeing. A minute later the man came out of the room across from us. Then he turned and looked at our door.

He's coming, I thought.

Taylor leaned back and whispered into Jack's ear.

The man touched our doorknob; then I heard something metallic slide inside the lock. I glanced over at Taylor, who had moved to my left side so the man wouldn't see her before he entered.

Don't reboot him until he's inside the room, I thought.

Taylor nodded.

The lock clicked. The doorknob slowly turned; then the door began to open. The man was halfway inside the room before he saw Taylor and me crouched down behind the door.

Now, I thought.

Taylor bowed her head. The man froze with confusion. Jack grabbed him by the front of his shirt, then pulled him forward, slamming him face-forward to the ground. I pushed the door shut with my foot as I grabbed the man's leg and pulsed. His body went limp.

Jack pulled the man's gun from its holster, pinning the man down with his knee in the small of his back. "We got him."

"Ostin, let's get out of here," I said.

"Still working on it," he said.

"Work faster," I said. "Taylor, open the window."

Taylor tried to open the window but couldn't. It had been painted shut.

"You better help her," I said to Jack, keeping my hand on the prone man. "Ostin, hurry!"

Jack got up and, after several attempts, pushed the window open. Then Ostin and the others came out of the bathroom carrying their makeshift rope. Ostin tied one end of the sheets around the radiator, then threw the opposite end out the window.

"You sure those knots are tight?" Jack asked.

Ostin nodded. "It will hold. I'd bet my life on it."

"Good," he said, turning back. "Because you're going first."

Jack came back over and put his knee into the small of our prisoner's back. The man was wearing cargo pants and a black, long-sleeve shirt, but nothing with the Elgen insignia. He also wore a knit mask with slits for eyes.

"I want to see this guy's face," I said to Jack. "Let's roll him over."

We rolled the unconscious man to his back; then Jack pulled off his mask.

Taylor gasped.

"I don't believe it," Jack said.

"Better hold up," I said to Ostin, who was nervously straddling the windowsill, about to climb out.

"What?" He looked back at the man. "Do you know who it is?"

"Yes," I said. "Let's lift him onto the bed."

"You know this guy?" Nichelle asked.

"His name is Gervaso. And he's not supposed to be alive."

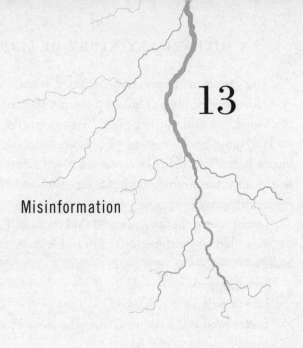

13

Misinformation

McKenna turned the room light on while Jack and I lifted Gervaso up onto one of the beds. Jack checked him again for weapons and this time found a Special Ops knife in a sheath strapped to his right shin. Jack unstrapped the sheath and slid it into his own belt while everyone else gathered around the bed.

"How do you know him?" Nichelle asked.

"He was our trainer from the resistance," McKenna said.

"Then he's a good guy?"

"He was," Ostin said. "We don't know what he's doing here. Or why he's alive and everyone else is dead."

"Maybe he betrayed the others," Nichelle said.

"He wouldn't betray them," Jack said. "He was awarded the Distinguished Service Cross. He's above reproach."

"Then why did you just take his weapons?" Nichelle asked.

Jack looked a little awkward. "Better safe than sorry," he said.

"Taylor, keep your hand on him. When he comes to, I want to interrogate him," I said.

Gervaso was out for only a couple of more minutes before he began to stir. As soon as he came to, he instinctively went for his gun, and froze when he saw Jack pointing it at him.

"Just stay still," Jack said. "Don't try anything."

Gervaso looked back and forth between us, his eyes stopping on me. "Michael, it's me, Gervaso."

"We thought you were dead," I said.

"Do I look dead?" He stared at me. "What happened to your arms?"

"Just answer the question," Jack said. "Why are you still alive?"

"Because I didn't die," he said. Then he slightly grinned. "Well, at least not yet." He said to Jack, "You can put my gun down. I came here to rescue you."

Jack looked over at me, and I nodded. He lowered the weapon.

"Where are Scott and the others?" Taylor asked.

"They're safe. This town is crawling with Elgen informants. That's why I came back alone. We need to get you out of here." He sat up. "You don't need to keep touching me, Taylor. You know I'm not lying."

Taylor looked a little embarrassed as she removed her hand. "He's telling the truth," she said to me.

"What's going on?" I asked.

"Are my parents dead?" Ostin asked.

Gervaso looked at him. "No," he said.

"But we saw the ranch," I said.

"We knew the Elgen were coming. We evacuated before they came."

"My mother's alive?" I asked.

"Everyone is safe. Your mother"—he turned to Ostin—"your parents, the council."

I put my hand over my eyes, overcome with relief. "She's okay."

Taylor took my hand. "I knew there was hope."

When I looked up, Ostin's eyes were filled with tears. He furtively brushed them away. McKenna put her arms around him.

"Dude, it's okay," Jack said. "Even warriors cry."

Ostin just nodded.

"I don't get it," Jack said to Gervaso. "If you knew the Elgen were coming, why didn't you ambush them?"

"There's brave courageous; then there's brave *stupid*," Gervaso said, looking at Jack. "You know what I mean?"

Jack nodded. "Yeah, I get it."

"Even with the intelligence we had, the Elgen still have a lot more firepower at their disposal than we do. They also have an army, which we don't. But even if we had somehow defeated them, there would have been lives lost. And, as far as I'm concerned, we don't have any to spare." He looked at me. "Would you agree?"

"Yes, sir," I said.

"I thought so," he said. "But that's just one of the reasons we didn't attack. The main reason was that fighting back wasn't our strategy. We want them to think we've been destroyed."

"If no one was at the ranch," Ostin said, "how did we bring down one of their helicopters? We saw it."

Gervaso smiled. "That was pretty good, wasn't it? Remember the robotic sentry system we used in Peru? Same thing. I also fired up our helicopter from here in Douglas. We gambled that they'd never put boots on the ground, so I created just enough action for them to believe we'd been caught unprepared."

"Smart," Ostin said. "Very smart."

"So what about the Elgen guard we found?" Jack said. "What do we do with him?"

"Scott briefed me about him," Gervaso said. "He provides us with an interesting opportunity. And risk. The Elgen don't know that he's still alive, and from what I've been told, he's bitter enough to tell us everything he knows. I don't blame him. The Elgen not only abandoned him; they dropped napalm on him and his buddies.

"Fortunately, his uniform was mostly burned off. Otherwise word

of his survival might have already gotten back to the Elgen, but that doesn't mean we're safe. Every Elgen guard is implanted with an RFID—radio-frequency identification—so he can still be traced. Probably the only reason they haven't already found him is that they aren't looking.

"In the morning, a doctor we know will be removing the RFID device. Then I'll be less worried. In the meantime, he's in serious condition. It will be weeks before he'll be stable enough to move."

"I still don't get it," Taylor said. "Why did the voice tell us there were no survivors at the ranch?"

"Because there weren't," Gervaso said. "Everyone was gone."

"Why didn't they just tell us that in the first place?" she asked. "Don't they care how we suffered?"

"I know it must have been awful for you," Gervaso said. "To think your parents and friends were dead. But we sacrificed our main headquarters just so the Elgen would believe we were wiped out. All we needed was one intercepted message for that sacrifice to have been in vain. The greater good dictated that we employ *misinformation*."

"That's a military way of saying 'lie,'" Ostin said.

"He's right," I said. "They did the right thing."

"So where is everyone?" Ostin asked. "Where are my parents?"

"Until we're out of danger, it's best that you don't know. But they're safe, and you'll see them soon enough. Let's leave it at that."

"So now what?" I asked. "Is our plane really gone?"

Gervaso nodded. "It wouldn't have been difficult for the Elgen to track down our plane, so we had Boyd fly it out shortly after you landed. We tried to stop you from going to Mexico, but we were two hours too late."

"What do you think we should do?" I asked.

"We're going to drive to Tucson, then wait for directions from the voice on where we need to go. There are a lot of pieces in play right now. We need to see our opponents' next move."

"What do you mean by that?" I asked.

"You saved Jade Dragon and escaped. Hatch isn't going to be very happy about that. And when Hatch is unhappy, heads roll.

The question is, whose heads and how high up are they? If we can get some high-level defections, it could turn the tide against him. Hatch's electric youths were in charge of guarding you. It will be interesting to see if he holds them responsible."

"Hatch isn't afraid to punish his kids," Nichelle said.

Gervaso looked over at Nichelle, suddenly realizing who she was. "You're Nichelle, aren't you?"

"Yeah, that's me."

"Hatch's favorite torture device."

"Yeah, that's also me," she said. "Or was."

"So you know, Hatch has imprisoned and tortured his own, but he's never executed one of them. But his kids are getting older now, and it's only a matter of time before one of them rebels. Of course if they turn against Hatch, it could be good or bad for us, depending on what they want.

"But there's even more in play. The Elgen still need a land base to carry out their plans of global domination. They've recently purchased two new warships that are, right now, sailing to Tuvalu, as are the *Faraday* and the rest of the Elgen fleet. It looks like Hatch is going to finish what he started."

"They're going to declare war on Tuvalu?" Ostin asked.

Gervaso frowned. "I wouldn't call it a *war*. The people of Tuvalu have no army and no weapons. It's going to be a complete surrender or a complete slaughter." He looked back at me. "So, if it's okay with you, it's time we got out of here. I've got a van parked out back."

"Of course," I said.

Gervaso stood. "May I have my weapons back?" he asked Jack.

"Sure." Jack handed him back his gun.

"And my knife?"

Jack smiled somewhat guiltily as he produced the knife, still admiring its blade. "I was hoping you wouldn't miss it."

Gervaso looked at him for a moment, then said, "All right. You keep it."

"Really?" Jack asked.

Gervaso nodded. "You pinned me. No one's ever pinned me before. You should get some prize."

"Thank you," Jack said. "This is the best gift I've ever been given."

"You earned it," Gervaso said. He turned back to me. "By the way, congratulations on your success in Taiwan. I knew you could do it."

"It was close," I said. "Hatch almost had us."

Gervaso nodded again. "Yes, but fortunately you're on the right side of 'almost.'"

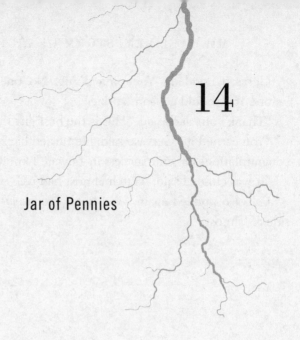

14

Jar of Pennies

We followed Gervaso down the stairwell to the main floor, then crept out the back doors of the hotel to where he had parked his van. It was still dark as we drove off.

The drive to Tucson was just a little over two hours, though I slept for most of it, waking just as we reached the city limits. I had fallen asleep in the backseat of the van, lying against Taylor. As I sat up, she combed my hair back from my face with her fingers. "Your hair is getting long."

"Not a lot of time for haircuts," I said.

"Too busy saving the world," she said.

I sighed. "Yeah."

We both looked out over the desert terrain and the approaching skyline. "That must be Tucson," I said.

"The Old Pueblo," Ostin said.

"The what?" McKenna asked sleepily.

"Old Pueblo. That's Tucson's nickname."

"What's a pueblo?" McKenna asked. "A Mexican city?"

"No," Ostin said. "It's an American Indian settlement."

"It looks Mexican to me," she said.

"'Old Pueblo' is a lame nickname," Nichelle said.

"You think that's bad," Ostin said, "in the eighties the local newspaper ran a contest for a new nickname. The winner was 'Tucson: The Sunshine Factory.'"

"That's even more lame than 'Old Pueblo,'" Jack said from the front. "Sounds like a kids' cartoon."

"Yeah," Ostin said. "It never caught on."

"How does he know all this stuff?" Taylor asked. "His brain is like Google."

"He should be on a game show," Nichelle said. "He'd win like a billion dollars."

"Then the Elgen would find him and kill him," Taylor said.

"Yeah, that too," Nichelle said. "But at least he'd die rich."

The sun was rising above the eastern horizon as Gervaso drove past a rectangular freeway sign that read WELCOME TO TUCSON.

"What's the plan?" I asked Gervaso.

"I think everyone's pretty tired, so first we'll stop at a hotel and get some rest. Then we'll see from there."

"I've got to walk around today," McKenna said. "After all this travel I'm going stir-crazy. If the Elgen don't kill me, I'll die of boredom."

"Too much talk of death," Taylor said. "It must be on our minds."

"It's always on our minds," I said.

"Can we stop and get some bagels?" Abigail asked. "Before I die of hunger?"

"More death," Taylor said softly.

"No problem," Gervaso said. "I'm sure you're all hungry."

"Isn't there a university in Tucson?" Taylor asked.

"The University of Arizona," Ostin said. "The Wildcats."

"We could hang out on campus," I said.

"That's a good idea," Gervaso said. "You'll blend in."

"It's like that thing Ostin always says," Jack said. "'The best place to hide a penny is in a jar of pennies.'"

"I said it *once*," Ostin said.

"When are we going to meet up with Ian and the others?" I asked.

"Not for a few days," Gervaso said. "They're not in Arizona."

"Where are they?"

"Someplace safe," he said. "Someplace no one will find them."

"New York?"

"No," he said. "Utah."

We stopped for breakfast at a local bagel shop called the Bodacious Bagel. The place was crowded with college students. Even though a few of us looked a little young, Gervaso was right, we blended in. Afterward we drove toward the university looking for a hotel. We didn't have to go far.

"This looks right," Gervaso said, pulling off the busy street into the hotel's driveway. The University Inn. He parked the van in front of the lobby doors, and we all got out. Gervaso opened the back of the van, then walked inside the hotel.

As Jack threw us our bags, Taylor said, "Oh, gross."

"What?" I asked.

"I think I got Elgen *guard* on my bag."

There was a dark brown-and-white stain on the side of her canvas bag. "Is that . . . pus?"

"I'm going to throw up," McKenna said.

"I just threw up in my mouth," Taylor said.

A few minutes later Gervaso walked out of the hotel. "We're set. Everyone, two in a room. Jack, would you mind rooming with me?"

"It would be my honor," Jack said.

As Gervaso handed out room keys, he said, "Everyone, let me know if you go anywhere. I'm in room 211."

"You can share a room with me, Nichelle," Abigail said. Hearing this made me happy. I had really come to like Nichelle and her dry, self-deprecating sense of humor. I was glad Abigail had forgiven her, or was, at least, trying to.

"What do you want to do?" Taylor asked.

"Sleep," I said.

"Me too," she said. "I'll see you in a couple of hours."

When I got to my room, I was more tired than I'd realized. It seemed like I always was these days. I lay down on top of the sheets and hadn't even gotten my shoes off before I fell asleep. Four hours later I was awakened by Ostin.

"Hey, we're burning daylight. Let's go do something."

I sat up, rubbing my eyes. McKenna was in our room, standing slightly behind Ostin.

"McKenna wants to walk over to the university," Ostin said. "Then get some pizza."

"Where's Taylor?" I asked.

"She's still getting ready," McKenna said. "She just got out of the shower. She'll be here in a minute."

"Is anyone else coming?" I asked.

"I don't know," Ostin said. "Jack left with Abi about an hour ago."

"What about Nichelle?"

"I haven't seen her," McKenna said. "She's probably just in her room."

"Ask her if she wants to come with us," I said.

"Okay," she said. "I'll be right back." She walked out of the room.

While McKenna was checking on Nichelle, I called Gervaso's room. He answered immediately.

"Gervaso."

"Hi, it's Michael. We're walking over to the university."

"Who's we?"

"Me, Taylor, Ostin, and McKenna. Maybe Nichelle."

"All right. Just report by twenty hundred hours."

"When?"

"Eight p.m.," he said.

"Sure," I replied.

A few minutes later Taylor came up to my room, followed by McKenna and Nichelle. The University of Arizona was less than a mile from our hotel. The weather was scorching, with a dry breeze and a few puffy clouds in the sun-bleached sky.

In the center of the campus was a large, grass mall lined with tall palm trees on both sides. There were students everywhere, and it felt good to be out in the open without worrying that someone might be watching us.

Taylor took my hand. "Wouldn't it be nice to actually be here, going to school, our biggest worry in the world our next midterm?"

I nodded. "Unless you're Ostin. Midterms are like Christmas morning."

"Christmas?" he said. "No, that would be finals."

I squeezed Taylor's hand. "Yes, it would be nice."

As we walked toward the union building, we passed two hipsters with hair even longer than mine. One had muttonchop sideburns and a beret, and both of them had multiple tattoos. They were both a few years older than me. They were staring at me *and* Nichelle. One of them was sitting on the concrete rim of a trash receptacle, and the other was leaning against it. As we neared them, the guy sitting on the garbage said to me, "Hey, lightning dude."

I looked at him. "What did you call me?"

He raised his hands as if in surrender. "No worries, bro. I called you 'lightning dude.'" He pointed at my arms. "In reference to your awesome tat."

"Yeah," his friend said. "*Killer* tat. And yours," he said, turning to Nichelle.

"They mean our 'tattoos,'" Nichelle said.

"Yeah, I got that," I said.

"Where'd you get inked?" the second guy asked.

I hesitated. "Mexico."

"Agua Prieta?"

I had no idea what he was saying. "What?"

"Yeah," Ostin said. "Agua Prieta."

"Lucky's Tattoos," the first said. "Lucky did this one." He pulled his sleeve up over his upper arm, revealing two Chinese characters. "Cool, right? But he never showed me that design you're styling. I've been thinking of getting a sleeve like that. Next time I'm gonna have to get me one of those."

"Yeah, do that," I said.

"You guys want . . ." The guy stopped midsentence. He looked at his buddy. "What were you saying?"

"What were *you* saying?"

"I wasn't saying anything."

"What are you talking about, dude?"

"Bye," Taylor said.

As we walked away, I said to Taylor, "Did you do that?"

"Yeah. I couldn't stand it anymore."

Ostin started laughing.

"What's so funny?" I asked.

"That tattoo that dude showed us."

"What's so funny about that?" Nichelle asked.

"The Chinese characters said 'pig face.'"

After walking the campus for a while, we stopped at a pizzeria named Magpies that was obviously very popular with students, as the line for a table was nearly to the door. It took us a half hour before we finally sat down and ordered our pizza.

Lined up across the front counter were a couple dozen bottles of assorted hot sauces.

"Look at these hot sauces," Taylor said. "Toxic Tick."

"I should get that," I said. "I tic."

"I think it's the bug tick, not the Tourette's tic," Ostin said.

"Look at this," McKenna said. "It's just called Hell."

"Wait, this one's Hotter Than Hell," Nichelle said.

"I just beat you all," Taylor said, holding up a bottle. "Scorned Woman." She looked at me. "Hell hath no fury like a woman scorned."

"You win," I said.

"No," Ostin said. "McKenna wins. She's hotter than all of them. Literally. And figuratively."

Taylor and I looked at each other.

"Did Ostin really just say that?" she whispered.

I nodded. "He did."

"Well played," she said. "Surprisingly well played."

Fifteen minutes later our waitress brought out our meal—two medium pizzas, one cheese and sausage, the other, the Whole Bird, was loaded with about everything on the menu. We also got an order of garlic bread and a large tossed salad with ranch dressing.

It was late, almost eight o'clock when we finally all met back at the hotel. Jack and Abigail were alone swimming in the hotel pool, and they waved us over.

"Hey, guys. Where have you been?" Abigail asked.

"We walked over to campus, hung out," Ostin said, trying to sound cool.

"How was it?" she asked.

"We had some good pizza," Taylor said.

"You can always find good pizza near a college," Abigail said.

"Yo, Michael," Jack said. "Gervaso said to call him when you got here. There's a phone in the lobby."

"What room is he in again?"

"My room—211."

I walked across the parking lot to the front office and called. Gervaso answered after just one ring. "Hello."

"It's Michael. We're back."

"All of you?"

"Yeah."

"Where are you?"

"We're by the pool with Jack and Abi."

"I'll be right down."

A few seconds later Gervaso came down the outside stairs and crossed the parking lot to the pool. He looked around to make sure we were alone, then said, "I've heard from the voice. The Elgen are on the move. They're about to launch their attack on Tuvalu."

I shook my head. We had almost died trying to stop them. For nothing.

"Can't we warn the people there?" Taylor asked.

Gervaso shook his head angrily. "We've already warned them. You risked your lives by sinking the *Ampere* and bought them the time

they needed to react. They chose to disregard the threat, so now they'll have to suffer the consequences."

"There must be something we can do," Taylor said.

"We've sent messages to the CIA, Britain's MI6, and the United Nations. Beyond that, our hands are tied."

"So now what?" I asked.

"The voice wants us to rendezvous at our secondary headquarters. Christmas Ranch."

Taylor cocked her head. "Where's Christmas Ranch?"

"It's in southern Utah near Zion National Park," Gervaso said. "That's where everyone's gathered. Ian, Zeus, and Tessa arrived there this afternoon."

I was glad to hear they were safe. "How long will it take to get there?"

"Las Vegas is about six hours from here. From Vegas it's about a two-and-a-half-hour drive north."

"I've always wanted to see Las Vegas," Abigail said.

"I've seen it," Nichelle said. "That's where I got my nose and ear pierced. The first time."

"We're not going to have time to play," Gervaso said. "We're just driving through. If we leave early and don't make too many stops, we should reach the ranch by early afternoon."

"What time do we need to leave?" I asked.

"We should leave here by six thirty. We'll stop in Phoenix for breakfast. Everyone good with that?"

"We're good," I said.

"All right. Get some sleep. You all look like you're sleep deprived."

"Yeah, I wonder why," Jack said.

Gervaso walked back up to his room. After he was gone, I asked Taylor, "Do you want to swim?"

"No," she said. "I don't have anything to swim in."

Neither did I for that matter. I turned back to Jack and Abigail. "Where did you guys get your swimsuits?"

"The hotel lost and found," Abigail said. "They let me take one."

"That's resourceful," Nichelle said. "Kind of gross, but resourceful."

"What about you?" I asked Jack.

"I'm just wearing my boxers."

"You're in your underwear?" Taylor asked.

Jack smiled. "It's all cloth, man."

"All right," I said. "Good night. See you bright and early."

We went back to our rooms and slept.

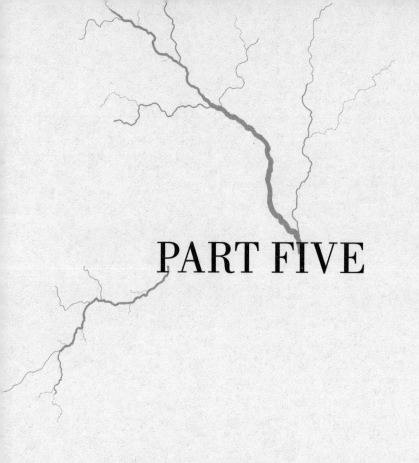

PART FIVE

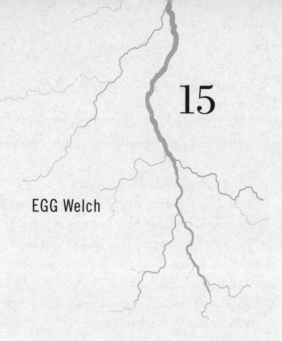

15

EGG Welch

Lido Deck of the ES *Faraday*
Kaohsiung Port, Taiwan

"**Y**ou're killing me," Tara said.

"No I'm not," Quentin said, looking over the chessboard between them. He had already captured more than half of Tara's pieces. "I'm just slowly torturing you."

For the last half hour they had been playing chess in the game room of the *Faraday*'s Lido Deck. The remaining three of Hatch's Glows were also in the room. Kylee was reading a Hollywood gossip magazine, Torstyn was practicing throwing some Chinese stars he had just purchased at a night market in Kaohsiung, and Bryan, as usual, was playing a video game.

They had been back on the ship for only a few hours after spending the day cruising the malls in Kaohsiung. Admiral-General Hatch had informed them that later that night they were setting sail to Tuvalu and it would be a while before they saw civilization or any of its comforts. They did their best to stock up.

Tara groaned as Quentin took her second rook. "This is hopeless. I always lose."

"Life is a game of chess," Quentin said. "The pieces are always in motion. If you don't plan three to five moves ahead, you lose to the one who does."

"That's profound," Torstyn said.

"Dr. Hatch taught me that. Did you know that there are more than a trillion possible play options in the first ten moves of chess?"

"No wonder I suck," Tara said. "I can barely handle one move at a time."

"You should make yourself look like Bobby Fischer," Quentin said. "At least you'll look like you know what you're doing."

"Who's Bobby Fischer?" she asked.

"Don't worry about it," he said.

"I don't get why we had to be on the boat so early," Bryan said. "We don't leave until ten."

"It's wartime procedures. They can't be holding up an invasion because Kylee couldn't decide what color nail polish she wants on her toes."

"Thanks for making me the failure in your story," Kylee said.

"If the shoe fits," Bryan said.

"My shoe will fit up your butt," Kylee said. She set down her magazine. "I wish we didn't have to travel in this piece of crap. I miss the *Ampere*. If Vey were here, I'd slap him. Twice."

"If Vey were here, I'd *kill* him," Torstyn said.

"Good luck with that," Bryan said.

"Dr. Hatch told me that our new yacht is almost complete," Quentin said. "Then we'll finally be able to move out of this pigsty."

"They can build boats that fast?" Torstyn asked.

"No, fortunately, Schema had ordered it three years ago. Probably the only smart thing he's ever done."

"What's it going to be called?" Kylee asked.

"The *Westinghouse*," Quentin said.

Tara said, "I heard it's even nicer than the *Ampere*."

"Nicer. Faster. Stronger," Quentin said. "It has two heliports, double

the surface-to-air missiles, a surround sound theater. It even has a climbing wall and skateboard park."

"And it's not sitting at the bottom of the ocean," Bryan said without looking up from his video game. "That's a plus."

"I wish you were sitting at the bottom of the ocean," Kylee said.

"Is that where Dr. Hatch went?" Tara asked. "To pick it up?"

Quentin was still studying the board as he shook his head. "No. He flew to Jakarta to pick up a different boat. It's our new warship, the *Edison*. He'll meet us in Tuvalu." Quentin eyed Bryan severely. "Keep that to yourself; that's confidential information."

"Why did you only say that to me?" Bryan asked, raising his palms. "Besides, who would I tell? It's not like I know anyone besides you guys anyway."

"Don't tell *anyone*," Quentin said. "We don't need Vey and his terrorists blowing up another of our boats. He's taken out enough of them."

"Ha!" Tara laughed. "I just took your horse-guy."

"It's called a knight," Quentin said, moving his bishop. "And I just took your queen."

Tara groaned. "Why do I even play this with you?" Suddenly she turned into the president of the United States. "Because it's the prudent thing to do," she said in the president's voice.

Quentin grinned. "That's so cool."

"Hey, Tara, why don't you turn into Scarlett Johansson and we'll go out on a date?"

"Hey, Bryan," Tara said, "why don't I throw up in my mouth?"

"Idiot," Bryan said.

Torstyn laughed. "You had that coming, dude."

Bryan went back to his video game. A minute later he said, "Any of you hear about Welch?"

"*EGG* Welch," Quentin said, without looking up. "Show some respect. And what about him?"

As Hatch had turned over more responsibility to him, Quentin had become more concerned with protocol and order. But this was more than a formality. EGG Welch was one of Quentin's best friends. During Quentin's early years at the academy, Welch had taught him

to golf and ski and oftentimes took him hunting on weekends. Welch was the closest thing Quentin had to a father.

"Well, the *egg* is scrambled now," Bryan said, grinning.

"What are you talking about?" Quentin said, looking up from the chessboard.

"Dr. Hatch sent him to the brig. When we reach Tuvalu, he's going to be rat feed."

Quentin suddenly looked panicked. "Who told you that?"

"Everyone's talking about it."

"Did you hear that?" Quentin asked Torstyn.

"No."

"I heard it," Tara said. "So did Kylee."

"He's down in the brig," Kylee said. "I passed the guards escorting him.

For a moment Quentin was speechless. "Do you know why Dr. Hatch had him arrested?"

"I heard it was because of Vey's escape," Tara said. "And the Chinese girl."

"Glad it's not me," Bryan said.

Quentin looked even more upset. "Did it occur to any of you geniuses that Jade Dragon was *our* responsibility and that we might be next?"

Everyone stopped what they were doing.

"Dr. Hatch wouldn't do that," Kylee said, though the way she said it sounded more like a question than a statement.

"Why didn't someone tell me about Welch?" Quentin asked angrily.

"I just did," Bryan said.

"I'm sorry," Tara said. "I thought you already knew. You know everything."

"Apparently not," Quentin said, standing. "I'm going to my room." He stormed out.

"You idiot," Tara said to Bryan.

"Why am I an idiot?" Bryan said. "He said he wanted to know."

Torstyn stood up and walked out after Quentin, followed by Tara.

Kylee just looked at Bryan and shook her head. "Nicely done, moron."

"Shut up," he said.

A few minutes later Tara and Torstyn knocked on Quentin's door. "Q, it's me and Torstyn. Can we come in?"

"It's unlocked," Quentin said.

They stepped inside. Quentin was lying on his bed, looking up at the ceiling.

"What are you thinking?" Tara asked.

Quentin hesitated. He had often suspected that his room was bugged, and now, just to be safe, he pulsed hard before speaking. "I'm thinking Dr. Hatch might be planning on punishing us, too."

"Won't be the first time," Torstyn said.

"I mean mortally," Quentin said. "He might feed one of us to the rats. Just to send a message that no one's immune."

Torstyn blanched. "Let them try. I'll microwave them like popcorn."

"You don't think they'll be expecting that?" Quentin said. "They'll attack without warning. They'll shoot us with darts, put RESATs on us to drain our power, and drag us away."

"All of us?"

"No. Just one of us. To make an example. It's how Hatch works." He breathed out. "It's probably me. I'm the leader."

Torstyn looked at Tara, then back at Quentin. "Won't happen, bro. If he comes after you, we'll rescue you."

Quentin nodded. "Thanks. That's the way it's got to be. For all of us."

"Except Bryan," Tara said.

Quentin shook his head. "Even Bryan. If they can take any of us, they can take all of us."

"What about Welch?" Torstyn asked.

"I'm not going to let it happen to him, either. I need to talk to him."

"That's impossible," Tara said. "He's in the brig. You know no one's allowed down there except Dr. Hatch."

Quentin looked at Tara. "Then Dr. Hatch will need to visit him."

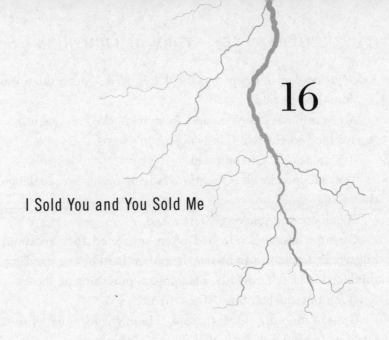

16

I Sold You and You Sold Me

The two Elgen guards stationed outside the brig's entrance stood at attention as Quentin, Torstyn, and Tara approached.

"Admiral-General, sir," they said in unison, sharply saluting. The guards didn't know it was Quentin they were saluting, as Tara was using her powers to make him appear as Hatch.

"Open the door," Quentin said.

"Yes, Admiral-General," the first guard said. He ran an electric key over the pad and the lock clicked. The other guard opened the door.

"Do not let me be disturbed," Quentin said. "Do you understand me?"

"Yes, Admiral-General."

"These are sensitive matters. Level C10. I want complete privacy. If I am disturbed, there will be consequences. Do you understand?"

"Yes, Admiral-General."

Quentin and Tara stepped in through the door, leaving Torstyn alone with the guards in the hallway. Tara pulled the door shut behind them. Before coming down to the cell, Quentin and Tara had gone up to the ship's bridge and taken out the brig cameras. Still, Quentin glanced up to the cameras again just to be sure they were dead. Then he looked at Welch sitting on the floor of the small cell. He had been there for less than twenty-four hours, yet he already looked haggard and defeated.

"Stand up!" Quentin shouted at Welch.

Welch quickly climbed to his feet. Like the guards outside the brig, he also believed Quentin was Dr. Hatch. "Jim," Welch said. "Can we talk about this?"

"Don't ever speak that name," Quentin said. "Jim Hatch no longer exists."

Welch lowered his head. "My apologies, Admiral-General," he said weakly. "Please don't do this."

"Quit sniveling," Quentin said. "It's unbecoming of an Elgen guard, especially an EGG."

"Yes, sir. I thought you had already left for Jakarta."

"My plans have temporarily changed," Quentin said, taking a few steps closer, his eyes locked on the prisoner. "Because of you."

Welch just stared at him.

"I'm in a quandary, Welch. A quandary. You were my first. My most trusted. You have been with me since the beginning."

"Yes, sir."

"Which is why you understand better than anyone else why mercy is not an acceptable strategy. To show mercy is to allow weakness. And to allow weakness is to promote more weakness. As soon as people think I'm getting soft, they'll start testing the waters. Then the trust of my army is like water in my hands." He took a deep breath. "But still . . . there might be a way around this."

"Sir?" Welch said.

"Don't get too excited," Quentin said. "It involves a choice on your part. Perhaps a difficult one."

"Please, sir. Whatever you ask."

"You were in charge of Operation Jade Dragon. But you were not alone in this assignment. You and the electric youths were in charge. And Quentin is in charge of the youths. For reasons I've already explained, I can't let this failure go without punishment. But the one I punish doesn't necessarily need to be you. So I came to ask you, EGG Welch. Should I feed Quentin to the rats instead of you?"

Welch stared at him. "I don't understand."

"This is not a difficult question," Quentin said. "It's you or Quentin."

Welch didn't answer.

Quentin continued. "On the way to your cell this evening, I realized that, in this circumstance, life is imitating art. You are familiar with George Orwell's book *1984*?"

"Of course, sir."

"Then you must see the irony of what is happening here. In the book we have Winston in room 101 facing his greatest fear—his primal fear of rats. Do you remember what he does to save himself?"

"Yes, sir."

"And what is that?"

Welch swallowed. "He betrays his love, Julia."

"Exactly," Quentin said. "'Do it to Julia,' he says. 'Do it to Julia.' Now here you are facing a nearly identical fate. The rat bowl. You and Quentin have always been close, haven't you?"

"Yes, sir."

Quentin moved closer to the bars. "So what is it, Welch? Who should I feed to the rats? You or Quentin?"

Welch gritted his teeth as he stared at the man he thought was Hatch, then he said forcefully, "It's my fault. I'm the only one to blame."

Quentin stared at him in disbelief. A weak, frightened part of him had hoped that Welch would betray him, as it would make his path easier, as crooked as that path might be. But deep down inside, in a part of his heart that had been kept shrouded for too long, he wanted his friend and mentor to be true. Welch was. Now the burden of action was back on his own shoulders. Quentin looked at

him for a moment, then said softly, "'Under the spreading chestnut tree, I sold you and you sold me . . .'" He looked back at Tara. "You can stop."

Tara released her power, and Quentin suddenly appeared to Welch as who he was. "You didn't betray me," Quentin said softly.

Welch looked at him in disbelief. "Quentin?"

"I came as soon as I found out."

Welch didn't speak for a moment, then he said, "Thank you. But I'm afraid that there's nothing that can be done. It's dangerous for you to even be here."

"There's always something that can be done," Quentin replied.

Welch looked up at the camera. "You need to go. You've already taken too great a risk. . . ."

"They can't see us," Tara said, furtively glancing at the dark security camera. "We took out the cameras before coming down."

"We're safe," Quentin said. "For a few more minutes. Tell me what you know about what Hatch plans to do to you and when."

"He plans to keep me locked up until we reach Tuvalu, then, after the revolution, send me to the bowl."

"That's not going to happen," Quentin said. "I won't let it."

"He won't change his mind," Welch said.

"Then we'll help you escape."

"You can't do that. He'll punish you instead."

"Then we'll come with you," Quentin said.

"It's no use. They'll find you. You've been implanted with tracking devices."

Tara looked at Quentin. Quentin had suspected as much, but it was frightening to hear it was true.

"We have tracking devices inside us?" Tara asked.

"You were implanted years ago," Welch said. "When they gave you your immunizations. They'll track you down in a matter of hours."

"Then we'll have to fight him," Quentin said.

"Fight Dr. Hatch?" Tara repeated as if Quentin had just blasphemed.

"Yes," Quentin said. "He's always talking about the extermination of the nonelectrics, but he's a Nonel. He's not one of us."

"I can't believe we're talking about this," Tara said.

"We knew it had to come to this someday," Quentin said. "We always knew."

"So did Hatch," Welch said. "He's always been paranoid, but he's especially afraid of you kids. He's like a man who has raised baby tigers knowing that they could turn on him when they grew up. He's talked to the EGGs for years about what would happen if any of you turned against him. He's prepared."

Quentin frowned. "Hopefully he won't be prepared for all of us." He looked into Welch's eyes. "What do you think we should do?"

Welch was quiet for a moment; then, in a rare show of emotion, his eyes welled up. "You should go back to your rooms before anyone finds out you've been here."

"But what about you?" Quentin asked.

"I knew the risks when I joined Hatch."

"That's not an option," Quentin said. "I refuse to accept that."

"As powerful as you are, you can't beat him," Welch said. "Even if I somehow escaped, the Elgen would hunt me down until they found me. They have the men, the money, and the power."

"Michael Vey has beaten Hatch," Quentin said. "Three times. I'm just as smart as he is. And Hatch doesn't know that we're not on his side. That gives us an advantage."

"Don't be too sure," Welch said. "Hatch knows that you and I are close. He's going to be watching how you deal with this."

"He must not be too suspicious," Tara said. "Or else he would have taken us with him. Or at least Quentin."

They were all quiet for a while; then finally Welch sighed. "No. No matter how you look at it, it's too big a risk. You need to get out of here."

Quentin shook his head. "It's already too late for that. The guards saw Hatch come in. They'll report that visit. Their superiors know that Hatch is gone. It won't take an Elgen scientist to figure out what really happened."

Tara turned white with fear. "You didn't tell me. . . ." She began to tremble. "He'll feed me to the rats." She grabbed Quentin's arms. "He'll feed all of us to the rats."

"No one's getting fed to the rats," Quentin said calmly. "At least not any of us." He turned back to Welch. "I need your help. You know Elgen protocol. What do we do to get you off the ship?"

Welch looked at him for a moment, then finally relented. "We need to get rid of the guards before they file their shift report."

"How do we do that?"

Welch thought about it for a moment, then said, "It might be easier than we think." He turned to Tara. "We'll just have Hatch give them a different order."

"To do what?" Tara asked.

"Have them transfer a Taiwanese prisoner off the ship." He looked at Tara. "You can make me Taiwanese?"

"I can make you a dolphin," she said.

"Taiwanese will do. Can you change more than one person at a time?"

"No. It takes too much focus. It would be like playing two different songs on the piano at the same time."

"All right. We'll just have to think around this." He looked down for a moment, then back up. "Okay, I know what we need to do."

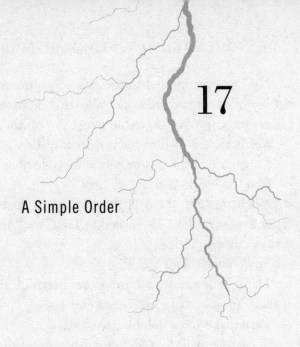

17

A Simple Order

The guards stood at attention as Quentin, still disguised as Hatch, walked out of the brig. Quentin nodded to Torstyn, then turned to the guards. "I have spoken with the Taiwanese government. They are ready to take Mr. Yin into custody. We will oblige them."

The guards glanced at each other. "Who, sir?" the first guard asked.

"Don't you even know who you're guarding?" Hatch bellowed. "Didn't you check your prison log?"

"My apologies, sir. I must have missed the name."

"Indeed. Tara will finish interrogating Mr. Yin; then you will escort him, unfettered, off this boat to the Taiwanese officials. They will be waiting for you on An Ping Road. Do you understand?"

"Yes, sir," the guards said simultaneously.

"An Ping Road. Do you think you can handle this?"

"Yes, sir. No problem, sir."

"I don't want to be bothered any more concerning this matter. I'm angry enough that we have to return this criminal. I'm going back to the bridge."

"What about EGG Welch?" the senior guard asked.

Quentin spun around. "What did you say?"

The guard cowered. ". . . EGG Welch. I was just wondering, who will . . ."

"Citizen Welch is no longer an EGG, and he will not be called one. The penalty for using that term for him is imprisonment. Do you understand me!"

"Yes, sir."

"Now, I gave you a simple order. If my orders are too difficult for you to follow, then perhaps your rank should be changed to something a little more basic, like GP."

Both men shuddered. "No, sir. We'll see that everything is done as requested."

Quentin looked back and forth between them. "We'll see. Tara will call for you when she is ready. This prisoner exchange is an embarrassment to me. I want you to take Mr. Yin out the back of the boat and avoid all guards. You must hurry; we are about to set sail. If you are asked what you are doing, you will tell them you are following specific orders from higher up. Do you understand me?"

"Yes, sir."

Quentin turned to Torstyn. "Torstyn, you and Tara will escort these men until they are off the *Faraday*; then you will report to me. You have ninety minutes before we set sail."

"Yes, sir," Torstyn said.

Quentin turned and walked away.

The guards looked at each other fearfully. Less than a minute later Tara called over the intercom, "We're ready. Open the door."

"Yes, ma'am," the senior guard said, unlocking the brig. The door opened, and Tara walked out ahead of a Taiwanese man. "Mr. Yin is ready to be escorted to the Taiwanese officials," Tara said.

"Yes, ma'am. Admiral-General Hatch has given us our orders."
They stepped to either side of their prisoner. "Let's go."

Torstyn fell in behind them.

Welch, of course, didn't speak. As they walked him out of the
brig, one of the guards stopped at a kiosk.

"What are you doing?" Tara asked.

"We're checking him out. It's required procedure."

Just then Quentin walked back, as himself, down the hallway. He
pulsed, killing the kiosk. "Did Admiral-General Hatch tell you to follow procedure, or did he tell you to avoid further embarrassment?"

The guards looked up at him. They were speechless.

"I just spoke with the admiral-general. He was not happy, and
he was very specific with his orders." Quentin lifted his cell phone.
"Shall I notify him that you think you know better?"

"No, sir," said the second guard. "We'll escort the prisoner immediately off the boat."

"I would recommend that. The Admiral-General mentioned something to me about a rank change."

"There's no need to threaten us, sir," the first guard said. "We will
follow orders."

The two guards took Welch by the arms and hurried him down
the corridor, while Tara, Quentin, and Torstyn followed from a distance. The guards led Welch to the second floor, where the staff was
completing the loading of food. When the group reached the loading
ramp, Quentin said, "Give me your weapons. You won't need them."
The men disarmed. To the guards' surprise, Quentin handed one of
the pistols to Welch.

"Be quick," Quentin said to the guards. "The Taiwanese officials
will meet you on An Ping Road near the front of the mall. That's two
miles due east. I recommend you take a cab."

"Yes, sir."

They hurried off. "How far can you hold the illusion?" Quentin
asked Tara.

"I'm not sure. No more than a few blocks."

"Won't they be surprised."

"What if they try to return him?"

"They won't. Welch is armed; they're not. And they just broke three Elgen protocols and are now guilty of aiding an Elgen fugitive. Discipline will be execution. I guarantee we won't ever see either of them again. At least not alive."

"What about EGG Welch?"

"I don't know," he said. "I don't know." He turned back. "Let's get back to our room before anyone discovers that the prisoner's missing."

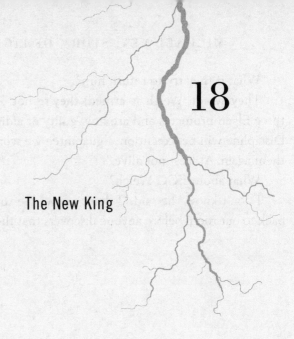

18

The New King

The *Faraday* set sail from Kaohsiung that evening a little after ten o'clock. The captain of the ship, Captain Bradshaw, set a course southeast to Tuvalu, through the Philippine Sea, and docked four days later in Papua New Guinea to join up with the other Elgen ships.

Three days later the two new Elgen ships, the *Franklin* and the *Edison*, arrived, completing the fleet. It would take just thirty-six more hours to reach Tuvalu.

The night before their final voyage to Tuvalu, Quentin was lying on his bed reading a book when someone rapped on his door. "Come in," he shouted.

Tara walked into his room. "Hey, Q."

"Hey," he said, looking up. "Where you been?"

"Just hanging out on top with Kylee. What are you reading?"

Quentin held up his book.

"*The Once and Future King*," Tara said, nodding. "Good book. Though, I disagree with the premise. Might *is* right."

Quentin looked at her quizzically. "So what's up? You look upset."

"Dr. Hatch is back."

Quentin was quiet a moment, then said, "Good. I heard he might be coming back tonight."

"He's already back on the ship. EGG Smythe said he wants to meet with you ASAP."

Quentin's brow furrowed. "Meet with me about what?"

"I'm not supposed to know this, but he said Welch's escape. I'm sure he wants to know if we had any involvement in it."

Quentin didn't flinch. "Why would he wonder that?"

"Why wouldn't he? Who else could have gotten him off the ship?"

"The guards helped him off."

Tara looked at him quizzically. "But what if he thinks you were involved? Welch was like a father to you."

"He *was* like a father," Quentin said. "But now he's a deserter and a traitor. No Elgen leaves their post without Admiral-General Hatch's permission. No one. Not even us. Friend or not, Welch knew the consequences when he made his decision. And anyone who helped Welch is a traitor and deserves the same punishment." Quentin went back to his book. "Don't worry. Dr. Hatch will find him. He'll find all of them. And we'll see them in the rat bowl."

"I'm so relieved to hear you say that," Tara said. She suddenly turned back toward the door. "All right. Let it go."

Quentin looked back up as Tara transformed into Dr. Hatch.

"I'm not Tara," Hatch said. "I'm sorry for the ruse. I just needed to be sure."

"Dr. Hatch," Quentin said, setting down his book and sitting up. He still looked puzzled. "Sure of what?"

"That you weren't involved in Welch's escape."

"You thought I would betray you?"

"I knew how close you were to Welch. I wanted to make sure your friendship hadn't clouded your judgment. Especially on the eve of battle."

"I know where I stand, sir."

"So you do." Hatch walked over to Quentin's wall and read a quote.

Mankind will only perish through eternal peace.
—Adolf Hitler

He smiled as he turned back. "So, matters at hand. The overthrow of Tuvalu will happen quickly. The Tuvalu defense, if you can 'call it that, will offer about as much resistance as a tree does to lightning. We will strike them hard and splinter them into shavings."

"How can I help, sir?"

"I want you to accompany the first squadron's landing on Funafuti. It is your mission to take out all possible communication devices in the area. Captain Steele has the coordinates; he and his men will lead the advance and protect you and the other youths."

"Yes, sir."

"You will take control of the Tuvalu radio station before they can broadcast an emergency message to the world. We are jamming frequencies from the plant, but there is still danger of word getting out. Take out their computers, but do not do too much damage to their broadcasting equipment. We will need to use the radio to broadcast the next morning."

"Yes, sir. I'll focus on tech wiring."

"Very good. By dawn our forces will have secured all communication and all weaponry, and crushed all rebellion, if there is any. Their tiny police force will be locked up in their own jails."

"You mentioned the other youths."

"Actually, just Bryan will be traveling with you. In the event that the radio operators try to lock you out, Bryan will cut through the locks."

"Yes, sir. What about Torstyn?"

"He and Tara will assist me inside the Starxource facility. We'll be flying out in the morning. Kylee will serve with the fourth division. Her gifts will be valuable in disarming their police force. Once you have taken the station, Captain Steele will cordon off the facility.

I want you and Bryan to maintain possession of the station until I arrive in the morning for the first broadcast."

"Yes, sir."

"There's another reason I want you at the radio station."

"What is that, sir?"

"I want to introduce the citizens of the Hatch Islands to their new king."

"You, sir?"

"No, *you*."

Quentin looked at him in surprise. "Me?"

"This is what I've been grooming you for since the beginning. Someday you will rule the world in my stead. I want you to begin your apprenticeship by overseeing this island nation. You will be the king of Tuvalu."

For a moment Quentin was speechless. "I don't know what to say. Thank you, sir."

"I'm pleased that I can count on you. You have no idea how pleased I am that you had nothing to do with this Welch business."

"Me too, sir. So, what do we know about Welch and the guards?"

"We're tracking their RFIDs right now. We've already found one of the guards."

Quentin hid his fear. "You have?"

"At least his body. It would appear that his companions turned on him."

"It's just a matter of time before we find the others, sir."

"Yes, it is. And you have my word, Welch will have company in the rat bowl."

19

The Puppet Dictator

Around one in the morning Tara snuck into Quentin's room. Quentin had been asleep for more than an hour. "Quentin." She knelt next to his bed and shook him. "Q."

Quentin's eyes opened. He jumped when he saw the shadow next to him. "It's just me. Tara."

"Tara," Quentin said, rubbing his eyes.

"How did it go with Dr. Hatch?"

Quentin just stared at her.

"Did it go all right?"

He hesitated a moment more, then asked, "What were we doing when Torstyn told us about Welch?"

"What?"

"You heard me. What were we doing?"

"We were playing chess. And it was Bryan who told us, not Torstyn."

Quentin breathed out. "It *is* you." He rolled away from her. "Now get out of here. I have nothing to say to you."

"Quentin."

"Leave. Now."

"Look, I don't blame you for being mad. But he made me do it. I had no choice."

Quentin rolled back over. "That could have been my death."

"No, I did it for us. If I had refused, he would have known we were involved. That includes you. Did you say anything in, incrim . . ."

"Incriminating," Quentin said. "No. I knew it was Hatch."

Tara looked both relieved and surprised. "How did you know?"

"He quoted from *The Once and Future King*. The day you read a book, let alone quote from it, is the day I eat it."

"So basically my illiteracy saved you," she said, trying to soften Quentin's anger.

"Your illiteracy saved *us*," Quentin said. "You would have been on the rat chute right next to me."

Tara swallowed. "It's a good thing he didn't go to Torstyn. He's not as smart as you."

"Did you tell Torstyn?"

"Yes. I told him that if anyone, including us, says anything to him about it, he knows nothing."

"Good," Quentin said. "We need to come up with a sign so that never happens again. A handshake or something."

"Torstyn and I leave in the morning," Tara said. "We're flying to the island."

"Yeah, Hatch told me. Did he tell you that he's making me the king of Tuvalu?"

"No. Congratulations, I guess. How does that make you feel?"

"Elagabalus was only fifteen when he became Roman emperor, and Ptolemy XIII was only twelve when he became Egypt's thirteenth pharaoh."

"I've never heard of either of them."

"Ptolemy was Cleopatra's brother."

"I've heard of Cleopatra."

"Unfortunately, things didn't work out for either of them. Elagabalus was assassinated when he was eighteen. And Ptolemy's forces were defeated by Caesar, and he drowned in the Nile while trying to escape."

"Then let's hope you have better luck," Tara said.

"You know I'm just a puppet dictator," Quentin said. "Dr. Hatch will still be in charge."

"I know. For now. But someday you will run all of this. And I'll be there with you." She leaned forward and they kissed. "I am loyal to you," she said. "Don't forget that."

"Thank you. Now you better go back to bed."

Tara stood. "All right." At the doorway she breathed out slowly. "If something had happened to you, I wouldn't have been able to live with myself."

Quentin looked at her for a moment, then said, "Come back."

She walked back over and knelt down next to the bed. "Yes?"

"I understand that you did what you had to do. I forgive you."

"Thank you."

He clasped her hand in a peculiar handshake, the middle and index finger out, the other two pointed in, like a gun. "That's our handshake. That's how I'll know it's really you and vice versa. Can you remember that?"

"Yes."

"Good. Because our lives may depend on it."

She nodded and stood.

"One more thing," he said.

"Yes?"

"I'm loyal to you, too."

Tara smiled, then turned and walked out of his room.

PART SIX

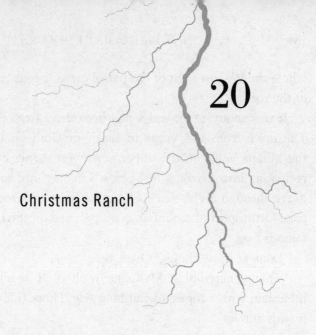

20

Christmas Ranch

Tucson, Arizona

We were on the move again. We left Tucson at six thirty, stopped a little after eight in Phoenix for breakfast, then continued on. Gervaso pushed the speed limit most of the way. He was eager to get us to the ranch. But, with the exception of Nichelle, who wanted to stop in Vegas to shop for some new clothes, we were all eager to get to the ranch too. We wanted to see our families and the rest of the Electroclan.

It seemed that the closer we got to the ranch, the more of a hurry Gervaso was in. A little past Kingman a highway patrol turned on its lights to pull us over, and Gervaso said to Taylor, "Can you take care of that?"

Taylor looked at the approaching police car nervously. "I'll try," she said. "I hope I don't make him crash."

"I can do it," Nichelle said. She looked back and extended her hand. Suddenly the flashing lights on the car's roof died, as did the

whole car. We lost sight of the patrol car as it coasted over to the side of the road.

It was about a four-and-a-half-hour drive from Phoenix to Vegas. The drive from Las Vegas to southern Utah on I-15 led through the Moapa Valley in the upper northwest corner of Nevada, briefly recrossing into Arizona. Just before crossing into southern Utah, we drove through a chiseled rock canyon that towered high above the pass. Ostin spotted mountain goats perched on the side of the mountainous crag.

"Look at those things," Ostin said.

"That's incredible," McKenna replied. "I wouldn't climb that mountain with a rope and climbing gear. Those things are walking on it with hooves."

"I wonder how many mountain goats fall," I said.

Everyone automatically turned to Ostin.

He shrugged. "Why would I know that?"

We drove through the borderline casino town of Mesquite before crossing over the Utah border. Then we continued on I-15 up to St. George, went about ten miles north, and turned off the highway, then headed east to the towns of Hurricane and Springdale, before entering Zion National Park. Our destination was just on the other side of the park, and the road through Zion was the shortest route. Peculiarly, something about the place seemed familiar. Like I'd been there before.

The place was crowded with tourists, and even though it was only twelve miles from the west gate to the east gate, it still took us about forty-five minutes to get across. Near the east end of the park our drive took us through a long, two-lane tunnel more than a mile long, carved through the mountain. The only lights in the tunnel were those from the headlamps of the cars in the opposite lane, so the whole way our van was brightly lit by our glows.

We passed through the east gate of the park and had continued on for about five miles when Gervaso slowed the van to turn north onto a dirt road. "This is the place," he said.

Not surprisingly, the entrance to Christmas Ranch was not obvious nor well marked, and if it weren't for a wood-post stop sign, you'd probably drive right past it. Just after turning off the freeway, Gervaso stopped the van and took a radio from beneath his seat. "This is Bauble Six, returning to tree."

"Roger, Bauble Six. Your ETA?"

"Ten minutes. We just pulled onto the road."

"We'll alert sentries. Welcome home."

Gervaso put the van in gear and started off again.

"Look at those," Ostin said, pointing out the window.

Outside there were two drones, one on each side of the van, hovering about fifty feet in the air, escorting us.

The road to the ranch was rutted dirt lined with cedar trees, twisted juniper, and small clumps of cacti and prickly pear. A deep, dry ravine ran along the road for much of the way, indicating that there had, at least once, been a lot of water in these parts.

As we made our way toward the compound, we passed several herds of cows and sheep. To our surprise we also saw several llamas. I hadn't seen a llama since Peru, and I felt an odd attachment to them.

"Lots of cows out here," McKenna said.

"Did you know that more people are killed each year by cows than sharks?" Ostin said.

"The Discovery Channel should change Shark Week to Cow Week," I said.

"Yeah, look at them out there," Jack said, grinning. "Plotting their next kill. Wild pack of killer cows."

"It's not a pack," Ostin said. "It's a herd."

"A what?"

"A *herd* of cows."

"Of course I've heard of cows," Jack said.

"No, a *herd*. A group of hoofed mammals that congregate together for—"

"Ostin," I said, stopping him. "He's just messing with you."

Ostin looked at Jack and stopped. "Oh."

"Killer cows," Jack said, shaking his head. "At least cows won't eat you. They don't even have sharp teeth."

"Neither do hippos," Ostin said. "But that doesn't stop them from killing more people than lions and crocodiles combined."

"Don't get him started on hippos," Taylor said. "I've heard this."

"Did you know hippos' mother's milk is pink?" Ostin said.

"I warned you," Taylor said, shaking her head.

"I really didn't want to know that," Jack said.

"What's with the llamas?" McKenna asked. "What are they doing here?"

"They're guard llamas," Ostin said. "Farmers use them to protect small sheep and chickens from coyotes and foxes. Llamas are aggressive animals and very territorial. Once they bond with a herd of animals, they get very upset when something comes near them."

"What do they do, spit on them?" Taylor asked.

"Exactly," Ostin said. "And scream at them."

"Llamas scream?" she asked.

"Yeah. It sounds like an amplified rusty hinge," Ostin said. "Or feedback on a microphone."

"That's just weird," Taylor said.

"Not as weird as pink milk," Nichelle said.

"I'd run from that," McKenna said.

"The llama scream or the pink hippo milk?" Taylor asked.

"Both."

"They're also good at kicking," Ostin continued. "They'll chase a coyote away from the herd and kick it. Some of them will even try to herd the animals together in a group to protect them."

"I didn't realize llamas were so smart," McKenna said.

"They are."

"Maybe Ostin's dad is part llama," Jack said.

Ostin frowned.

"That was a compliment," Jack said.

Ostin still didn't smile.

After several winding bends, Gervaso slowed to a stop in front of a large timber archway, then turned off the dirt road down into a

decline shrouded on both sides by towering cottonwood trees. The road was lined with a low barbwire fence held up by cedar posts. There was pasture on both sides of the road, with cows grazing beneath the shade of the cottonwoods.

"This is pretty," Taylor said.

"Welcome to Christmas Ranch," Gervaso said.

"It doesn't look as threatening as the last place."

"It doesn't need to be," Gervaso said. "We're in the U.S. But don't let it fool you. There are sentries and machine gun bunkers along the road, and missile launchers in silos. You just can't see them."

We drove past an orchard of apple trees next to a field of lavender. "It's nice. I could live here," Taylor said.

"For a long time," Gervaso said. "Just like our compound in Mexico, Christmas Ranch is completely self-sufficient and off the grid. We grow our own food, pump our own water, raise our own beef, and generate our own electricity. We even have beehives."

"I love fresh honeycomb," Taylor said. "With cheese. Especially with cheese."

"We make our own cheese as well," Gervaso added. "From goats and sheep. We keep busy."

"Do you have more llamas?" McKenna asked.

Gervaso smiled. "No. But we have around-the-clock snipers, so we don't worry about coyotes."

We stopped at a wooden gate that was reinforced with riveted steel plating. A man suddenly appeared. I have no idea where he came from. He wore a cowboy hat and boots. "Welcome back," he said. "You got them all?"

"Every last one of them," Gervaso said.

The man pushed a button, and the gate opened. "Go on ahead; everyone's waiting."

Gervaso drove ahead until the road curved left and turned to gravel, which crunched and spit out beneath our tires, pinging against the van's undercarriage. We climbed an incline for about a hundred yards past a large open aluminum-topped carport that was filled to the top with bundles of hay.

Then the road split into three different directions: left, straight ahead, and right. We took the right fork up a road lined by white vinyl horse fencing and columnar poplar trees nearly sixty feet tall.

The road opened up into a clearing with a large house and about a half dozen parked vehicles, mostly Jeeps and Hummers. To the left of us was a horse stable and corral, and to the right was a large tarp over a tractor. On the hill below that was an amphitheater with a large outdoor movie screen.

"I think I could live here," Taylor said again.

"It's beautiful," Gervaso said. "But it's not so great in the winter. We get a lot of snow. Enough to snow us in."

"I can do snow days," Taylor said, looking at me. "As long as I have someone to keep me warm."

Jack smiled at me and gave me a thumbs-up.

As we pulled up to the house, a group of people emerged from the front door onto the deck. Most of the people we'd seen before, but all I really cared about was seeing my mother and Ostin's parents. We didn't have to wait long.

Ostin's mother looked beside herself with joy. My own mother was, as usual, looking calm and happy. She was standing next to Joel.

Gervaso stopped the van. "Welcome home, Electroclan."

"Home sweet home," Taylor said. "Wherever that is these days."

"Home is where they don't want to kill you," Jack said.

We all climbed out. Not surprisingly, Ostin's mother was the first to greet us. She threw her arms around Ostin and began kissing him. Ostin was so glad to see her, he didn't even look embarrassed. She was followed by Mr. Liss, my mother, and Chairman Simon.

My mother wrapped her arms around me. She had tears in her eyes. "I'm so glad you're safe." After a moment she stepped back, examining my arms and neck. "What happened? What are those marks?"

I was going to get all technical and say something about Lichtenberg figures, but instead I just said, "I got too electric. It scarred me. It's on my chest and back, too."

She looked concerned as she ran a finger over the scars. "Does it hurt?"

"No."

She threw her arms around me again. "I'm glad you're safe. I've been so worried about you."

I stepped back. "You were worried about me? I thought you were dead."

"I know. I'm sorry. Things were crazy for a while. We got an advance warning that the Elgen were going to attack, and we had to evacuate in the middle of the night." She hugged me again. "I'm just glad you're safe."

After we parted, she looked over at Taylor. "Hello, Taylor."

"Hello, Mrs. Vey. We've been so worried about you all."

My mother hugged her as well. "Thank you for watching over Michael."

"I did my best."

"I knew you would."

My mother then went around and hugged everyone else, stopping at Nichelle, who was standing by herself near the back of the van. She had never seen any of these people before and I guessed felt like an outsider. "You must be Nichelle," my mom said.

Nichelle looked a little shy. "Yes, ma'am."

"Nichelle saved our bacon," I said.

My mother smiled. "Thanks for saving my son's bacon."

Nichelle grinned. "I was glad to save his bacon."

The chairman then stepped up and put out his hand to Nichelle. "Nichelle, I'm Chairman Simon. We've been following you for so long, I feel like I already know you. I'm so pleased to finally meet you."

"That's kind of creepy, but it's nice to meet you, too," she said awkwardly. "Are you the one who sent them to get me in California?"

"It was a decision made by the council, but it was my idea."

"Thank you for trusting me."

"Thank you for making me right."

"It's about time you guys got here," someone shouted.

I turned to see Zeus walking up from around the side of the house. He was followed by Ian, Tanner, Grace, and Tessa. "What took you guys so long?"

We man hugged. "You guys ditch us and then complain we're late?" I said.

"Ditched you? Man, it was intense. I thought we were under attack."

"Yeah," Ian said. "Zeus almost took out one of our own vans before I stopped him."

"Fortunately no one was hurt," Gervaso said.

A man I'd never seen before raised his bandaged arm. "What exactly do you mean by 'hurt'?"

Gervaso grinned. "By 'hurt' I meant 'killed.'"

"Then no one was hurt," he said.

I hugged Ian and Tessa as well. "How's the ranch?" I asked.

"I love it here," Tessa said. "It's awesome."

"Yeah, it's pretty cool," Ian concurred.

Tanner walked up to me. He looked the best I'd seen him yet. He looked healthy. "Hey, Tanner," I said, hugging him.

"Hey, Vey-dude. You're still alive. I was sure you were going down on this one."

"That's comforting," I said. "We almost did. How are you doing?"

"I'm doing all right," he said. "This place is healing."

"Healing's good," I said.

He nodded. "Yeah. Healing's good." He suddenly noticed Nichelle and his expression changed. "I can't believe she's here."

"She's cool," I said.

He looked at me as if I were crazy. "Nichelle's cool?" he said. "No, she ain't. We have history."

"Look," I said. "Hatch has made all of us do things we're not proud of. You can understand that."

For a moment Tanner was speechless. Then he nodded. "You're right, man."

"Forgiveness is part of healing. Just let it go. What happened with Hatch stays with Hatch."

Tanner looked a little ashamed. He nodded again. "That's good advice, Vey. Thanks."

We briefly hugged again. Then I looked over at Grace, who I knew the least of all the electric kids. "How are you?"

She smiled. "I'm good."

"They're taking good care of you?"

She nodded. "They're treating me like gold. You're going to like it here."

"I hope we get to stay awhile," I said.

"Me too. Welcome home."

"Electroclan," the chairman said loudly. "Welcome to Christmas Ranch. I am certain you're exhausted from your travels, so if you'll follow me, I'll show you to your rooms."

We grabbed our bags, then followed the chairman behind the ranch house, where there were two log cabins more than thirty feet long.

"We're staying in bunkhouses," Zeus said. "Women in that one, men in this one."

"See you in a minute," I said to Taylor. We quickly kissed, then split up. My mother led the girls over to their dorm.

The two bunkhouses looked the same, with stained log siding and a pitched, olive-green tin roof. Inside there was a loft that ran over two-thirds of the ceiling, looking out over the front. There were bunk beds extending out from the walls running the length of the room, four sets of two on each side, sleeping sixteen people.

The chairman said, "You can grab any of the bunks along the wall that don't already have sleeping bags on them. Or, if you want to sleep on the loft upstairs, that's available as well. There's no mattresses up there, but it's carpeted with thick padding. And there's plenty of extra quilts and pillows."

"How do you get up there?" I asked.

"That wood ladder at the end of the room," he said, pointing. "That door next to the ladder is the bathroom. There's a shower in there as well, but there's only one bathroom per house, so please keep your showers to a minimum." He stepped back toward the door. "That's it. If you have any questions, you can talk to any of the staff inside the main house. Also, I know it's late for lunch, but we have sandwiches and chili for you in the main house. If you're hungry, come over. They'll be closing the kitchen in about an hour. But there's always snacks."

"We'll be right over," I said. "Do the girls know?"

"Your mother will tell them," he said. "You'll have some time to wander around the grounds. We'll have dinner around six; then we're going to have a meeting."

"Where?" I asked.

"In the big room in the main house. We'll ring the bell when it's dinnertime. So don't eat too much, or you won't be hungry later, and we have fantastic dinners." He looked us over. "You have no idea how happy we are to see you." He walked out.

Ostin, Jack, and I climbed the ladder to the loft. The ceiling was low, maybe six feet at its pinnacle. There were gabled windows that looked out over the property.

"This is nice," Ostin said. "I wonder how long we'll be here."

"A long time, I hope," Jack said.

After a moment I said, "I wouldn't get used to that idea. You know that just when we get comfortable, Hatch will do something crazy. If he hasn't already."

"That's his way," Jack said.

"Crazy freakin' moron," Ostin said.

Jack and I grinned.

"Crazy freakin' moron," I repeated.

21

Simple Things

We piled our bags in the corner of the loft and laid out some quilts and pillows; then Ostin, Jack, and I climbed back down and went over to the main house to get something to eat. The only one in the kitchen was a woman stirring a pot. She was tall with long silver hair.

"I'm going to go find the girls," Jack said, walking back out.

The kitchen was small for so many people, and most of the counters were covered with food.

"It smells good in here," Ostin said.

"It's garlic," the woman said, smiling. "Garlic always smells good. Except on your breath."

"Is that for lunch?" I asked.

"No," she said. "It's dinner. I'm making Italian. This is my Bolognese sauce. I'm also making meatballs and spaghetti. The chairman asked for something special since we're having a celebratory dinner tonight," she said.

"What are we celebrating?" I asked.

She looked at me with an amused smile, then said, "You, of course."
She put a lid on a pot, then stepped away from the stove. "My name is
Lois. I'm the cook. If you need anything, just let me know."

"Where are you from?" Ostin asked.

"I live in town," she said. "In Orderville, just a few miles north. But
I was born near here in Kanab. It's about twenty miles from here. It's
where we do most of our shopping." She gestured to the food. "We're
having sandwiches and chili for lunch. Help yourself."

There was a sandwich bar with roast beef, sliced turkey, pastrami,
and salami, and chicken salad with grapes and walnuts in it. There
were all kinds of vegetables—tomatoes, lettuce, onions, cucumbers,
jalapeños—and at least four kinds of spreads.

On the next counter there were plastic bowls filled with coleslaw
and potato salad, and a cooler filled with ice and drinks—soda, juices,
and bottled water.

Ostin and I grabbed paper plates and made sandwiches, then sat
down at the table to eat. Jack, Abi, Nichelle, Taylor, and McKenna
walked into the kitchen about five minutes after we'd started eating.

"Not waiting for us?" Taylor said.

"Sorry," I said with a full mouth. "I didn't know if you were coming."

"Of course I was coming," she said. "There's food, isn't there?"

Lois introduced herself, then handed them all plates. They made
sandwiches, got bowls of chili, and then came over and joined us.

"I think my mom must have made this potato salad," Ostin said.
"It's definitely her recipe."

"As a matter of fact, it is," Lois said. "So is the chili. How is it?"

"It's good," Jack said. "But it's not very hot."

"I'm sorry," Lois said. "I forgot to turn the heat back up. I can
warm it up if you like."

"No worries," McKenna said. "I'll take care of it." She put her hand
above Jack's bowl, and her hand began to turn bright red. Lois stared
in amazement. It took less than ten seconds before the chili was bub-
bling. Almost habitually, Ostin handed her a bottle of water.

"Thank you," McKenna said. She quickly downed half the bottle.

"That was amazing," Lois said. "I was told that you kids had special abilities."

"You have no idea," Nichelle said.

Jack took back his bowl of chili. "Thanks."

"My pleasure," McKenna replied.

Taylor had made herself a chicken salad sandwich that looked really good.

"How is it?" I asked.

"Beats swamp eel," she said.

"My shoe beats swamp eel," Jack said.

"How're your rooms?" I asked.

"It's just one big room," Taylor said.

". . . and one bathroom," McKenna added. "That's not going to work for twelve women."

"There are two bathrooms and showers in here," Lois said, smiling. "You're welcome to use them anytime."

"Thank you," McKenna said.

Zeus and Tessa walked into the room. "Hey, guys," Zeus said. "After you eat, we'll take you on a tour of the ranch. We've got ATVs."

"I think you should walk," Lois said. "It's much nicer. There's a nice path down to the pond."

"There's a pond?" McKenna asked.

"It's more like a small lake. You can swim if you like. There's also a canoe. It's just down at the end of the dirt road behind the bunkhouses."

"Just watch out for rattlesnakes," Tessa said.

"Rattlesnakes?" Ostin said, looking suddenly afraid.

"We found one yesterday," Tessa said. "It was huge, like five feet long."

"A Mojave Green," Zeus said. "Pretty wicked."

"What's a Mojave Green?" I asked. I turned to Ostin, who now looked even more terrified. The only things that scared Ostin more than an empty refrigerator were sharks and snakes.

"It's bad news," Ostin said. "Only the most venomous rattlesnake

in the world. Not only does it have the usual venomous proteins, but it's venom also contains a presynaptic neurotoxin. Think cobra, man. Be very afraid."

"You don't need to be afraid, just cautious," Lois said. "No one here has ever been bitten, but we have antivenom just in case. Just respect them and keep your distance. And don't play with them."

"Who would be dumb enough to play with a rattlesnake?" Taylor asked.

"You'd be surprised," Lois replied.

"What did you do with the snake you saw?" Ostin asked.

"Fried it," Zeus said. "I'm much faster than any snake."

"I'm sticking with you or Michael," Ostin said.

"What's the matter with me?" McKenna asked. "Or don't you like being protected by a girl?"

Ostin seemed stumped. "I just . . . I should be protecting you."

"We protect one another," McKenna said. "In whatever way we can."

Ostin nodded. "That's intelligent," he said.

After lunch, Taylor and I walked out the back of the house down a small, stone-set walkway past an outdoor pizza oven piled high with cut wood. I took Taylor's hand, and we walked about a hundred yards down a tree-lined clay trail, over two cattle guards, to the pond. The pond was about three acres in size. Its water was bright blue, and there were ducks floating in it. One edge was covered in sunflowers and cattails. There was a boat dock on the south end, and on the east side a large platform hung out over the water. Tied to the dock was a long, green canoe with two oars inside.

"Want to go for a boat ride?" I asked.

Taylor smiled. "Sure."

We walked down onto the narrow floating dock, which rocked slightly beneath our weight. I held the canoe steady while Taylor climbed into the front and balanced herself. Then I untied the rope from the dock's cleat and climbed into the back of the canoe. The canoe rocked a lot, and I nearly tipped us over trying to get to my seat.

We paddled to the middle of the pond, the canoe gliding easily

over the water. There was a light breeze, and the ducks took flight as we approached them.

Taylor laid down her oar, then carefully slid back toward me until I could hold her.

"I could live like this for the rest of my life."

"Like what?" I asked.

"A pioneer life. Simple. I mean, I know it's physically hard, but the challenges are different. Milking cows, planting, harvesting . . . you know, simple."

"Simple is good," I said.

"The world has gotten so complex. I sometimes wonder if all these labor-saving devices actually just make our lives more difficult. You know what I mean?"

"Yes."

"It's not like all these gadgets and appliances have slowed people down or anything. It just means they have to do more. The whole world just keeps trying to go faster and faster." She sighed. "Except for here. Nature is never in a hurry. You can't make a flower bloom faster. They don't read magazines to make themselves prettier; they just know they are."

I looked at her and smiled. "How do you know flowers think they're pretty?"

She smiled. "I can tell."

For a moment we were both quiet, listening to the soft, whistling breeze and the rhythmic tin squeak of an aged windmill. A dragonfly buzzed by above our heads, chased by another. Taylor looked up at me. "Why do you think Hatch does what he does? With all his money, he could live anywhere, do anything. Instead he makes himself and everyone else miserable."

"I don't think people like Hatch can find joy in simple things anymore. All that matters is power."

"I don't get that. I mean, what's power? Let's say he's suddenly the king of the world. What is he going to do with it that he can't do now? Is his food going to taste better? Is the weather going to be nicer? Will love feel better? I just don't understand that mentality."

"I think deep inside, people like Hatch are afraid. So they try to control everything. If they can control everything, nothing can hurt them. At least that's what they think."

"But he's in much more danger than if he just enjoyed life. Kings are never safe. There's always someone who wants their throne."

I nodded. "He's in much more danger," I said. "Just like we are."

"It's not fair. We're not after power. Why should we have to change our lives just because he does?"

"So he doesn't take away our lives," I said. "But you're right, it's not fair."

We were both quiet again. Then Taylor asked, "Did your mom say anything about my parents?"

"Not yet," I said.

"I wonder if my mom's told my dad yet." She shook her head. "How would she even begin? My dad's so skeptical about everything. He doesn't even believe that man really landed on the moon. I'm not sure that he'd believe her if she told him about me, you, or the Elgen. He'll probably just think she's crazy."

"Well, he's going to have to believe her sometime."

"I just hope they're safe," she said.

We stayed out on the water for another half hour, until the wind pushed us into the cattails on the far side of the pond. Then we paddled back to the dock, and Taylor climbed out first. I secured the boat to the cleat, then climbed onto the dock. Taylor started laughing.

"What?" I said.

"I just had the meanest thought. I almost rebooted you as you were climbing out."

"I would have fallen in."

She grinned. "Exactly."

"You have a mean streak," I said.

"Everyone does," she replied, laughing. "Some just hide it better than others."

After the pond we walked several miles around the grounds, climbing over barbwire fences and stepping over cow pies. There were entire fields of lavender and peppermint. Along one fence was a

hedge of raspberry bushes laden with berries, which we stopped and picked. They were plump and sweet.

As we crossed the middle of a pasture, several cows started walking toward us. After what Ostin had told us about cows killing people, it made me a little nervous until I remembered the bull in Peru that I had brought down. *I could take down one of these cows*, I thought. *Bring it on.* Fortunately for them, they never attacked.

On the west side of the ranch, about fifty yards from the horse stables, we came across a dozen white boxes about five feet high. As we got closer, we could hear the buzz coming from them.

"What are those?" Taylor asked.

"They look like beehives," I said.

Taylor squealed as she swatted at a bee. "Okay, I'm not going any closer."

"I want to check them out," I said.

"They'll sting you."

"No they won't." I increased my electricity until I could feel all the hairs on my arms stand up. A bee flew near me, and there was a light blue snap of electricity.

"You're a bug zapper," Taylor said.

"More and more each day." I looked at her. "Want some honeycomb?"

"Yes. But you better not. They'll swarm you."

I walked closer to the hives. "They can't hurt me."

"But you might end up killing them all."

I stopped. "You're right. That wouldn't be good."

"Wait," she said. "I wonder if I could reboot them."

I was curious. "Try," I said.

She bowed her head, and I walked up to the closest box. A few of the bees ran into me, but I don't think that they were trying to sting me. I think they were just confused.

I lifted the top off the box. There were trays inside covered with wax and bees. It took effort, but I pulled one of the trays out, then broke off a piece of honeycomb about half the size of my hand. Fresh,

golden honey dripped down my fingers. A few bees tried to sting me, but they basically disintegrated before they could land on me.

I shut the hive back up, then walked over and handed the honeycomb to Taylor. "Try it."

"Thank you," she said. "That was really weird."

"What?"

"You know how, when I get into someone's mind, their thoughts become part of me? It's like . . . I could understand them."

"You could read the bees' minds?"

"Sort of. I just . . ." She looked at me. "I could feel what drove them and their concerns."

"Bees have concerns?"

"Yes, they do, especially when you take their honey. But it's not individual. It's like they're all part of the same mind, and I could read their collective mind." She looked at me and smiled. "That makes me the queen bee."

"Yes, you are," I said.

She tasted a piece of honeycomb. "This is amazing." She handed me a piece. I put it into my mouth and chewed.

"That is like the best honey I've ever tasted."

"It's perfect," Taylor said. "It's been a perfect day."

The sun was setting, lighting the plateaus to the east in bright golden-pink hues. As we finished off the honey, we heard the clanging of the dinner bell.

"Must be dinnertime," I said. I took Taylor's hand, and we walked back to the house. As we were walking up the dirt road, we ran into Gervaso, who was walking toward us. "I've been looking for you," he said.

"What's up?"

"I was just making sure you were coming to dinner. There's going to be a meeting afterward. It's very important."

"We'll be there," I said.

The kitchen was crowded, as people walked past the front counter dishing food onto their plates. Lois and both of Ostin's parents

were serving from the kitchen. My mother was pouring drinks—lemonade, sweet tea, and water. Joel was next to her, helping.

"Do you need any help?" I asked my mother.

"No, we're good. How was your day?"

"It was nice," Taylor said. "We went canoeing."

"And we got some honey," I added.

My mother cocked her head. "How did you get honey?"

"From the hives."

"Yes, I know where it is, but how did you get it?"

"We have superpowers," I said.

She smiled. "Of course you do. Would you like some lemonade?"

"Love some," Taylor said.

"Should we wait for you?" I asked.

"No, go ahead and eat."

Lois had prepared spaghetti in Bolognese sauce with meatballs, garlic bread, green salad, and a vegetable soup.

We loaded up our plates, then went out back to the patio, where there were six long picnic tables. There were about forty of us in all. Taylor and I sat at the middle table with Zeus and Tessa. They had gone hiking and found some Anasazi ruins, including a large piece of a painted clay pot.

A few minutes after everyone had been served, Ostin's parents came around to all of the tables with a tray of German chocolate cake and homemade vanilla ice cream, which they scooped out of a round metal canister. The sun had fallen by then, and the back patio was lit by large flood lamps on the back of the house that were swarmed by bugs.

After we ate, Ostin and McKenna came around carrying a large white plastic bucket and a garbage bag. They scraped the leftover scraps off our plates into the bucket, then put the plates into the garbage bag.

"How'd you end up with this job?" I asked.

"Ostin's mom and dad are on kitchen duty tonight," McKenna said. "So we volunteered."

"What's the bucket for?" Taylor asked.

"They put all the leftover food in it. It's pig slop."

"It looks gross."

"It looks like the inside of your stomach," Ostin said. "Except it's not chewed and soaked in hydrochloric acid, which is, by the way, the same stuff found in some toilet-bowl cleaners."

"That's not making it more appetizing," Taylor said.

"Then just think of it as unprocessed bacon," Ostin said.

The chairman walked outside. "I hope you're all enjoying your celebratory dinner," he said. "I'd again like to welcome our guests of honor. But even more I'd like to congratulate them on their recent success rescuing Jade Dragon. It was a risky mission, to put it lightly. But, once again, they succeeded."

Everyone applauded.

"Now, if you're done eating, we'd like to invite you to come inside for a debriefing with the council of twelve."

Except for the staff, everyone, including my mom and Ostin's parents, went inside to the main room, an open space with a tall, stone-hearth fireplace at one end. Taylor and I sat down next to my mother. The chairman had a microphone.

"Welcome," he said. "As I said before, we are so grateful for the safe return of the Electroclan. We can't thank them enough for their heroism. The entire world could never adequately repay them for what they've done." He looked around. "Unfortunately, the world is blind to their own danger and has no idea what these young people have accomplished on their behalf, so our thanks will have to suffice.

"We would also like to welcome the newest member of the Electroclan, Nichelle. Would you mind standing so everyone can see you?"

Nichelle shyly stood. She looked both embarrassed and honored.

"We are so glad to have you with us. Thank you for your valor."

"You're welcome," she said, quickly sitting back down.

He turned back to us. "We have received reports from Ben, our Asian agent, as to what happened in Taiwan. The Electroclan performed bravely and brilliantly. They also barely escaped with their lives. I'm pleased to report that their efforts were successful and they

rescued Jade Dragon. Had they not, we are certain that the Elgen would have broken her by now and would already have begun their work rebuilding the MEI and creating a new race of electric children. We are very fortunate that this isn't the case.

"So that takes us to where we are now. Yes, we have lost our primary facility, but that's all. Our sources tell us that the Elgen now believe that we have been destroyed, which is precisely what we hoped for. But there's more. Two important events have occurred, or are about to occur, that are of great concern to us right now.

"First, the Elgen are preparing to move ahead with their original plan of overthrowing the island of Tuvalu. They have acquired two new ships, both with battle capabilities. At this point, there is nothing we can do to stop them.

"The second event may, in the long run, be even more consequential. Every despot has a weakness. Hatch's is hubris."

"What's hubris?" I whispered to Ostin.

"Ego," he said.

"Hatch sees any Elgen failure as an act of defiance against him, and he responds accordingly.

"After the Electroclan rescued Jade Dragon, Hatch decided to punish his top man, sentencing his senior EGG Welch to the rat bowl as an example to the rest of his force. Welch was being kept locked up in the brig of the *Faraday*, but somehow, while the Elgen were still docked in Taiwan, he managed to escape. We assume that he's still somewhere on the island. The Elgen are hunting him as we speak.

"What's most important about this twist is that we have reason to believe that his escape was facilitated by Hatch's own youths, in particular, Hatch's chosen, Quentin. If this is true, there's a major fracture in the Elgen hierarchy. And that's exactly what we've been hoping for. A house divided against itself must fall. If Welch and the Elgen electric youths combine forces, they might be able to defeat Hatch and take control of the Elgen.

"This might be the opportunity we've been waiting for. Up until now we've been like sailors in a sinking ship, running from one hole in the boat to the next, when what we really need to do is stop the

person making the holes. If Hatch's youths have turned on him, we have a chance to take Hatch down."

"So what do we do?" Gervaso asked.

"First, we need to find Welch," he replied. "We need to find him before the Elgen do. Rather than risk another escape, Hatch has commanded them to shoot him on sight."

"How can we help?" I asked.

"Right now you can't. Ben has organized a search. He knows Taiwan's underground and streets. We're confident that he'll find him. Other than that, it's Hatch's move. So right now we do what's most difficult of all. We wait."

"Wait for what?" Jack asked.

"For Hatch to screw up."

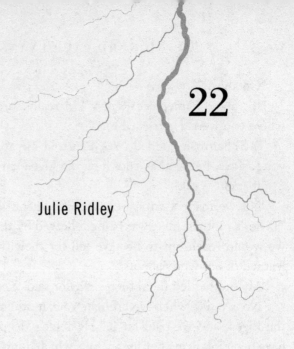

22

Julie Ridley

As everyone left the room, the chairman approached Taylor and me. He was flanked by Joel and Gervaso. "Michael, we need to talk with you and Taylor."

"You need me?" Taylor asked.

"Especially you. What we have to show you concerns you most of all."

We followed them down a short hallway into a room with a large television mounted to the wall in front of an oval conference table. The television was on, frozen to a newscast. I recognized the woman on the screen. She was Gretchen Holly, a popular news anchor on the Boise evening news.

"Have a seat, please," the chairman said.

"It's okay, I'll stand," Taylor said.

"It's best if you sit," he said.

After we were seated, I said, "Before we start, I need to say something."

"Go ahead."

"It's about Timepiece Ranch. I'm really sorry that I told Hatch where you were. He tricked me."

The chairman nodded. "Yes, Ben told me about that. If it makes you feel any better, that's not how the Elgen knew where we were."

"It's not?" I said.

"No, we made a critical error in judgment." He looked at Taylor. "Taylor's mother, Julie, was being followed by the Elgen, hoping that we would reach out to her. We fell for their trap. That's how they learned of our whereabouts."

"My mother led them there?" Taylor said.

"No, we did, when we brought your mother. We underestimated the Elgen, and we paid for it." He took a deep breath. "The Elgen have been following her for a while, which, unfortunately, is what we need to talk to you about." He nodded to his assistant, who pushed a button on a remote, and the video started to run.

"Tonight's breaking story, an Idaho woman has been arrested in connection with the disappearance of her daughter. Meridian resident Julie Ridley was taken into police custody after authorities provided evidence linking her to her daughter's disappearance. Mrs. Ridley has refused to cooperate with authorities and is currently being held pending bail. Ridley's husband, Charles Ridley, is an officer for the Boise police department and has been suspended following an internal investigation to assess his involvement."

I looked over at Taylor. She was staring at the screen in shock. When she could speak, she said, "When did this happen?"

"Two days ago. Your mother went back to Idaho to tell your father and prepare to come back with us permanently, but then the Elgen attacked the ranch and threw off our timetable. We had to delay our plans and they beat us to her."

"I need to go to Idaho," Taylor said. "I need to show myself to them."

"Absolutely not," the chairman said. "That's what the Elgen are hoping you'll do. It's a trap. You can be sure that the information the police are working off was provided by Elgen."

"I don't care; they have my mother," Taylor said.

Gervaso said, "Taylor, right now your appearance will raise far more questions than it will answer. And we're certain that you'll disappear again as soon as the Elgen find you."

"They can't charge your mother with murder or kidnapping without a body," Joel said. "How can they prove a murder's taken place without a body?"

"There's more," the chairman said, motioning to his assistant.

The woman advanced the DVD to another news clip.

"In an ongoing investigation, Boise police discovered more than two kilograms of heroin in a car belonging to Meridian resident Julie Ridley."

There was footage of a police officer standing before a row of microphones holding aloft a plastic bag filled with white powder. "This is one of the biggest drug busts in the history of the Boise DEA. This much heroin has a street value in excess of a half million dollars. We're happy to keep this off the street."

The clip returned to the anchor. "In addition to the drugs, Idaho forensic investigators have found traces of blood matching the DNA of Mrs. Ridley's daughter, Taylor Ridley, who was reported missing nearly four months ago. Mrs. Ridley is currently being held in the Boise jail. Bail has been set for a quarter million dollars."

There was video footage of people screaming at Mrs. Ridley as she was led in handcuffs into the jail by police.

Taylor was crying. "How could it be my blood?"

"They took our blood in the academy," I said.

"This is bad. Really bad." She looked at me. "Michael, we've got to do something."

Joel interjected. "We will. But in the meantime, you don't need to worry. She'll be safe in jail."

"They can't protect her in jail," Taylor said. "If the Elgen have someone in there, she's as good as dead."

"They won't hurt her," the chairman said.

"How do you know that?"

"Dead bait doesn't draw fish."

Taylor's lips pursed with anger. "My mother's not *bait*."

"In this case, she is," Joel said. "They're using her to lure you to them. If they wanted to kill her, they would have done it already."

"He's right," I said. "They could have easily done it." I looked at the chairman. "But we can't leave her in jail."

"No, we can't," the chairman said. "And we won't. We need to extract her and Taylor's father. We've asked Gervaso to come up with a plan."

We both turned toward Gervaso. I wondered how long he had known about this and not told us.

Gervaso looked at Taylor. "First, we're going to get your mother out. I promise. But it's going to be tricky." He looked back at me. "You've both broken in and out of much more secure facilities. The challenge here is, we need to rescue Julie without the Elgen or the police knowing we've rescued her."

"How do we do that?" Taylor asked.

"We need to get your father to post your mother's bail; then, after she's out, we disappear with both of them. This won't be easy since it's not likely the Elgen will let your mother out of their sight. And, of course, we have the Boise police to worry about. Which brings up another problem. Your father is a police officer, and we're pretty sure that he still doesn't know anything about you or the Elgen. From what I understand, he's a stubborn man."

"As stubborn as a brick," Taylor said.

Gervaso nodded. "This is going to be a small, clean operation. In and out. My plan involves you two and Ian. Also, I have a friend we can trust in Idaho who will be helping us out with logistics. No one else. The more moving parts there are, the more that can break down."

I nodded. "Okay. When do we start?"

"Timing is critical. I'd like to be in contact with Officer Ridley by tomorrow evening. Boise is a nine-hour drive from here, so we'll leave early tomorrow morning."

"We'll be ready," I said.

"Good. We'll meet in front of the main house at oh-six-hundred hours." Then he added, "That's *six a.m.*"

The chairman looked at us. "Good luck."

As we walked out, Taylor said to me, "Thank you for helping me rescue my mother."

"I owe you. You helped me rescue mine."

Taylor frowned. "My mom must be terrified."

"We'll get her," I said. "And your father."

"My father," she said. "It's been so long since I've seen him."

"He's going to be happy to see you."

"Yes," Taylor said. "And he's going to be totally freaked."

PART SEVEN

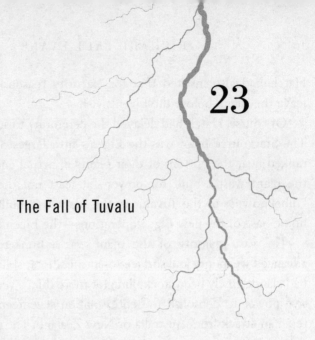

23

The Fall of Tuvalu

Funafuti Island, Tuvalu

The Polynesian island nation of Tuvalu consists of four reef islands and five atolls, a total of about ten square miles in area. The islands are isolated in the Pacific Ocean, a coral oasis more than five thousand miles northeast of Australia and forty-one hundred miles southwest of Hawaii. The nation's population is less than ten thousand, making it the third-smallest populated country in the world. It also attracts few tourists, due to its remoteness and inaccessibility. The nation has one of the best of the Pacific island economies, with a peculiar source of income—their .tv Internet domain suffix, which generates millions of dollars a year.

The Elgen had built their Starxource plant on the largest and chief island, Funafuti, then dragged power cables north and south to five of the other islands. Even though the plant had already been operating for more than four months, the natives had delayed the ceremonial ribbon cutting to honor Admiral-General Hatch's wishes.

Hatch had also insisted that for "security reasons," all non-natives leave the island before the Elgen's visit.

Of course, Hatch had delayed the ceremony to suit his own plans. The Starxource plant was the Elgen's fifth largest in the world, yet ranked near the bottom of their plants in actual energy output. But the plant wasn't built for power—at least not the electrical kind. Unbeknownst to the Tuvaluans, the plant was built to serve as the home base of the new Elgen operations—the Elgen Kremlin.

The vast majority of the plant was a bunkered fortress, with advanced weaponry and surface-to-air missile capability that the Elgen had clandestinely been stockpiling for more than a year, enough explosive power to demolish the entire nation seventeen times over and repel an attack from Australia or New Zealand. The plant also had an extensive prison, with more than two hundred cells and an advanced reeducation center patterned after the center in Peru.

While the people of Tuvalu slept, the Elgen fleet sailed through the cover of darkness, securing the waters surrounding the islands. At three in the morning the *Faraday* docked off the coast of Funafuti and, using the *Tesla* as tender, began shuttling soldiers onto their base. The *Edison*, the Elgen's new battleship, had taken up a defensive position off the southwest coast of Funafuti, and Elgen helicopters kept surveillance over the waters.

Tuvalu spent no money on military, and the small police force, dressed in British uniforms, typically didn't carry guns. In fact, the total number of firearms registered to civilians was twelve, and the entire police force owned just twenty-one guns, which meant a single Elgen patrol carried more weaponry than the entire nation. The peaceful Tuvaluan people were vulnerable to the extreme.

The Starxource plant's ribbon-cutting ceremony was attended by the entire Tuvalu administration—the governor-general and staff; prime minister and staff; deputy prime minister; chairman of the Public Service Commission; assistant secretary-general; secretary of foreign affairs; chief immigration officer; the police commissioner; the ministers of education, finance and economic planning, health, natural resources, energy and environment, trade, tourism and com-

merce, and foreign affairs; and the ambassador to the United Nations.

The UN ambassador was the one Tuvaluan official who had already been brought into the Elgen ranks and had, for some time, been receiving payment for his service.

The ceremony began a little after noon at the nation's capital, with a Tuvaluan proclamation of friendship followed by a traditional ceremonial dance. Then the party moved, at Hatch's insistence, behind the walls of the Starxource plant.

While Hatch, his personal bodyguards, and nine of his twelve EGGs led the delegation on a tour of the facility, the plant's electricity was shut down across the rest of the islands and throughout most of Funafuti. A small commando squad of Elgen frogmen commandeered the sole Tuvaluan naval ship—a Pacific-class patrol boat—taking the captain and crew as prisoners.

All radio frequencies were jammed, and the Elgen's new amphibious vehicle, the *Franklin*, began the landing assault on Funafuti and two other islands, Nanumea and Nukufetau.

As Hatch had planned, inside the Elgen facility the leaders of Tuvalu were completely isolated from the outside, oblivious that their country was under attack.

After an hour-long tour of the facility, the delegation was seated for dinner in the large, crescent-shaped observation room above the rat bowl. The metal blinds were drawn so that the dignitaries could not see the actual bowl, and as Hatch had planned, they still had no idea how the electricity was generated, outside of the Elgen's standard explanation of a hybrid form of cold fusion and organic composting.

Two roast pigs were served for dinner, along with grass-fed Australian beef and lamb, salad, and sweet potatoes. For dessert the Elgen served two Australian–New Zealand favorites: Pavlova, a large meringue filled with fruit and cream, and Lamingtons, a cubed sponge cake coated in chocolate and coconut.

Hatch made sure that the best regional wine was available and had purchased three cases of a Penfolds Grange at nearly eight hundred dollars a bottle. The Tuvaluan dignitaries were well fed and slightly inebriated when the dinner was over, and a dozen Tuvaluan women,

wearing ceremonial outfits with grass skirts and crowns woven from palm leaves, performed another traditional Tuvalu ceremonial dance.

As the dance concluded, one of the young women approached Hatch, dropped to her knees, touching her forehead on the ground between them, and then offered the admiral-general a flowered lei. Hatch accepted the lei but did not put it on.

Afterward the prime minister of Tuvalu, a slim, silver-haired man dressed in a white short-sleeved shirt, approached the lectern near the center of the room. He turned to face Hatch.

"Our esteemed benefactor and friend. In the Tuvaluan anthem we sing,

> *"Tuku atu tau pulega*
> *Ki te pule mai luga,*
> *Kilo tonu ki ou mua*
> *Me ko ia e tautai.*
> *'Pule tasi mo ia'*
> *Ki te se gata mai,*
> *Ko tena mana*
> *Ko tou malosi tena.*

"Please, esteemed admiral-general, allow me to translate to your language.

> *"Let us trust our lives henceforward*
> *To the king to whom we pray,*
> *With our eyes fixed firmly on him*
> *He is showing us the way,*
> *'May we reign with him in glory'*
> *Be our song for evermore,*
> *For his almighty power*
> *Is our strength from shore to shore.*

"You, esteemed Admiral-General Hatch, have come as a gift of the God above to bless our humble island nation. The gratitude of

our people will forever shower down to you from heaven. I hereby bestow upon you, esteemed admiral-general, our greatest honor, the Tuvaluan star, and declare you a citizen of Tuvalu."

The crowd broke out in applause, then stood in an ovation. Hatch almost looked moved by the gesture. Then, at the prime minister's bidding, Hatch rose and walked to the lectern while the prime minister returned to his table.

Hatch looked out over the congregation, then slowly raised a glass of wine to toast the assembly of Tuvaluan dignitaries. "To a new day," he said.

"To a new day," the audience repeated, clinking their glasses.

Hatch set down his glass without drinking from it. "Prime Minister, dignitaries, friends, I am very much entertained by your ceremony and hospitality, as primitive as it may be. You have come here to celebrate the completion of a new Starxource plant, our thirty-sixth in the world. I say 'you,' because we, the Elgen, are here to celebrate an entirely different matter." He looked around the room, and his expression darkened. "Guards."

At Hatch's word a force of more than a hundred Elgen guards ran into the room with drawn automatic weapons. At first the confused guests watched with curiosity, as if the display of force were just another part of the day's entertainment. But as the moment dragged on, their amusement turned to fear. A few of the dignitaries attempted to leave, but they were forcefully returned to their seats. The noise in the room grew as the Tuvaluans began talking with one another in their native tongue.

"Silence!" Hatch shouted. After all were quiet, he continued. "Today, you, the *former* leaders of Tuvalu, came to celebrate a new power in your country. In this you are correct. But it is not electrical power as you supposed, but political power. We are celebrating a new regime.

"While you have been here in our facility, our Elgen forces have been at work. Of course, our work started more than a year ago when we demolished your last diesel power plant and took complete control of your electricity.

"This afternoon, we seized your lone radio station, destroyed your

phone towers, and jammed all communications. You are now completely cut off from the outside world. There will be no broadcasts and no phone calls.

"Our takeover continued this afternoon when we overthrew your navy, if I might be so presumptuous as to call it that. No one will be allowed on or off the islands. All seacraft have been confiscated or sunk, and our fleet is patrolling the islands, destroying anything that enters or attempts to flee these waters. Now you understand the true reason we insisted that all non-Tuvaluan residents be sent off the island weeks ago. We did not want any foreigners meddling.

"Your police force has been imprisoned in their own jails, and my Elgen guard has taken control of this nation. I would say the nation of Tuvalu, except it is no longer to be known as such. From this time forth Tuvalu shall be known as the Hatch Islands. Speaking the word 'Tuvalu' will be punished by public flogging.

"In this time of transition there will be many floggings. Those who do not attend the floggings, which will become my nation's prime amusement, will be dragged from their homes and flogged themselves. In other words, you will enjoy the entertainment or become it.

"From this time forth the nation of Hatch is a dictatorship, and I, as supreme commander and president, declare your constitution null and void. My Elgen forces have authority to make and enforce all civil and criminal laws as they see fit.

"To ensure that we have your utmost cooperation, we have established reeducation camps, where all of you, beginning right now, will be admitted.

"Prime Minister, you will now again come forward and bow down to me as your new sovereign and kiss my hand as a token of your allegiance."

The man, visibly shaken, stood. He looked over his own bewildered and frightened subjects. Then he turned to Hatch. "I will not bow to you or any man. I bow only to God."

"God," Hatch said, smiling. "Where is your God in your time of need?" His eyes narrowed. "I will tell you where your God is. You are looking at him.

"As to you refusing my order, I was hoping you would. I made you the offer out of mercy, not desire. I had a much better plan for you.

"You will be stripped of your clothing, bound, and your tongue will be cut off; then, for the rest of your life, you will be kept in the central square in a cage with monkeys. You will sleep with the monkeys, you will be fed with the monkeys. And the good people of Hatch will be brought to see your humiliation and mock you." Hatch turned to the audience. "From this time forth, this man will be known not as the prime minister of Hatch, but as the Prime Monkey of Hatch." Hatch turned back to the prime minister. "For the rest of your life, you will live with the monkeys, and, someday, you will die with the monkeys. If you try to take your life, your sons and daughters will take your place. Do you understand me?"

The prime minister's face flushed bright red with anger and fear.

"Do you understand me?" Hatch repeated.

"Yes," he said bitterly.

"Mr. Prime Monkey, you are an educated man, so you have, no doubt, studied history. You will recognize that I have much in common with another great man who changed the world, the great Spanish explorer Hernando Cortés.

"We both came from the sea to a primitive culture who welcomed us as their savior. Like them, you, and your people, did not know that I came to rule you and claim your land as mine.

"But I am more merciful than Cortés. I will spare you and your subjects their lives. This revolution has taken place without a single shot. And even as it was with Montezuma, the great Aztec king, it will be with you. In the end, your own people will turn on you. They will mock you in your new cage and stone you with their insults. They will sell T-shirts with pictures of you in your cage."

"The joke is on you, Hatch," the prime minister said. "Our nation is sinking into the ocean. There will be no Tuvalu in thirty years."

"In thirty years," Hatch said, leaning forward, "we won't need Tuvalu. The entire world will be my footstool. Washington, London, Tokyo, Beijing, New Delhi, Moscow—these will be my capitals."

"The world will never allow this," the prime minister shouted.

"Of course they will," Hatch said dully. "And they have. We do have our enemies. And they warned the UN that we were going to attack Tuvalu, and no one listened. No one. Including you. You were warned, and you didn't listen, did you?"

The prime minister hung his head.

"The 'world' doesn't even know that you exist. And they wouldn't care if they did. The world has their own problems, not the least of which are their economies and the financial and environmental cost of energy, a problem to which only I hold the key." Hatch looked around. "Speaking of economies, will the minister of finance please come forward."

A small, thin young man timidly walked up to Hatch, his knees shaking and his eyes averted, afraid to look into Hatch's face.

"On your knees," Hatch said.

The man immediately dropped to the ground. "Yes, Your Excellency."

"Promising," Hatch said, nodding approvingly. "You, sir, should have been the prime minister. You're obviously much wiser." Hatch looked back over his terrified audience. "So, in addition to the changing of my country's name, the official currency has also changed. Your money, the Australian dollar and the Tuvaluan dollar, is now useless. We have printed a new currency that we will, starting this week, exchange with the citizens of Hatch. Only the Elgen Mark will be recognized as currency. It is illegal to accept or to use any other currency. To attempt to do so is punishable by flogging, prison, or death."

Hatch looked over the delegation. "It is now time for each of you to make a decision, one that will have lasting repercussions, so consider your choice carefully. You must decide whether or not you will accept my supreme command.

"You have two options. Though, in truth, they have the same destination, just a different path. Option one, you may accept fully, by choice, an Elgen oath of allegiance with a covenant to follow and obey your Elgen masters. For those who make this wise choice, you will be treated with respect and kept in comfortable lodgings for the next six weeks as you are educated in the Elgen ways and groomed for Elgen leadership and success.

"Option two is for those who do not accept the oath of allegiance. They will be imprisoned for the next year in the Elgen reeducation facility, the portion of this facility that you did not tour. They will be subjected to an extreme physical and psychological barrage designed, and proven, to break both mind and will. In the end these former dissenters will, on their knees, beg to take the oath of loyalty.

"This is not exaggeration. We have reeducated thousands of minds already, of many who believed they could not be changed. These newly enlightened converts are among our strongest enthusiasts.

"But even after their conversion, they will forever be regarded as a lower caste, an untouchable. We will brand on their foreheads the letter *F*, signifying to all that they are a fool and a failure. They will be a pariah.

"So, to be clear, the only choice you really have is not whether or not to swear an oath of fidelity to your new monarch, as you will all eventually do this. Rather, the choice you have is what path you will take to that destination. I leave that decision to you.

"In just a moment we will take all of you, one at a time, into these side rooms to hear your decision. *All* except for you, Mr. Prime Monkey. Your vocation has been chosen for you. You will serve as an example to your people for the rest of your tortured days. You are clearly a man of the people. I'm certain you would have it no other way."

24

Hatch Islands

By midnight, all but two of the forty-six Tuvaluan officials had taken Hatch's oath of allegiance. The prime minister, after a brief struggle, was stripped of his clothing, bound, and led away to a cell to await the surgical removal of his tongue. Hatch wanted the procedure performed immediately, as he wanted the man to have recovered enough to be in the cage the following day.

Outside the Starxource plant, the Elgen had overthrown the island nation. Hatch's plan of attack, which he called "the trident" for its three prongs, consisted of knocking out all communications, quarantining the island, and overthrowing the police force.

The Tuvaluan Navy had been the first Tuvaluan force to be overthrown, while, nearly simultaneously, Squad Captain Steele and his men, along with Quentin and Bryan, had stormed the radio station. Other than the station's simple security already in place—an

electric door lock, which Bryan quickly cut through—there was no attempt to stop them. When they broke into the studio, they found two employees huddled with fear in the corner of the room, while a third, the station's technician, was behind the control panel trying to figure out why their machinery had stopped working.

The three radio employees were handcuffed and driven off by two of the guards to the Starxource plant for reeducation. The remaining guards took positions around the station, including one sniper on the roof, to ensure that no one got near.

Concurrent with the attack on the radio station, three other squads blew up the country's cell phone towers, disabling all phone communication.

Ten squads, a force of more than a hundred guards, subdued the police force and confiscated their weaponry, all of which was sent back to HQ. Since half the force was not on shift during the attack, several Tuvaluan traitors guided the Elgen to the remaining police officers' residences.

Another force was sent to capture members of the Tuvaluan elders, the cultural leaders of each district, whom the people looked to for guidance.

With their first objective met, the Elgen guard swarmed across the island like a cloud of locusts. As Hatch had predicted, there was little resistance, outside of a group of drunken natives on the smallest island of Niulakita, who were quickly tased and handcuffed and locked in the village center under guard.

The country's weapons registry led the guards to the homes of those with guns, and they were subdued and jailed. A squad was left to patrol each city block, in the event that the people began to gather in large groups.

At two a.m., the Elgen began transmitting a looped radio message to the people of Tuvalu.

> *Good people of Tuvalu. Do not be alarmed. Thanks to the aid*
> *of our allies, the Elgen, an attempted overthrow of our country*

*by the Philippines has been averted. Prime Minister Saluni has
declared martial law and authorized the Elgen forces to seek out
those traitors who were involved with this planned coup. They may
be your neighbors. We apologize for the inconvenience and expect
your full cooperation in these perilous times. Those who do not
cooperate will be arrested on suspicion of conspiracy.*

The message, broadcast on the radio and played from Elgen PA systems, repeated every thirty seconds for the rest of the night. At six a.m.,
as the sun rose above the eastern Pacific horizon, the message changed.

*People of Tuvalu. Prime Minister Saluni and the Tuvaluan defense
forces have commanded all citizens to gather on the runway of the
Funafuti International Airport by twelve noon. Anyone who does not
attend will be arrested on charges of treason and aiding the enemy.
We repeat, all citizens must gather on the runway of the Funafuti
International Airport by twelve noon. Anyone who does not attend
will be arrested on charges of treason and aiding the enemy.*

By noon, four companies of the Elgen guard, consisting of more
than five hundred men, lined up along the airfield, heavily armed
with automatic weapons. The Tuvaluan people were herded in like
cattle being driven to market. A raised platform had been constructed near the middle of the airfield, with the Elgen insignia hung
behind it, on tall strips of draping fabric. The Elgen motto, *Absolutum
Dominium*, was plain for all to see.

Outdoor speakers nearly twelve feet high flanked both sides of
the platform, which was surrounded by an Elgen company of a hundred and fifty guards.

About thirty feet in front of the platform, to the left side, was
a rectangular structure about eighteen feet long, twelve feet high,
and twelve feet wide. It was covered with a large sheet, with guards
standing at each corner. On the opposite side of the platform was a
wooden pole, about the diameter of a telephone pole, sticking up
about ten feet out of the ground.

Waiting beneath the hot sun, the Tuvaluan crowd grew unruly, shouting out their displeasure. An hour later, at one o'clock sharp, the Elgen anthem played loudly as Hatch and his entourage arrived. Hatch walked directly up to a lectern with a microphone. He was flanked by four EGGs on either side, and Quentin, Tara, and Torstyn.

"Good morning," Hatch said calmly to the jeering crowd. "May I have your attention please."

The people continued shouting their disapproval.

"Your attention please," Hatch repeated softly.

Still the noise continued, even rose. Unmoved, Hatch nodded to the captain of the guard in front of the platform, who shouted out an order to his men. The guards fired their machine guns just above the heads of the crowd. The people all fell to the ground in fear. Not surprisingly, the shouting stopped.

"I thought that might get your attention," Hatch said. "I am Admiral-General Hatch, leader of the Elgen force. I realize that many of you feel displaced and inconvenienced. But trust me, those of you who are here right now are the fortunate ones. Because those who have not come, whether from disobedience or ignorance, are, at this moment, being hunted down. When they are caught, they will be marked as criminals, tagged, and jailed. Those who resist will be executed on the spot. We will not waste time in these matters."

Someone cried out from the crowd, "My sons!"

Hatch turned toward the voice. "Who said that?"

A woman raised her hand.

"If your sons are not here, they are criminals of the state. Pray that they do not resist arrest." He turned back to the crowd. "The island nation of Tuvalu is no more. From this moment on you are citizens of the Hatch Islands."

Another shout went out from the crowd. "Where is Prime Minister Saluni?" Then hundreds of voices echoed the query. "Where is the prime minister?"

Hatch looked at them with an amused smile. "You would like to know where *former* Prime Minister Saluni is? He's right here with us. Captain Page, please unveil our display."

The guards at the back of the covered box near the platform lifted the sheet while those in front pulled it forward until the drape fell in a pile to the ground. The crowd silenced. Inside the cage were about a dozen bald-faced rhesus macaque monkeys and, in one corner, the naked prime minister huddled in the fetal position. He looked pale and sick, his mouth swollen from the amputation of his tongue.

"The man who was once the Tuvaluan prime minister is now the Prime Monkey of Hatch. This is where he will reside for the rest of his life. Let his fate serve as a testament of our resolve. Those who oppose our regime will meet similar fates. Those who speak against the Elgen regime will speak no more. Those who *think* against the Elgen regime will be taught to think differently.

"I now welcome to the microphone someone you know well, the honorable Nikotemo Latu, your former ambassador to the United Nations."

The ambassador walked up to the microphone. He tapped on it twice, then leaned forward, countering the blank stares of the Tuvaluan people.

"Citizens of the Hatch Islands. Relax, this is a marvelous day for us, the people of Tuvalu. Our culture and customs, our *tuu mo aganu Tuvalu*, our way of life, is a new way of life. A better way. Welcome to a new world.

"The Elgen have come to rescue our sinking island, to bring us an improved quality of life. We are fortunate to be benefactors of the benevolence of the Elgen generosity. For those who feel uncertain, I bring a message of hope and wisdom. Accept the change. I know that change is sometimes difficult, especially when you are elderly. But are you satisfied with all that our island holds? Is our health care enough? I think not.

"For those of you who think to resist, do not foolishly hold on to hope that someone might come to your aid. We have no contact with the outer world. This is your new world. Accept it willingly, and you will come to love it.

"Those who do not resist will be treated with respect and will

have a better future. Those who refuse to accept this great change will face much pain and difficulty. If you care about your families, your children, your aged parents, then you will do the right thing. There is no choice. All of this island's leadership has signed an oath of allegiance to the new Elgen government. All except for the Prime Monkey. He has foolishly, selfishly, betrayed all of us and tried to cling to power. That is why his punishment is so severe. And he will be here, as a reminder, every day, all day."

"You have betrayed us!" a large, older man near the platform shouted. He stuck his finger out at the ambassador. "You are no longer a Tuvaluan. You are a traitor."

Two squads of Elgen guards rushed the man, while one of the squads stood with guns pointed toward the crowd, should anyone come to his aid.

The protestor was able to knock down just one of the guards before he was tased by three different guns, then beaten nearly unconscious by truncheons. The guards then dragged the man out before the crowd. He was lifted to his knees and pushed up against the pole next to the monkey cage. His arms were bound behind the pole, and a belt was cinched tightly around his waist to hold him up.

"Let this be a lesson for all of you," Hatch said. "This man will not hear. He does not need his ears." He looked down. "Captain."

The Elgen squad captain brought out a long, serrated knife and cut off the man's ears as he screamed in agony. Then the captain stepped back so all could witness.

"Does anyone else have a complaint?" Hatch asked.

Nobody spoke. Only the sound of crying could be heard in the audience.

"Very well. You learn quickly. Now I would like to introduce your new sovereign, the monarch of the Hatch Islands, King Quentin. You will obey and honor your new king, even as you would obey and honor me. He will explain to you the procedure you are to follow today."

Quentin stepped up to the microphone as Hatch put his hand on Quentin's shoulder.

"Greetings," Quentin said nervously. "I am certain today might be

difficult for you. But all good changes begin with difficulty." Quentin lifted the paper that Hatch had given him and began to read. "We desire that all of you become citizens of the new nation of the Hatch Islands. The procedure to gain your citizenship will be simple. All you need to do is sign a few forms, declare your allegiance to me and the new government, and have your picture taken for your citizen card. It is that simple. Then, in celebration of your new citizenship, we offer a delicious, celebratory meal.

"With a new government there will, of course, be changes. One of these changes involves the currency you are currently using. The Elgen Mark will replace the Tuvaluan dollar. This will not be a difficult process. You will simply exchange your money at the Hatch central bank. You have two days to turn in your Tuvaluan currency. So go to the Hatch bank as soon as possible.

"Only citizens will be allowed to exchange currency, and you must have your citizen card with you, the one we will provide you with today. In seven days from now it will be illegal to use Tuvaluan currency. No store or place of business in any of the Hatch Islands will accept it. To do so is a crime punishable by imprisonment or flogging. The previous currency, just like the previous government, is extinct. Tuvaluan dollars will be worthless and burned.

"For those of you who have bank accounts, your money has already been converted to the Elgen Mark. And I have more good news. Those who sign the declaration of citizenship will receive an additional five hundred Elgen Mark, which can soon be spent at a new Hatch department store that will provide many goods and products that you have previously gone without. For this we have Admiral-General Hatch to thank for his generosity."

Quentin paused for applause, but none came. He continued. "We expect that some of you might choose *not* to sign the declaration of allegiance. As long as you are obedient to the new laws of the land, you will not be punished for your decision. But be aware that rejecting citizenship has its consequences.

"Noncitizens will not be allowed in any of the Hatch Islands community buildings, stores, medical clinics, or hospital. This also means

that if you are now, in any way, employed by the government, your employment will be terminated.

"Noncitizens will not be allowed to travel abroad or even between the islands. Noncitizens will have no right to vote on issues that concern the people of Hatch. Noncitizens will also have no rights before the Elgen courts. If they are found guilty of an infraction by the Elgen guard, they will be punished immediately without trial.

"Noncitizens will not have access to electricity. And, finally, noncitizens will defer to citizens in all circumstances. You will ride in the back of the bus, stand in the back of all lines. You may not drink out of the same water fountains as the citizens. You are, simply put, inferior.

"As you see, the choice is yours. But once you make this decision, it is final. So decide wisely. For those wishing to declare citizenship, you will line up in one of these twelve queues to my right. When you reach the front of the line, you will raise your hand to the square and read the declaration you will be shown, in which you will renounce your Tuvaluan citizenry and declare your allegiance to the new Elgen government. Your photograph will be taken and added to our database, and you will be given a citizen card and number.

"For those foolish few who choose not to join the new government, you will go to the line at my left." He pointed to the side. The line began next to the pole where the man, the lone protestor, lay bound and bleeding. "You will be marked as a noncitizen and injected with a device so that we can track your movements at all times. You will then be free to return to your primitive and impoverished lifestyle."

Some of the people began moving toward the citizenship lines.

"Wait, please," Quentin said, holding up his hand. "Do not move yet. In one minute I am going to give you the opportunity to make your decision. A life of prosperity and happiness, or one of poverty and deprivation. As we make this transition, it will be wise for you to stay tuned to your radio for further instructions. Do you all understand?"

"Yes!" someone shouted.

Hatch stepped back up to the microphone. "I would like to hear your acclamation for your new king. All hail King Quentin, three times."

The people began shouting. "All hail King Quentin. All hail King Quentin. All hail King Quentin."

When they had finished, Hatch said, "There is one more thing. The first fifty people in each line who swear allegiance will be given another five hundred Elgen Mark. You may line up now."

The scene looked like the start of a marathon race as people sprinted for the lines. Some of the older people who were closer to the lines were knocked down or trampled by others rushing from the back. Quentin looked over at Hatch, who was nodding with approval.

"Just like you said it would be," Quentin said.

"*Exactly* as I said it would be," Hatch said without smiling.

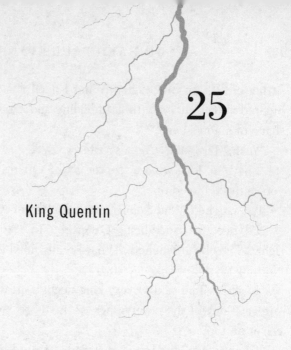

25

King Quentin

Over the next week King Quentin and the other Glows moved from the *Faraday* into the royal palace, which, by Elgen standards, was modest and in need of renovation. Quentin, at Hatch's instruction, began building his cabinet—a group of counselors—to help him run the nation.

Early on the morning of the eighth day, Quentin was in his office looking over a résumé when Tara walked in. She sat down in one of the chairs facing his desk. "Are you growing a beard?"

Quentin looked up. "Yes. What do you think?"

Tara nodded. "It looks kingly," she said. "So how does it feel to be a king?"

"It's not what I thought it would be," he said, his voice dull. "You get these pictures in your head of what it's supposed to be like—probably from old King Arthur movies. But the truth is, it's mostly just interviewing people and paperwork. I mean, look at what I'm

sitting on. It's an office chair. What I need is a throne, one of those big, red velvet chairs with gold leafing and a tall back carved in the shape of a lion's head."

"Yeah," Tara said. "And a scepter."

"I have no idea what a scepter is for," Quentin said, grinning. "But you're right. I need one."

Tara laughed. "And a court jester. You've got to have one of those."

"I'd need a court first," Quentin said. "And we've got Bryan, right?" They both laughed. "What I really need is a crown. It's iconic. Nothing says 'king' like a crown."

"Exactly," Tara said. "Every king needs a crown. What kind would you get—one of the pointy ones, or the more roundish kind with red velvet on top?"

"I don't care. As long as it's made of pure gold and inset with a few million worth of jewels."

Just then Dr. Hatch walked into the room. "So it's a crown you covet," he said.

Quentin flushed. "Sorry, sir. We were just being . . . stupid."

"If every fool wore a crown, everyone would be king," Hatch said. He sat down, glancing over to Tara. "Would you excuse us, please?"

"Yes, sir," Tara said, immediately standing.

"See you," Quentin said.

After she was gone, Hatch said, "Quentin, have you wondered why I would make you king of a tiny nation when I could have just as easily turned all of the Tuvaluans into slaves?"

"Yes, sir. I have."

"This is not a kingdom," he said. "It is your classroom. These backward natives are not subjects; they are *practice*. If you are to rule millions, you must first learn to rule thousands. Kingship is an art to be mastered—like the foil or the chessboard—and the only certainty of kingship is that someone is always standing behind the throne, waiting to take your seat. If you wish to maintain a throne, there are certain rules that must be followed."

"What are those, sir?"

"The greatest threat to a dictator is not from without but from within. The first rule is, you must keep your subjects divided. A united people is a smoldering revolution. A divided people is a conquered people."

"How do I do that?" Quentin asked.

"You make them hate one another. Before World War Two, Hitler was amazed and disgusted by the hate the German people exercised toward one another. He harnessed their animosity and directed it to his own ends."

Quentin took out a pad of paper. "Do you mind if I take notes?"

"I would be disappointed if you didn't," Hatch said.

Quentin set his pen to the paper. "How do I make them hate each other?"

"You begin by teaching them that they have been wronged by one another—that they are victims of a grave injustice—and encourage them to embrace their victimhood."

"What if they haven't been wronged?"

"Everyone has been wronged," Hatch said. "Everyone. And if you can't find a potent enough current injustice, then borrow someone else's. Find one that happened to someone else long ago and make your citizen a supposed crusader for justice. Imbue them with a sense of moral superiority as they trample the rights of others beneath their feet. Righteous indignation is the alibi of mobs and murderers."

Hatch leaned back in his seat. "Unfortunately, the Tuvaluan people are of the same race and culture, as cultural disparity is the easiest way to divide a nation. But divisions in humanity can always be found. Turn men against women and women against men. Divide the young from the old, the rich from the poor, the educated from the uneducated, the religious from the nonreligious, the privileged from the underprivileged. Teach them to shame others and to use shame as a tool to their own ends.

"Make the ridiculous ideal of 'equality' their rallying cry. Let them get so caught up in their supposed moral superiority that they'd

rather see all men grovel in poverty than rise in differing levels of prosperity.

"Do not let them see that there has never been nor ever will be true equality, in property or rights. Equality is not the nature of the world or even the universe. Even if you could guarantee everyone the same wealth, humans would reject the idea. They would simply find a different standard to create castes, as there will always be differences in intelligence, physical strength, and beauty.

"Don't worry if your propaganda is true or false. Truth is subjective. It's as easy to tell a big lie as it is a small one. And any lie told enough will be regarded as truth. In dividing the young from the old, do not teach the youths the error of their elders' ways, as they may see through your propaganda. Instead, mock their elders. Mocking requires neither proof nor truth, as it feeds the fool's ego. You will see that when it comes to the masses, the stupider the individual, the more they want to prove it to the world.

"The second rule is to keep the people distracted from the weightier and more complex matters of liberty and justice. Keep them obsessed by their amusements—just as the Roman emperor Commodus gave the Roman people games to distract them from his poor leadership. A championship soccer team may do more to ease a public's suffering than a dozen social programs. If your subjects can name a movie star's dog but not the president of their country, you have no need to fear.

"The third rule is to teach them not to trust one another. An ancient proverb says, 'Kings have many ears and many eyes.' You must build a web of informants from within the population. Openly reward those who report on their neighbors. If your subjects don't know who is an informant and who isn't, they will never risk speaking their grievances."

Quentin finished writing, then looked up. "Thank you, sir."

"You will learn," Hatch said, "that human nature is a game. Learn to control the few, and you will someday control the masses." Hatch stood. "Give them hate. Give them games."

"I will start this afternoon."

"Very well." He took a step toward the door, then turned back. "I like the beard. Work on it."

"Thank you, sir."

As soon as Hatch walked out of his office, Quentin called his new minister of public planning. "I want to build a stadium."

PART EIGHT

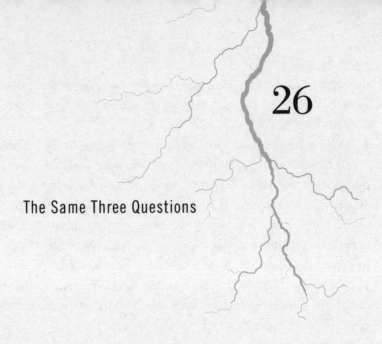

26

The Same Three Questions

**Ada County Jail
Boise, Idaho**

Julie Ridley stared back at her husband from behind the glass partition of the jail's visiting room. Her usual meticulously styled blond hair was disheveled and slightly matted, and instead of a carefully accessorized outfit, she was wearing an orangish-red jumpsuit that hung formlessly on her frail frame. In just three days she had already lost almost five pounds, and her face looked pale and gaunt. Her eyes were puffy from lack of sleep. She didn't have to sleep to have nightmares. She was living one.

The Boise police had arrested her as she'd walked from her car to her home. They had searched her, handcuffed her, and then driven her to jail while detectives and a forensic team combed over her car and residence. Their search bore fruit—they found a large quantity of drugs, and traces of her daughter's blood.

It took two days for her arraignment and the judge to set bail. Because she was considered a flight risk, and in consideration of the

quantity of drugs they had found in her possession, the bail was set high, at a quarter million dollars—almost enough to guarantee that she wouldn't get out.

During her time in jail she had been kept mostly isolated and was interrogated repeatedly by detectives who asked the same three questions a thousand different ways: *Where did you get the drugs? Where is your daughter? Why did you go to Mexico?*

Today was the first visit she'd been allowed since her incarceration, and her husband, Charles, sat on the other side of the thick, bulletproof glass window of a visitation booth, holding a telephone. He also looked like he hadn't slept in days. Over his career he had put more people in this jail than he could remember, but he had never expected to be visiting his wife here.

"Are you okay?" he asked.

"I'm in jail, Chuck."

"Dumb question," he said. "Sorry."

She didn't respond.

"Julie, you've got to tell me what's going on."

"I wish I could."

"What's stopping you? You're going to have to talk sometime. Do you have any idea what kind of trouble you're in?"

"I know exactly what kind of trouble I'm in. More than you do."

"What does that mean?"

She just breathed out slowly. "It doesn't matter."

"Yes, it matters!" Charles said. He leaned up to the glass. "Julie, you need to give me some answers, here. You owe me that."

Julie looked at him angrily. "I owe you?"

"I'm sorry. Please. I want to help."

"What do you want to know?"

"To begin with, why were you in Mexico?"

She slowly shook her head. "I can't tell you."

Charles groaned with frustration. He looked into her eyes. "Were you there to buy drugs?"

Julie's eyes narrowed. "We've been married for twenty-six years and you ask me if I'm a drug dealer? Who do you think I am?"

"Honestly, these days, I don't know, Julie. You tell me you're going to Scottsdale, and then you secretly fly off to some stronghold for drug cartels in Mexico and then won't tell me why. The police find a half million dollars of heroin in your car. . . ." His eyes welled up. "Then they find traces of Taylor's blood. . . ." He raked a hand back through his hair. "I don't know who you are anymore. I wish you would tell me."

"I wish I could," she said. "But the less you know, the better."

"No, the less I know, the less I can do to help."

"You can't help me, Chuck. No one can. They're just using me. And after they get what they want, they'll kill me."

"What are you talking about? No one's going to kill you. Who do you think is using you?"

"The people trying to get Taylor."

"Taylor is gone, honey."

Julie didn't speak.

"You need to tell me something. Do you know where Taylor is?"

She shook her head. "No."

"Did you do something to her?"

Julie slammed her hand against the glass. "How dare you!"

The police officer standing against the wall behind her yelled, "Control yourself, Ridley. Or I'll terminate your visit."

"Sorry," she said. She turned back and took a deep breath, then looked up at her husband. "How dare you ask me that?"

"They found traces of her blood in your car. What am I supposed to think?"

"You're supposed to think that I love my daughter, because you know I do. You know her blood was planted."

"Planted by whom? Who would do this? *Why* would they do this?"

"Bad people," she said. "It's a conspiracy."

Charles sighed. "Julie, when you say that, you sound . . ."

"Crazy? Paranoid?"

"I didn't say that."

"But you almost did." She breathed out. "Chuck, you know me. I'm not crazy. And I'm not lying to you. Have I ever lied to you before?"

Charles was quiet for a moment, then said, "Not until now."

"You know I've been framed."

"By whom? The same person who's leaving drugs in your car?"

"Yes."

"Then tell me who they are. Give me something to go on here."

Julie just put her head against the glass. "I can't. You wouldn't believe me if I did."

"You're telling me that someone just randomly picked some woman in Meridian, Idaho, to frame? Why would they willingly lose a half million dollars to frame you? It makes no sense."

Julie breathed out slowly in resignation, covering her eyes with her hands. "You're right. It makes no sense. Nothing makes sense anymore."

Charles just stared at her for a moment, then said, "You need to start giving them some answers, or things aren't going to go well for you. You could be in real trouble. We both could."

Julie slowly looked up at her husband. Her eyes were strong and cold. "My dear Charles, you have no idea what kind of trouble we're *really* in."

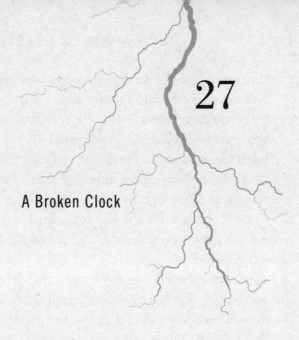

27

A Broken Clock

Chief Davis looked over as Officer Ridley opened the door to the chief's car. He waited until Charles was seated to talk. "How'd it go?"

Charles looked over at him. "Not well. She's suffering. She's afraid."

"I'm sorry," Davis said. "Did she tell you anything?"

"Nothing worth anything. She just kept saying that someone planted everything, and that someone is going to kill her."

Davis's brow furrowed. "Who's going to kill her?"

"She wouldn't say."

"Does she need a psychiatric evaluation?"

"I don't know. She seemed . . . normal."

"Normal, huh? We just found blood spatters and a half million dollars of heroin in her car. Hardly normal."

"No, I meant, she didn't sound crazy."

"Paranoid schizophrenics can be very convincing."

"I just don't get it. Julie's always been solid. She's as levelheaded a person as you'll ever meet."

"What other explanation could there be?"

"I don't know. I mean, the woman's a Girl Scout. She yells at me if I go a mile over the speed limit. She once drove a mile back to the grocery store because the guy at the register gave her a quarter too much in change." Charles shook his head. "It makes no sense. No sense at all. I don't even think she would know what to do with the drugs they found."

"That could work in her favor, you know. If we could show that she was forced into this, the judge could show leniency. As long as she cooperates. She could lead us to some major dealers."

"She's sticking to her claim that she knows nothing about where the drugs came from."

"What about your daughter?"

"Same thing. She says she knows nothing."

"Do you believe her?"

"I don't know what I believe anymore."

The chief was silent for a moment, then said, "I'm sorry, this has got to be really tough on you."

"Nothing compared to how tough it is on her," Charles said. "I just wish I could get her out of there. She's a mother, not a convict."

"A lot of convicts are mothers," Davis said. "I heard about the bail."

"A quarter million dollars," Charles said, shaking his head. "That's more than the equity we have in our home. I don't know how I can get my hands on that much."

Davis anxiously eyed Charles. "You're not going to try to raise it, are you?"

"She's my wife. I can't let her just sit in jail."

"Until we figure out what's going on, jail might be the best place for her. If she gets out, she may just run off to Mexico again."

Charles exhaled loudly. "I don't know what's happened to her, but I do know that I still love her. She's my life. I just don't know

what to do." He looked into the chief's eyes. "If it was your wife, what would you do?"

Davis shook his head. "I don't know. We married for better or worse, right? Bottom line, it's a man's job to protect his wife. The real challenge is knowing how best to do that. You've been on the force for fifteen years; you know as well as anyone that sometimes we need to protect people from themselves."

Charles just sat quietly thinking. "Yeah, you're right."

"Every now and then I'm right." He smiled sadly. "Even a broken clock is right twice a day, huh?" He leaned forward and started the car. "Let me buy you some pie."

"Thanks, but it's been a long day. I just want to go home."

"I understand," Davis said. He pulled the car out of the jail's parking lot and into traffic. Twenty minutes later they drove up into Charles's driveway.

"Home sweet home," Davis said.

"Not anymore. Not without her." He looked at the chief. "I can't help but feel guilty. I just feel like I should try to post bail."

"Chuck, listen to me here. I know you love Julie, which is why you need to be especially careful right now. Give her some time to get her head back on right, you know? If you post bail and she runs, then there's no turning back for her. If she's caught, no judge will let her out again. If she's not caught, you'll never see her again. It's a no-win situation."

"Yeah." He groaned. "You're right. Again." For a moment neither of them spoke. Then Charles said, "I'm going crazy just sitting at home. How long are you going to keep me suspended?"

"At least until her first court date," he said. "Look, heaven knows you can use the time off. Take a trip or something. Go see your boys. Or go up to Coeur d'Alene. There's some great fishing up there. You've given your all to the force for fifteen years; you deserve the break."

Charles took a deep breath. "All right. Maybe I will." He opened the car door. "Thanks for the ride."

"That's what friends are for. See you."

Charles saluted him, then got out of the car. He stepped back as the chief backed out of his driveway, then drove down the street.

As soon as he was down the road, Davis took out his phone and dialed a number.

"It's me. We just left the jail. She didn't tell him anything. He's thinking about posting bail, but I'm pretty sure that I talked him out of it. . . . Yeah, I know. Don't worry, it won't happen. He'll talk to me first. If he tries to post bail, we'll arrest him, too. She's not going anywhere. . . . Yes, sir. . . . We still have his place staked out, a man on both ends of the street. If anyone tries to visit him, I'll let you know. If anything happens, I'll call. And please thank Captain Marsden for the bottle of Scotch. No one knows Scotch like an Elgen." Davis hung up his phone. "And no one pays like one either."

PART NINE

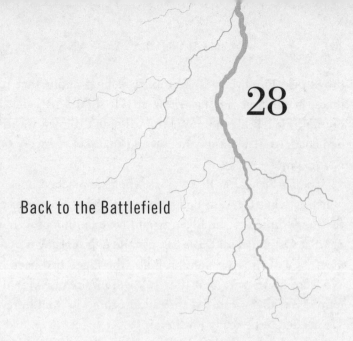

28

Back to the Battlefield

Earlier that day

The sun was just dawning when the four of us—Taylor, Gervaso, Ian, and I—pulled off the ranch road onto the freeway. The night before, while Gervaso had been packing the car, Jack had tried to talk Gervaso into letting him come with us, but Gervaso wouldn't budge. This was a covert operation, the fewer along the better. And, with Jack, there was the added risk of someone recognizing him. The same was true for Ostin, who had also asked to come. This was the first mission I'd been on without him.

Gervaso provided Taylor and me with hats and sunglasses to help conceal our identities once we reached Idaho. We couldn't take the odd chance of running into a former classmate or neighbor or even a stranger who recognized us. For all we knew, our faces had ended up plastered on milk cartons.

The drive from southern Utah to Boise took a little less than ten hours. It felt strange being back in Boise, especially when Gervaso

drove past PizzaMax. I had mixed feelings about that place. I had mixed feelings about the whole city. It should have felt like home, but nothing felt like home anymore. I didn't think it was the city that had changed. It was the whole world that had changed. Or maybe it was just me.

It was a little after five o'clock when we reached Boise, rush hour, which is what Gervaso had planned on. The more cars there were, the more difficulty the Elgen would have finding us. I thought again of what Ostin had said. *The best place to hide a penny is in a jar of pennies.* The last time we were in Boise, the Elgen had been hunting us. We were pretty sure that they still were. Why else would they have framed Taylor's mother if they didn't think it would draw us back? We needed to be ready for them.

On the way to Taylor's house we drove past Meridian High School. The marquee read:

CHEERLEADER TRYOUTS
WED–THURS AFTER SCHOOL

Taylor didn't say anything. Just past the school, Gervaso stopped the car on a side street, and Ian and I changed places—he got in back with Taylor, and I got in front with Gervaso.

"I'm first going to make a slow pass down the street to check things out," Gervaso said. "The Elgen set this trap, so we should assume they're watching. Ian, I want you to watch closely for anyone suspicious. Also for any cameras panning license plates. This car's plates won't set off any alarms, but it's not an Idaho plate, and that still might cause them to take a second look."

"I'll recognize an Elgen guard," Ian said. "But if they're not in uniform, I won't know if someone belongs around here or not."

"Taylor can touch him and see what he sees," I said.

"Brilliant idea," Gervaso said. "Look for anything out of the ordinary. We also need to see if Taylor's dad is home before we break into the house."

"What if he is?" Taylor asked.

"We'll come back at night after he's asleep," Gervaso said.

"Put your sunglasses on," he said to me. "Taylor, you and Ian need to duck down."

"Then I won't be able to see," Taylor said.

"Ian will see for you," Gervaso said.

Ian took Taylor's hand, and they both lay sideways in the backseat, with Taylor lying against Ian. I looked ahead, trying to act normal.

Gervaso slowly turned onto Taylor's street. "Here we go," he said.

"That tan car on the right," Ian said. "It's a police officer. He's got binoculars."

"Why would the police be watching their house?" I asked. "They wouldn't be expecting anyone."

"What is he doing?" Gervaso asked.

"He looked at us, but he's not concerned."

"That's my house up on the right side," Taylor said. "The tan one with aspens on the side."

"There are two cars in the garage," Ian said.

"That's my mother's van and my father's truck," Taylor said.

"I can't slow down any more without looking suspicious," Gervaso said. "So look quickly."

"I can't see anyone in the house," Ian said. "The lights are all off, so I don't think he's there."

"It looks empty," Taylor said. "But that's my father's only car. He wouldn't have left without it."

"Maybe he went for a walk," I said.

"Or maybe someone picked him up."

"All I know is that the house is empty," Ian said after we'd passed. "The front dead bolt is locked."

"Anything else?"

"Looks like we've got another one of Boise's finest up ahead," Ian said.

"Why would there be police here?" Taylor asked.

"Maybe they think the drug cartel will come looking for the drugs that went missing," I offered.

"That's a possible explanation," Gervaso said.

"Wait," Ian said.

"What?"

"I'm not positive, but it looked like that cop was holding an Elgen handbook."

"Are you sure?"

"No."

As we drove past the officer's car, he glanced up at us but showed no concern. I pretended not to see him.

"If they're working for the Elgen, they're most likely looking for Taylor, not us."

"I was right," Ian said. "It's an Elgen book. The Elgen guard insignia is on the cover."

"The Boise police are working with the Elgen?" I said.

"My dad isn't with the Elgen," Taylor said angrily.

"I never said he was," Gervaso said, trying to calm her down. "If he was, the Elgen wouldn't be staking him out." We reached the end of the street, then kept going.

"Now what?" I said.

"We wait until it's a little darker; then we sneak into the house." He asked Taylor, "Is that the school behind your house?"

"Yes."

"What's the best way to get to your house without being seen?"

"There's a gate for the school along Hampton Road. We can park there, then follow the fence up to my house. There's an opening in my next-door neighbor's fence that we used to climb through. It comes out behind a row of bushes, so we can sneak into my backyard and go in through the back. My parents keep a key under a rock near the door."

"That gives us about an hour before dark," Gervaso said. "Anything you want to do while we're here?"

No one spoke for a moment; then I said, "Can we go to PizzaMax?"

"Is that a pizza place?" Gervaso asked.

"Yes. We passed it on the way here."

"We can't go inside," he said. "But we can order to go and eat in the car."

"I'm good with that," I said.

"How can you think of food at a time like this?" Taylor asked.

"How can you not?" I replied.

She frowned. "Now you sound like Ostin."

"I'll take that as a compliment."

Even though it was almost twilight, Taylor and I still wore our sunglasses as we drove into the restaurant's parking lot. Being back at PizzaMax filled me with unexpected emotion. I realized that I hadn't really asked to go there for the pizza. I was hungry, but there was something psychological driving me there. In many ways, PizzaMax was where everything changed. It's where I first met Dr. Hatch and Zeus and Nichelle. It was where my mother was kidnapped. Nothing in my life was the same after that night . . . especially me. It was the place where my fantasy of security was finally shattered.

I once watched a show on the History channel about old men going back to battlefields where they had fought as young soldiers. There's something in us that wants to see the place where we once battled.

Gervaso parked our car backward in the parking spot to facilitate a quick getaway should we require one. Then, leaving us there to wait, he went inside, and returned twenty minutes later with an extra-large pizza with garlic bread and sodas.

"That's a busy place," Gervaso said. "It holds more people than you'd think."

"It's always crowded," I said. "My mother and I used to come here for special occasions. This is where I was when I first met Dr. Hatch."

"It was on your birthday," Taylor said. "I was supposed to come too. But I'd already been kidnapped."

"You really met Dr. Hatch here?" Ian asked.

"Right over there by the light pole," I said, pointing. "Hatch wanted to see my powers in action, so he sent a GP to steal our car. As I handed the GP the keys, I shocked him. Then Hatch appeared out of nowhere, clapping."

"Creepy," Ian said.

"Yeah. Then Nichelle did her thing and I passed out. That's when they kidnapped my mother."

"Why didn't they take you?"

"I think they wanted both of us. But before they could take me, Ostin and a bunch of people came out of the restaurant."

We sat in the car and ate, though Taylor didn't eat much. She was too upset.

Gervaso seemed especially anxious, carefully eyeing everyone coming in and out of the restaurant. By the time we finished eating, the sun had fallen behind the mountains.

Gervaso looked back at us. "Everyone ready?"

"I'm ready," Taylor said.

"Me too," I said.

Ian nodded. "Yeah, let's do this."

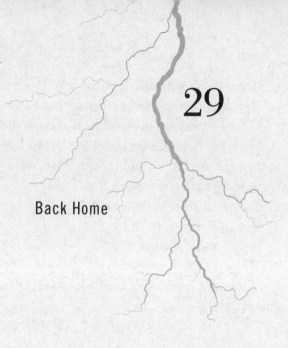

29

Back Home

Two undercover police cars were still parked on Taylor's street when we returned, though not the same cars or officers. I figured that there must have been a shift change.

We turned onto the road past Taylor's, drove to the end of the street, turned, and then again passed Taylor's street, parking on Hampton Road, which ran along the south side of Meridian High. Fortunately there was enough light from the moon that the three of us wouldn't be standing out like walking glowsticks.

Ian took one last long look around as we got out of the car and made our way along the school's wood-slat fence to Taylor's backyard, about seventy-five yards from our car.

"It's right here," Taylor said. She walked up to the wooden fence and ran her hand down it until she found the loose slats and pulled two of them aside. "I can't believe that after all these years no one's ever fixed this thing."

"Do they have a dog?" Gervaso asked.

"No dogs," Ian said before Taylor could answer.

"There's a woman inside playing the piano. And a cat."

"That's Mrs. Glad," Taylor said. "She teaches piano to half the kids in the neighborhood. Her husband owns some kind of metalworking place, so he's always working late."

"Is anyone in Taylor's home?" Gervaso asked Ian.

"No. Still vacant."

"What about their cars?"

"They're still there."

"I wonder where he is," Taylor said. "If he's at work, his car wouldn't be there."

"He's not at work," Gervaso said. "Remember, he's been suspended."

"What if he doesn't come back tonight?" I asked.

"If he's not back by tomorrow, we'll have to hunt him down," Gervaso said.

"Maybe he went on vacation," Ian suggested.

"With his wife just incarcerated?" Gervaso said. "I doubt it. Not if he loves her."

"Of course he loves her," Taylor said tersely.

We crossed the back of the neighbor's yard, then, on all fours, crawled into Taylor's backyard behind an overgrown hedge. It appeared that all the lights were off except for one—a small dome light in the kitchen.

"Are we still safe?" Gervaso asked.

"Still safe," Ian said.

"Does your home have an alarm system?"

"It didn't," Taylor said.

"If they installed one, they would put stickers on the windows," Gervaso said. "Ian, can you see an alarm?"

"I don't see any wires around the door."

"How about motion detectors?"

"Not that I can see."

"All right," Gervaso said. "Just be prepared."

"I'll get the key," Taylor said. She crept up to the back door, then squatted down and looked under a stone, lifting the key from beneath it. Then she got up, unlocked the door, and went inside.

"You're next, Michael," Gervaso said. "Then Ian."

"Okay," I said. I stood, ran to the door, and slipped inside.

There was a single light on above the kitchen sink. Taylor was standing to the side of the kitchen, looking at a large family photograph on the wall.

"I can't believe I'm finally home," she said. Then she reached out to me. "Come with me. I want to see my room."

I took her hand, and we walked out of the kitchen and down the hall. For a moment she stood in her room's doorway, just staring inside. I looked over her shoulder. "What are you thinking?"

"It looks exactly the way it did the day I left." She turned back to me. "They were expecting me back. They never gave up on me coming back."

"Of course not," I said. "They love you."

I followed her into her room, which was only illuminated by our glow. It was feminine, with a four-poster bed and pink-and-red polka-dot wallpaper adorned with large pictures of Taylor cheerleading. Pinned to the wall above her bed were two felt flags, one goldenrod, the other purple, with the word "WARRIORS" next to a picture of Meridian High School's mascot.

On top of her bed was a mountain of pillows and her cheerleading outfit, which looked freshly pressed and laid out, as if it were just waiting for her to return and put it on. Against one wall was a white antique three-drawer writing desk beneath a cork message board. The desk had a pewter desk lamp on one side hanging over a framed picture of Taylor and her two older brothers.

I picked up the picture. "Do you think about them very much?"

"All the time," she said softly. "I'd give anything to talk to them." She corrected herself. "I guess anything but risk everyone's lives." She breathed out slowly. "Why do I have a feeling I'll never see this again?"

I didn't know what to say. Finally I took her hand. "We better get back with the others."

We walked back out into the hallway and out to the front room, where Gervaso was standing near the front door. He held a small penlight in his teeth. He had taken the cover off the light switch and was doing something with the wires. Ian was sitting backward on the couch, staring at the wall, which would seem weird for anyone but him. To Ian pretty much everything was a window.

"Anything?" I asked.

"The cops are bored," he said. "That one keeps picking his nose."

"Thanks for sharing that," Taylor said. She sat down on a love seat.

"How does it feel to be back home?" Ian asked.

"It feels sad," she said. "Like a morgue."

"That's because no one's here," he said.

"Or maybe because I've buried so many of my memories here," she replied.

"What are you doing?" I asked Gervaso.

"Just throwing him off a little when he gets here. Sometimes the simplest distractions are the best."

He put the switch plate back on and had begun to screw it into place when Ian said, "Someone's coming. A police car."

"One of the undercover police?"

"No. It's a third car. This one's marked and has a rack on top."

Taylor walked over and took Ian's arm. "That's my father in the passenger seat."

"Who's that with him?" Ian asked.

"I think that's his boss. The chief."

"They're pulling into the driveway."

"I'm going to the kitchen," Taylor said.

"They're in the driveway," Ian said. "He just shut off the car. They're talking."

"What do we do if the chief comes in with him?" I asked.

"We go out the back door," Gervaso said. "Ian, tell us if the chief starts to get out of the car.

"Will do."

For a moment none of us spoke. Then I asked, "What's going on?"

"They're just talking."

"Can you read their lips?" Gervaso asked.

"No. Now they're shaking hands. Taylor's dad just opened the car door."

"Is he armed?"

"No. He's not in uniform."

"Give us the step-by-step," Gervaso said.

"He's getting out. They're still talking . . . still talking. . . . He shut the door. . . . The chief's pulling out of the driveway; Taylor's dad is waiting . . . waiting. . . . He waves. . . . Okay, he's walking to the front door. He's taking out his keys." His voice fell to a whisper. "He's on the front porch. . . ."

Gervaso raised his hand to stop Ian from talking. We could hear the sound of Mr. Ridley's key enter the doorknob. The handle turned, and a moment later the door opened. Mr. Ridley stepped inside, reaching for the light switch. He flipped it several times.

"What the . . ."

Still in the dark he shut the door and locked it. Then, as he turned, he saw us. Or at least our glows. For a moment he froze; then he reached for his gun before realizing that he wasn't carrying it.

"We're not here to hurt you," Gervaso said. He turned on the lamp on the sofa's end table.

Mr. Ridley looked at us anxiously. "Who are you?"

"We're your friends."

"I know my friends," he replied. "I don't know you."

"Still, we are your friends," Gervaso said.

"Why is their skin glowing like that?"

"We'll explain later," Gervaso said.

"Mr. Ridley, you know me," I said.

Mr. Ridley's eyes narrowed. "Vey. What have you done with my daughter?" His hand clenched into a fist.

"You should have a seat," Gervaso said, motioning to an armchair across from us. "Please."

Mr. Ridley stood for a moment, as if not sure what to do. Then he slowly went to the seat and sat down. He looked at us for a moment, then asked, "What cartel are you with?"

"We're not with a cartel," Gervaso said.

"Are you the people my wife said are going to kill her?"

"No. We're here to protect her from those people. Like I said, we're friends."

Mr. Ridley just looked confused. "Did you take my daughter?"

"Again, you're confusing us for the other side. Michael rescued your daughter. We're the ones who brought her back."

"Back? Back where?"

"I'm right here, Daddy," Taylor said, turning the hall light on. Tears were running down her face.

Mr. Ridley swung around. For a moment he just stared in disbelief. Then he said, "Taylor!" They ran to each other and embraced. "My girl. Oh, my girl."

They held each other for several minutes. "I've missed you so much," Mr. Ridley said. "I can't believe you're really here."

"I've missed you, Daddy. More than I can say."

He leaned back, kissed her on the forehead, then hugged her again. "I just can't believe you're really here." After another minute he looked into her eyes. "Please don't ever leave us again."

"She didn't leave you," I said. "She was kidnapped. The day before you came to see me."

He looked back at me. "Who kidnapped her?"

"A group of people called the Elgen."

He looked back at Taylor. "Did they hurt you?"

She hesitated, then lied. "No."

"Thank God. I thought you ran away. The texts I read . . . they broke my heart."

"I'm so sorry. Michael told me the Elgen had done that. They must have made it look like I'd run away so you wouldn't get the police involved."

After a while he looked back at me. "You knew she'd been kidnapped?"

I shook my head. "No. I only suspected it."

"Why didn't you tell me?"

"It wasn't that simple," Gervaso said. "This organization is very

secretive and very powerful. It's also international. If the police had gotten involved, the Elgen would have taken your daughter to some remote part of the world where no one would ever find her again. Michael did the right thing."

Mr. Ridley turned back to Taylor. "Why would they kidnap you? They didn't even ask for a ransom."

"They kidnapped her because she's special," Gervaso said. "Just like Michael."

"What do you mean, 'special'?" Mr. Ridley asked.

Gervaso looked at him intensely. "What I'm about to tell you is going to be a little difficult to believe."

Taylor took his hand. "Dad, you need to listen very carefully. What we're going to tell you is really weird."

"How weird?"

"Like aliens, UFO weird," Ian said.

Mr. Ridley glanced back and forth between us. He looked skeptical. "You're going to tell me she was abducted by aliens?"

"No," Gervaso said. "Not aliens. Worse."

"All right, try me."

"We don't have time to explain everything, but your daughter was born different from other children. She's electric."

He looked at us, then back at Taylor. "I don't understand."

"Michael and Taylor are both electric," Gervaso said. "So is Ian. They are three of seventeen electric children who were part of a failed hospital experiment. Electricity runs through their bodies. That's why they glow. It also gives them special gifts."

"What kind of gifts?"

"Michael?" Gervaso said. "Show him something."

I held out my hand, then pulsed, creating a grapefruit-size lightning ball.

Mr. Ridley stared in disbelief. "How did you do that?"

"Like I said, they're electric," Gervaso said.

He turned to Taylor. "You can do that?"

"No. I have other powers."

"Like what?"

She took his hand. "Think of something."

"Like what?"

"Anything. It doesn't matter."

"All right."

Taylor closed her eyes. "You're thinking this is crazy. And you still want to hit Michael for not telling you I was kidnapped."

"That's good to know," I said. "I saved your daughter. You should want to hug me or something."

"That's not going to happen," he said. "And you could have guessed that."

"Then think of a number," Taylor said.

He looked at us all skeptically, then said, "Okay. I'll play along."

She closed her eyes for a moment, then said, "You thought of number three thousand, two hundred and sixty-eight, our address. Then you changed your mind and decided that you're not going to think of a number so you can ruin my trick."

Mr. Ridley looked at her. "How did you do that?"

"That's my gift. I can read your brain's electrical signals—your *thoughts*. I can also reboot people's brains."

"What do you mean?"

"Remember that time when Ryan was in the final round of the spelling bee and the best speller in the state suddenly choked and kept asking over and over again for the word?"

"Yes. . . ."

"That's because I kept rebooting him."

"You were only eight."

"That's about the time I was figuring out what I could do," she said.

Gervaso said, "The people who made these children electric have been hunting them down. Michael and Taylor were the last ones they found. They tried to kidnap Michael, but something went wrong and they took his mother instead. They knew if they had her, Michael would come after her, which is the same thing the Elgen did to your wife. Only they framed her and, we assume, leaked the information to the police. Probably an anonymous caller."

"You're right, it was an anonymous caller," Mr. Ridley said.

"They knew that if she was in jail, Taylor would come to save her. And that's when they planned to capture her."

"That's what Julie was saying," Mr. Ridley said. "She said they were just using her to get Taylor."

"She's telling the truth," Gervaso said.

"Do you know my wife?" Mr. Ridley asked.

Gervaso nodded. "I met her three weeks ago. In Mexico."

"So that's why she went to Mexico." He turned to Taylor. "Did you see her there?"

Taylor nodded. "Yes."

"Why didn't she tell me?"

"She was going to, at the right time."

"She said she didn't know where you were," Mr. Ridley said.

"She didn't. I left Mexico before she did."

"Your wife did as she was instructed," Gervaso said. "To protect you and her. Had you known the truth, you both would be in jail right now. Or worse."

Mr. Ridley raked a hand back through his hair. "This is unbelievable."

"The Elgen think we're going to try to break your wife out of jail. But we have a different plan. You're going to post bail and get her out."

"I don't have that kind of money. Not even if I put my home up as collateral."

"Which is what you're going to do," Gervaso said. "You'll still be about ten thousand short. But you're going to suddenly remember that you have a special investment account that has fifteen thousand dollars in it. Then, after she's out, we'll take all of you to a safe place."

Mr. Ridley thought a moment; then he said, "Just a sec." He walked over to the coat closet near the doorway and reached inside.

"He has a gun," Ian said.

Mr. Ridley turned back around, holding his police revolver.

"Daddy!" Taylor said.

"Just stay calm, honey," Mr. Ridley said. "I know what I'm doing."

He looked at me. "Let me tell you what we're going to do. I'm going to turn you in to the police, show them my daughter, and they're going to let my wife go."

"No they won't," Gervaso said calmly.

"Dad," Taylor said, "put the gun down."

"Six bullets in the chambers," Ian said.

"You're making a mistake," Gervaso said. "We are not your enemy."

"You've had my daughter, and now you're using me to get to my wife."

"We're trying to protect Mrs. Ridley," I said.

He scowled at me. "I don't know how old you are, Vey, but you're not too young to be tried as an adult for kidnapping."

"Dad, Michael didn't kidnap me. He rescued me."

"Put the gun down, Officer Ridley," Gervaso said.

"That's not going to happen." He pulled a cell phone out of his pocket. "You can tell your crazy story down at police headquarters."

"I'll take care of it," I said to Gervaso. I reached out my hand. "Your phone's no good. I've already scrambled it."

Mr. Ridley looked down at his phone, then back up. "What are you doing?"

I took a step toward him. "Now put the gun down or I'll take it from you."

He looked at me anxiously. "Stop right there. If you don't think I'll shoot, you're mistaken."

"No, I just don't care if you do." I put my hand out. "Try it."

He leveled the gun at my chest. "Don't try me, Vey."

"Dad, don't!" Taylor shouted.

"Go on, Mr. Ridley. Shoot me. At least try to."

His hand was trembling. Finally he said, "You're just a kid." Then he pointed the gun at Gervaso. "But he's not."

That's when I blasted him.

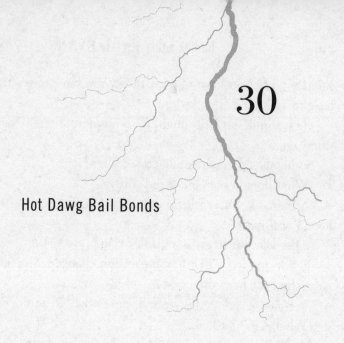

30

Hot Dawg Bail Bonds

Officer Ridley groaned out as he woke on the couch we had laid him on. He looked at me. "What did you do to me?"

"I did what I do. I shocked you. You gave me no choice."

"Could you have electrocuted me?"

I nodded. "If I had to."

He was quiet again.

"That was really stupid," Gervaso said. "Use your head, Officer. You're wasting valuable time."

"He's right, Dad, we don't have much time. You have to trust me. If you don't get Mom out of jail, the Elgen will kill her. You can't let that happen." Her voice cracked. "And you'll lose me again too."

"Trust me," Gervaso said to Taylor. "The Elgen will kill your father, too."

Taylor took her father's hand. "These are my friends, Dad. They've

saved my life. You have to trust them. You have to trust me. You just have to."

He was quiet as he thought for a moment; then he said, "Read my mind again."

Suddenly a pleasant smile crossed her face.

"What do you see?" he asked softly.

"A memory. I was a little girl. You're reading me a bedtime story. *Love You Forever.*"

"That was our story," Mr. Ridley said.

Taylor nodded. Then her expression changed. She let out a small gasp; then she began to cry.

"You really can read my mind, can't you?" he said.

"What is it?" I asked.

Mr. Ridley turned to me. "When Taylor was four, she fell into the water at Boise Creek Falls. I dove in and saved her."

"You've always been there for me," Taylor said. "Please, don't let me down now. I need your help to save Mom."

He looked at her for a moment, then took a deep breath. "I'm sorry. Everything's been so crazy lately, I don't know what to believe." He breathed out slowly. "But who should I believe over my daughter?"

I looked at Taylor. "Is he telling the truth?"

She looked at me. "Yes."

"What do I need to do?" Mr. Ridley asked.

"There's a bail bondsman on Cole Street," Gervaso said.

"Hot Dawg Bail Bonds," Mr. Ridley said.

"That's the one. Go there first thing in the morning and talk to Troy. He already has all your paperwork complete. He'll help you post bail. I'm sure you're familiar with the procedure."

"Of course."

"You'll have to go out the back and take our car."

"Why?"

"Because you're being watched."

Mr. Ridley looked surprised. "By whom?"

"By your own police," Gervaso said. "There are undercover police on both ends of the street. I'm surprised you didn't notice them."

Mr. Ridley looked upset. "So am I."

"One of them had an Elgen manual," Gervaso said. "They might be part of the system."

"That's not possible."

"Trust me, everything's possible. And nothing's what it seems to be."

"Including my daughter," Mr. Ridley said.

"Officer Ridley," Gervaso said, "timing is critical. You must be at the bail bond office by six forty-five. Troy will be opening early for you. Then come back to the house. At eight forty-five you'll take your car to the jail and wait for your wife to be released at nine o'clock. Everything will need to happen quickly. The moment you post bail, the Elgen will know. They'll be waiting for you when your wife steps out of the jail. You'll both be in danger. That's where we step in. Tomorrow morning I'll tell you the rest of the plan."

Mr. Ridley looked at us solemnly. "Whatever you say." He put his arm around Taylor and pulled her close. "Whatever it takes to protect my family."

"You can count on us to do the same," Gervaso said. "Now, I'm sure you'd like to spend some time with your daughter, so we'll leave you alone. We have some things to do to prepare for tomorrow." He turned to Ian and me. "Let's go. I need your help getting some things out of the car."

As we started to go, Mr. Ridley said, "Just a moment."

We all turned back.

"Thank you for bringing my daughter back. Especially you, Michael."

"It was my pleasure," I said.

"Good night," Gervaso said. "And don't stay up too late. You're going to need your rest."

PART TEN

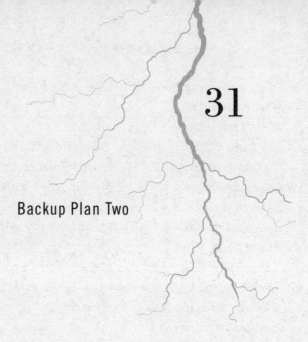

31

Backup Plan Two

**The next morning,
9:17 a.m.**

Chief Davis was sitting next to his wife at his kitchen table, drinking a coffee and reading the morning paper, when his phone rang. He didn't recognize the number but answered anyway.

"Davis here."

"We seem to have a problem, Chief," a voice said.

"Who is this?"

"This is Captain Marsden."

Davis was shocked. "Captain. It's an honor."

"No, it's a problem. It would seem that Officer Ridley has decided to post bail."

The news caught Davis off guard. "What? But he said . . ."

"I don't care what he said, Chief. He intends to post bail."

"That's no problem. It will take him at least an hour to do the paperwork and get to the jail. We'll arrest him on the way."

"He's already at the jail," Marsden said. "In fact, he's about to leave with his wife."

"That's not possible," Davis said.

"It's reality, Chief. Either you take care of this or we will."

"I'm on it," Davis said. "We'll initiate backup plan two. We have two men on Ridley's street, and we'll arrest Ridley the minute he pulls out of the jail."

"I suggest you hurry, Chief. Because, by my calculations, that's in about twelve minutes."

"I'll be right there. And don't worry. She's going to be wearing a GPS ankle bracelet, so they can't elude us, even if they try." He hung up, then set down his coffee. "I've got to run," he said to his wife.

"Something wrong?"

"Nothing I can't fix," he said.

Davis sped to the jail. As he pulled into the jail's parking lot, he saw Ridley's car parked up against the north retaining wall. He pulled his car into the lot opposite Ridley's, about forty yards from the jail's front door. As he put his car into park, his phone rang.

"Davis."

"Glad you could make it," Marsden said.

"Where are you?" Davis asked.

"That's not important. The paperwork is done. Ridley's wife has been released into his custody. She's changing her clothes. They're about to come out."

"We're ready," Davis said. "His home has been taken care of. I've got two officers on their way now. We'll arrest him as he pulls out."

"I'll be watching," Marsden said. "If you miss him, we'll blow up his car."

"Don't do that," Davis said. "You can't imagine the bureaucratic mess that will be."

"Then don't screw this up."

"Wait, I think that's them. Hold on." The jail door opened, and Officer Ridley stepped out with his wife. Charles quickly glanced around, then walked toward his car.

"That's him," Davis said, slightly slumping down in his seat.

"We have eyes on him too," Marsden said.

When Officer Ridley reached his car, he and his wife hugged and kissed. He opened the passenger door and waited for her to get in; then he walked around to the other side of the vehicle.

Just then a white police van drove up behind the car and stopped, temporarily blocking Ridley's car from view.

"I've lost visual," Marsden said.

"Doesn't matter," Davis said. "He can't pull out with that van behind him."

As the van pulled ahead, Ridley's reverse lights illuminated; then the car started to back out of the parking place.

"Okay, I'm on him," Davis said.

That's when the car exploded.

Almost every car alarm in the parking lot sounded off as the fire raged white-hot.

"What did you do?" Davis shouted at Marsden. "I said to give me a chance to arrest him."

"We didn't do that," Marsden said.

"Well, we sure didn't," Davis said. "If you didn't do it, who did?"

"Perhaps the resistance wanted them silenced."

"I thought you said the resistance was destroyed."

"Not everyone. Not the Electroclan."

"They're the parents of one of the Electroclan. The Electroclan aren't going to kill their own parents. Holy crap, how much explosive did they use?"

PART ELEVEN

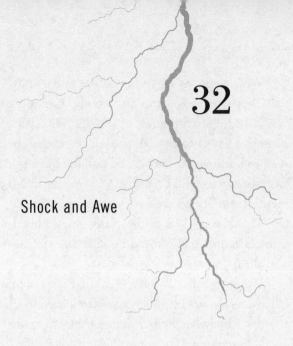

32

Shock and Awe

Charles held his wife tightly as Gervaso pulled the police van out of the jail's parking lot. She was crying, and all he could say was, "I'm so sorry. I'm so sorry."

I had already deactivated the ankle tracking bracelet she wore with a massive pulse that shorted out the device.

"Mom," Taylor said.

Mrs. Ridley turned back. "Taylor!"

They hugged over the seat. "You made it back. I was so worried," Mrs. Ridley said.

"We're together again. That's what matters."

"With a little luck we'll keep it that way," Gervaso said. "What's going on back there, Ian?"

Ian grinned. "Shock and awe, baby. Shock and awe. The Elgen are sitting in their cars on the east side of the building. The chief just got out of his car to survey the damage, but it's way too hot for him to get close."

"What happens when they don't find a body?" Mr. Ridley asked.

"They won't expect to find a body," Gervaso said. "We filled the car with two hundred pounds of rust thermite. It burns at four thousand degrees. That's hot enough to melt the asphalt beneath it. By the time it stops burning, the car will be nothing but a puddle of molten metal. Everything else will be ashes." He glanced at Mrs. Ridley in the rearview mirror. "It's good to see you again, Julie."

"Thank you," Mrs. Ridley said, still cuddled up in her husband's arms. "I didn't think you'd be able to save me—with all the police and all. . . ."

"Mom, you should have seen the Starxource plant in Taiwan. The jail's security was like a day care compared to that."

Mrs. Ridley laughed. "I'm just glad you made it back."

"Where are we going now?" Mr. Ridley asked.

"We're ditching the van," Gervaso said. "It was caught on video surveillance. They may suspect it of being involved with the explosion and start looking for it."

"Where do we do that?"

"Where we left the car this morning," he said. "It's at a warehouse in Nampa. We'll exchange cars, then head south to our ranch. The sooner we get out of Idaho, the better. The Elgen are cautious. They won't just automatically assume you were killed. If they don't find your bodies, they'll keep looking."

There had been an accident on the freeway, so the drive to Nampa took about ten tense minutes longer than it should have. As we drove, Gervaso scanned the radio until he found a news station reporting the explosion. A spokesman for the Ada County Jail stated that they believed the explosion had been perpetrated by a local gang who had threatened retaliation after one of their gang members had been arrested last month.

"We're doing everything in our power to bring the guilty parties to justice," the spokesman said.

A reporter asked, "Was anyone hurt in the explosion?"

The spokesman hesitated. "We have no comment on that just yet."

* * *

When we reached Nampa, Gervaso dialed a number on his cell phone, then spoke just two words, "We're here." We then drove slowly along a quarter-mile section of warehouses, mostly protected behind tall chain-link fences with razor wire on top. At one of the entrances a Hispanic man wearing a navy-blue mechanic's jumpsuit pushed open a gate as we approached.

"Everything look good?" Gervaso asked Ian.

"No one here but the man," he said. "He has a gun."

"As he should," Gervaso said.

Gervaso drove the van through the gate, and the man closed and chained it behind us. We then drove into an open warehouse, and a metal overhead door rolled down after us. After the door was shut, Gervaso turned off the van and said, "You can all get out."

As we climbed out of the van, the Hispanic man walked in through a side door. He wore a large grin. "*Hola*, Gervaso."

The two men hugged; then the man grabbed one end of the van's police decal and pulled it off.

"It looks very much real," he said. "I do good work."

"Yes, you do good work," Gervaso said. "Now destroy it."

The man looked at us. "Would your friends like something to drink? I have a soda machine." He pointed to an upright soft drink vending machine.

"Yes, please," Taylor said.

"Help yourself. You do not need coins," the man said. He walked to the side of the room and opened the front of a Coca-Cola machine. "Please, help yourself."

Ian, Taylor, and I walked over to the machine. I grabbed a cold root beer.

"There's no beer in that machine, is there?" Mr. Ridley asked.

"No, sir," the man replied. "I'm sorry."

"You want something, Gervaso?" I asked.

"Just some water."

"There's no water in here," I said.

"The water is in the small refrigerator," the man said. "On the ground."

I pulled out a bottle and threw it to Gervaso. He caught it. *"Gracias."*

"Señor Gervaso, I heard on the news that there was an explosion at the jail."

"Yes, we heard that too," he said.

The man nodded. "Very nice."

"Did they say anything about the police van?" Gervaso asked.

"No. Not a word."

"That's good," Gervaso said. "What did you get for us?"

"It's over here." The two of them walked over to a car covered with a canvas tarp. "If you'll give me a hand, please."

The men pulled the cover off, revealing a black Chevy Suburban with tinted windows. "This is what I have for you to drive. It is full of gas. The windows are bulletproof."

"Perfect," Gervaso said. "That will do nicely. Have you been paid?"

"Yes, they took care of me." The man reached into his pocket and pulled out some keys and handed them to Gervaso. "I think you need to leave quickly. It is always good to see you, Gervaso."

"My pleasure," Gervaso said. "Thank you for your help."

"That would be my pleasure. What would you like me to do with the money after I sell the van?"

"Keep it," Gervaso said. "But paint the van and hold off a couple months before you list it."

"Muchas gracias," he replied. *"Muchas, muchas gracias."* He looked at us. "Please, have more drinks on me."

I took an extra bottle of root beer as the man walked over to the warehouse door.

"Let's get back to the ranch," Gervaso said. "Everyone, get in."

I climbed into the very back of the car, while Taylor and her parents sat in the middle and Ian rode in front with Gervaso.

"I can keep you company back there," Taylor said to me.

"No, you and your father have a lot to catch up on," I said.

Gervaso thanked the man again, and we drove out of the small compound. As we pulled onto the freeway, Gervaso said, "Keep your eyes open for anything suspicious. We're not out of the woods yet."

"Look," Taylor said. "You can still see the smoke."

There was a thin gray column of smoke about ten miles from us.

"How long does thermite burn?" I asked.

"It burns quickly, but the heat will remain awhile. It will be an hour before they can really examine the wreckage. If there's anything left of it."

About two miles past the Utah-Idaho border, Gervaso's phone rang. He picked it up.

"Yes, we have them both. We're on our way back. We just crossed into Utah. Okay, we'll talk tonight."

He turned off the phone and set it back in his shirt pocket. After a moment he looked back. "They were preparing rooms," he said to the Ridleys. "They were making sure we'd gotten out all right. And that we were bringing back a couple extra guests."

"Thank you again," Mrs. Ridley said.

"How far is it to the ranch?" Mr. Ridley asked.

"Other end of the state. So you have some time to relax."

Mr. Ridley leaned back with his arm still around his wife. "We can't ever go back," he said softly. "Ever." He breathed out heavily as he looked into his wife's eyes. "In a blink of an eye my entire world has changed."

Mrs. Ridley shook her head. "No, honey. Your world changed long before today. You just didn't get the memo."

PART TWELVE

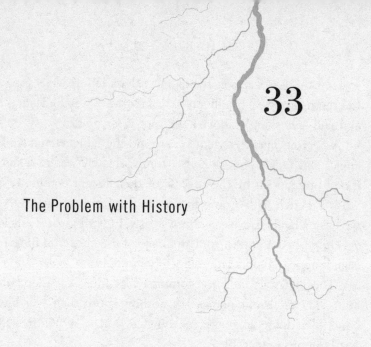

33

The Problem with History

Admiral-General Hatch stood at the front of the great meeting room in the Hatch Islands Starxource plant. Assembled around the long table were Quentin, the three remaining Elgen board members, and the eleven EGGs.

Hatch, who insisted on punctuality, had made them wait for more than an hour in silence to build their anticipation for what he had to say. As he walked into the room, flanked by two guards, everyone rose to their feet, snapping to attention. No one looked the admiral-general in the eye. To do so was to risk being singled out. Hatch walked to the front of the room and looked over his audience, then said, "Be seated."

Everyone sat.

"The problem with history," Hatch said softly, "is that it's written by the victors. It's a shame. Had Hitler won the war, as he nearly did, he'd be as beloved today as George Washington is in America. Or

was. So there is a lesson for us in Hitler's failure." His gaze panned the room, stopping briefly on each member. Then he leaned forward and said only slightly above a whisper, *"Don't lose."*

A nervous laughter went up around the table. Hatch smiled. "Go ahead and laugh," he said. "It's funny." Hatch was in a rare, jovial mood brought on by the success of their recent conquest. "So here we are," Hatch said. "About to rewrite the Tuvaluan history. Now that we have a land base, we can move forward with greater efficiency."

He pushed a button, and an image of the cluster of nine Tuvaluan islands appeared on a large screen behind him.

"The Hatch Islands are comprised of four reef islands and five atolls. Their current names are nothing more than worthless remnants of a dying language, meaningless and, as Quentin will attest, nearly unpronounceable."

Quentin blushed. There was more laughter.

"Henceforth I will bestow upon each island a new name, one derived from Greek mythology, to match our purpose.

"Funafuti will remain the capital of the Hatch Islands and shall be named after Nike, the goddess of victory.

"Nanumea, our northernmost atoll, will be called Hephaestus, after the god of fire and blacksmiths. This is where we will manufacture the equipment for our Starxource plants.

"Niutao will be named Hades, after the god of the underworld, and so it will be considered by its non-Elgen inhabitants. It will be our prison and work camp and source of GPs.

"Nanumaga will henceforth be known as Demeter, after the goddess of agriculture. This is where we shall raise livestock and where the bulk of our agricultural production will take place.

"Nukufetau, the island closest to Nike, will be called Plutus, after the god of wealth. This is where we shall build our bullion and currency depository and, in the meantime, dock the *Joule*. This construction is of utmost importance, and I will address it shortly.

"Vaitupu will be called Ares, after the god of war. This is where our warships will dock and our forces will be trained. It is close to Plutus, so it will be easy to staff and guard the depository.

"Nui, the centermost atoll, will be named Athena, after the goddess of wisdom, war, and useful arts. It is where the *Volta*, our science ship, will be docked, and where we shall build our laboratories and, eventually, perfect the MEI.

"Nukulaelae will be called Dionysus, the god of wine. This is where we will grow our vineyards and build, for the Elgen elite, our luxury retreat. Only the most beautiful of the Tuvaluan natives will be stationed here to serve the Elgen.

"Niulakita, our southernmost island, will be called Poseidon, after the god of the sea. This is where we will establish our fishing port, providing food for the Elgen guards and our rats in the Starxource plant."

Hatch turned back to his audience. "This, Elgen, represents our new temporary home. Effective immediately, these new names will be adopted by all Elgen and will be taught to the natives in the Hatch Islands schools. I have had maps printed to help you familiarize yourselves with these islands and their names."

Hatch's two guards began handing out maps to those at the table.

"Next, I present the architectural drawings of our bullion depository." A picture of a massive ten-story stone-and-concrete structure appeared on the screen. It resembled the Fort Knox depository in America.

"The architects of this impressive structure have, of course, been imprisoned. And, as with the pharaohs of old, once our building is complete, they will be executed along with the inner workers of the facility, so that no one will ever know its secrets.

"This vault will be more secure than Fort Knox, and someday it will hold more gold than Fort Knox ever could. Needless to say, this building is of utmost importance, which is why we will break ground on it tomorrow. But there are priorities of equal importance.

"From the beginning, our goal has been to take over the world's electric power supply. We've made tremendous progress. We are currently producing three billion kilowatt hours annually, providing thirteen percent of the electricity currently being created in the world. A lesser man might be pleased with this accomplishment. But, as you

well know, I am not a lesser man. My objective is to be producing more than half the world's electricity within thirty-six months.

"Unfortunately, we've hit a few snags. The attacks by the resistance and the Vey terrorists have slowed our progress some. I am pleased to announce that they will not be a thorn in our side any longer. The resistance has been annihilated."

The group broke out in applause.

Hatch held up his hand and continued. "It is just a matter of time before we have captured and executed Vey and his terrorists, but in the meantime, without the help of the resistance, they are impotent. The boy doesn't even have a driver's license."

Again there was laughter.

"But that does not mean that we don't still have great obstacles to surmount. Our greatest challenge is the nature of global politics itself. The largest countries in the world, the U.S., Russia, China, and India, have continued to keep us out. As shortsighted as the nations often are with their energy production, they are wise enough to realize that once we have complete control of their electrical power, we have control of them.

"For some time I have puzzled on how to overcome this challenge. I am pleased to announce that I have found a solution. We've been going about this all wrong. We have been relying on politicians, presidents, and prime ministers to invite us into their countries. Simply put, we've been talking to the wrong people. Big government is so inefficient and run by such myopic factions that any real company so run would soon go out of business. It is time we bypass the bureaucracy and go straight to the end consumers. Today I am pleased to present our newest initiative, the Nova Starxource Pod."

Hatch pushed a button on his remote, and the screen displayed the picture of a sleek white structure about the size of a suburban garage. The corners were slightly rounded, and the top rose in a dome. The walls were bright white, with the appearance of plastic. On one side, fastened to the circular construction, was a large control panel with gauges, lights, and LED screens.

"Starting today, the construction of massive Starxource plants will no longer be our primary focus. Our new focus is the corporation, whom we will reach by building sleeker, miniature versions of our Starxource plants—power sources just large enough to power a large hotel or business, even a condominium complex.

"Initially, for those who opt in to our system, power will cost, on average, just twenty-nine percent of what they are currently paying. Once the unit is paid off, which will take the average business owner about three years, the price will drop to eleven percent.

"As we unveil our new system, we will launch a half-billion-dollar advertising campaign extolling its virtues. This is one such ad designed to play during the Super Bowl." An advertisement began playing on the screen. A beautiful, intelligent-looking woman was sitting next to a replica of Thomas Edison's original lightbulb.

In 1879, Thomas Alva Edison invented the electric lightbulb, bringing illumination to a dark world. Today, Elgen Incorporated presents the biggest breakthrough in electricity since the lightbulb: the Nova Starxource Pod. Propelled by organic fuel with zero emissions, the Nova Starxource Pod is capable of producing clean, electric energy at less than twenty percent of what you're paying now. That's an eighty percent savings and one hundred percent clean energy. So what are you waiting for? Save money, save the environment, save the world. Contact Elgen today for a free demonstration. Let's keep America shining from sea to sea.

Everyone clapped at the commercial's conclusion.

Hatch continued. "Concurrent with our campaign, we will fund major conservation groups and lobbies to oppose all our competition—to fight offshore drilling and the creation of nuclear power plants and nuclear dumps, as well as additional coal mining sites.

"This will raise the price of energy for everyone else, making our alternative even more appealing. Then, as more and more consumers leave the grid for our Nova systems, the average cost of traditional energy per person will increase, making our alternative still

more appealing. Eventually our energy will become so inexpensive, and theirs so expensive, that we will control ninety-eight percent of the commercial and residential market."

EGG Despain raised his hand. "Once we've spread our mini-plants, how do we still make money?"

"By providing fuel, of course. Our special Rabisk."

". . . But what if people just start feeding the rats their own food?"

Hatch looked at Despain as if he were an idiot. "They won't know that our Nova plants contain rats. The units are completely self-contained, and the new Rabisk has been liquefied and looks like oil, which we've named Petrox.

"The consumer just inserts a canister, and the pod time-feeds the rats. If the proper canister isn't used, the rats die and the energy fails. As part of their contract, they will be fined a substantial amount for repairs."

"What if someone tries to take apart the pod?" EGG Bosen asked.

"Of course someone will try. The Nova Pod is marked with warning labels and double-secured with an intrusion trigger. The interior pod is lined with magnesium panels that will reach heat in excess of two thousand degrees if the pod is tampered with. Once opened, they will find nothing inside but ashes."

"This is brilliant," EGG Bosen said, clapping. Everyone else began clapping as well.

"Thank you," Hatch said.

EGG Grant raised his hand. "Sir, how can we be sure that corporate America will buy into our process?"

"Are you a fool or an idiot?" Hatch asked.

The EGG didn't answer.

"I asked you a question."

"I hope neither, sir."

"Then quit asking foolish, idiotic questions. Of course they will buy into our process. What part of capitalism do you not understand?"

Grant shrank with embarrassment.

"What we are doing is creating an unfair competitive advantage. Let me explain this so a five-year-old could understand. We have two bread companies, Bakery A and Bakery B. They both bake bread.

They both have the same basic expenses: material, labor, and energy prices. So the cost of their bread is roughly the same.

"But let's say that Bakery A installs a Nova Pod system. Their energy cost is now eighty-seven percent less than Bakery B. They can now produce bread for less money and make more profit.

"Bakery B is now in trouble. In order to compete with Bakery A, they have no choice but to come to us. Our success will fuel our success. And this ball will roll down the mountain until it covers the world." Hatch paused for emphasis. "Elgen, this is our path and our destination. This is the day of our glory. In the words of the great Russian leader Stalin, 'the capitalists will sell us the rope with which we will hang them.'"

The room broke into wild applause.

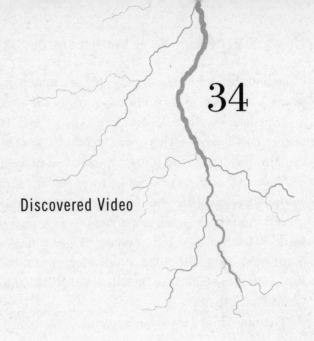

34

Discovered Video

After the meeting concluded, all the attendees went up to congratulate Hatch. Quentin and EGG Daines were the last to leave.

"Brilliant, sir," Quentin said. "Just brilliant."

"Thank you, Quentin," Hatch said, then added, "*King* Quentin. How are things progressing in your kingdom?"

"Well," he said. "We've started the remodeling of the palace, the construction of a stadium, and the new educational curriculum is complete and is being taught in the schools."

"Excellent," Hatch said. "Keep me informed of the progress." He turned toward his EGG. "I'm tired, Daines. What do you need?"

"A moment of your time, sir."

Hatch frowned. "Is it important?"

"Vitally," Daines said.

Hatch nodded. "All right. Proceed."

Daines glanced at Quentin, then said, "In private, sir."

"You're sure it can't wait?"

"It's best that it doesn't, sir," Daines said. The EGG was known to be a man of few words but much violence and action.

Hatch sighed. "Very well. We'll meet in my office." Hatch turned to Quentin. "Carry on."

"Yes, sir," Quentin said, walking off.

Hatch led Daines down the corridor to his private office. Once they were inside, Hatch asked, "What is it?"

"We've discovered video of criminal Welch leaving the ship, sir. He was, as we suspected, accompanied by the two guards, Hill and Rawlings."

"As we suspected," Hatch said. "Was Welch wearing some kind of disguise?"

"No, sir."

"And no one questioned them?"

"No, sir. They exited the boat through the aft loading dock."

"The place was swimming with guards," Hatch said angrily. "Someone must have noticed."

"The whole escape was very peculiar. No one they passed showed the least amount of interest in them."

"That is peculiar," Hatch said, rubbing his chin. "Very peculiar."

"There's more, sir."

"More?"

"They were not alone."

Hatch's eyes narrowed. "It was a conspiracy?"

"Yes, sir," the EGG said. "Three of the electric youths were with them."

"Which ones?"

"Quentin, Torstyn, and Tara."

Hatch's face turned beet red. "What were they doing?"

"They were walking behind him."

"How closely?"

"Within ten meters."

Hatch clenched his jaw. "That explains why no one paid attention.

Tara must have made him look like someone else. Probably a Taiwanese."

"That's a possibility, sir."

"It's not a possibility," Hatch shouted, slamming his fist onto his desk. "It's what happened." Hatch began to shake with anger. "I made him a king, and he repays me with betrayal? He will pay for this. They will all pay."

"What are your orders, sir?"

Hatch carefully thought over the situation. "We must proceed cautiously. Especially with Torstyn. He's very dangerous and loyal to Quentin. I want you to arrest all of the youths in their sleep, RESAT them, and then isolate them from one another."

"What of the two not involved?"

"All of them. The other two must have at least known what was going on. Instruct the guards to use the new RAVE to apprehend them and lock them separately in T block. But leave Quentin to me."

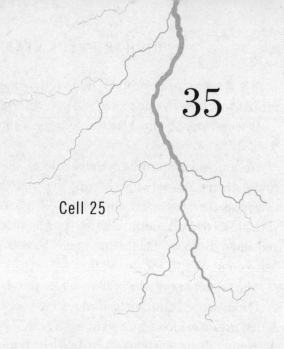

35

Cell 25

It was three in the morning and Quentin was fast asleep when Hatch opened his door and turned on the light. "Wake up, Quentin."

It took Quentin a moment to get oriented. He shielded his eyes from the garish light. "Dr. Hatch . . . what are you doing here?"

Hatch looked around the messy room, then walked to the side of Quentin's bed. "I think you know what would bring me to your room at three in the morning."

Quentin sat up. "No, sir."

Hatch sighed a little. "No, I didn't think you would be eager to confess your crime." He sat on the side of Quentin's bed. "So if you are insistent on playing this little game, I'll oblige you. I know what you did, Quentin. Unfortunately, Tara's powers don't work through video."

"I don't follow, sir," Quentin said.

"Of course you do. You know exactly what I'm talking about. I trusted you. I made you a king, and you betrayed me."

Quentin stared into Hatch's eyes for a moment, then shouted, "Guards!"

An amused grin crossed Hatch's face. "How optimistic of you. And pathetic. You actually thought that your guards would be loyal to you in the face of certain death? No, no one will be coming to your aid." His eyes narrowed. "I've taught you thousands of lessons, and now you have taught me one. There is no loyalty. Not even between us. You've shown me that."

"Sir, I don't know what you're—"

Hatch slapped Quentin hard enough to knock him back into his bed. A thin stream of blood dripped from his nose. "Quit lying to me! Tell me the truth. Tell me that you escorted Welch off the ship. Tell me now!"

Quentin held a hand to his stinging face. He was shaking with fear. "Yes. I saved him. He was like a father to me."

Hatch stood, then grabbed Quentin by the foot and dragged him off the bed. Then he kicked him while Quentin tried to protect himself from the blows. "*I* am your father," Hatch shouted. "And your king. And you turned on me. Your betrayal is worse than Welch's. And so your punishment will be worse as well."

Quentin coughed up blood. "How could it possibly be worse?" he said bitterly.

"You should know better than that by now. Things can always be worse."

Quentin, still on his back, feebly raised his hand to put out the power, but nothing happened.

Hatch shook his head. "And to think I had so much hope for you. Foolish, stupid boy. You didn't think I would be prepared for that? We have a new invention just for you. That slight headache you feel . . . that's me. The RESAT darts were too cumbersome. Too unreliable. So we invented this." Hatch brought out a small hand remote about the size of a bar of soap. "The scientists who invented it named it the RESAT 2.0, but I renamed it the RAVE. It's a remarkable improvement. I just slightly turn the knob . . ."

Quentin screamed out in pain.

"Think of it as a handheld version of Nichelle. We created it based on her powers. Do you remember her? She's one of the losers you let escape." He turned the dial up more, and Quentin screamed out even louder.

"Please, stop. Please."

"You're begging for mercy? Wasn't it you who said whoever helped Welch is a traitor and deserves the same punishment? You, of all people, should know that there is no mercy for kings. Kings are on thrones or in graves. There are no exceptions."

"Then kill me," Quentin said.

"Quick death would fall under the category of mercy. An example must be made of you. We will build a special monkey cage just for you, and that is where you will spend the rest of your life."

"Please. I'll do whatever you want."

"What I want is for you to not have betrayed me, but it's too late for that. Bad eggs don't get good again." He turned back toward the door. "Guards."

The room echoed with the clash of trooper boots on the marble floor as an Elgen patrol ran into the room, lining up at attention behind Hatch.

"Captain, take Quentin to cellblock T. Keep your RAVEs on six. I don't want him damaging any of the electronics on the way in."

Sweat dripped off Quentin's face. "What about the others?" he asked. "What are you going to do with them?"

"Your immediate accomplices have already been arrested and are awaiting their punishments. Bryan and Kylee have also been arrested until I can determine how much they knew."

"They didn't know anything."

"I'll determine that. As far as Torstyn and Tara, I haven't yet decided what their fates will be, but rest assured their punishments will be commensurate with the crime they committed. Treason is always punishable by death. It's the going rate. The only question is, how long and how painful will that death be?" He turned back to the captain. "Take him."

The guards quickly surrounded Quentin. They rolled him onto his stomach, secured his hands, then lifted him to his feet.

"Prisoner is secured," the zone leader said to Hatch.

Hatch walked up to Quentin until their faces were six inches apart. "So, Quentin. How did it feel to be *good*? Was it worth it?"

For a moment Quentin looked Hatch in the eye, then said, "I would do it again."

Hatch slugged him in the stomach, and Quentin fell to his knees, gasping.

"Get him out of here," Hatch said. "Lock him in Cell 25."

PART THIRTEEN

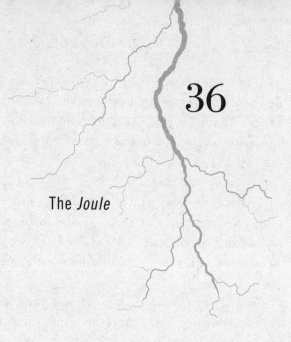

36

The *Joule*

The next few weeks at the ranch were the most peaceful we'd had in months. It was nice to have nothing to do. I mean, we helped out with chores and stuff; I even helped harvest honey, but there really wasn't that much they needed help with.

We played a lot. There was a sand volleyball pit down near the pond, which everyone spent a lot of time at. Even Ostin. What a sight that was. Ostin played volleyball about as well as I did advanced calculus. Bad, but entertaining to watch.

It was about two weeks after our return from Idaho when Taylor and I went on a hike in the nearby mountains. We had just started climbing the first small hill when I asked, "How are your parents doing?"

Taylor shrugged. "Not so well," she said. "My dad's still freaked. I wouldn't be surprised if he had a nervous breakdown."

"I'm not surprised. He just lost his job, his home, and everything he thought he knew about the world. I'd be freaked too." I put my hands into my pockets. "Actually, I *am* freaked."

Taylor was quiet a moment, then stopped walking. She turned to me. "Michael, what if this is it?"

"What do you mean?"

"What if this is as good as it gets? Seeing that marquee at Meridian High for cheerleader tryouts . . ." She shook her head. "Everything's just moving on without us. I feel like I've been waiting for everything to be good again so I could be happy. But what if that day never comes?"

"It will come," I said. "The Elgen can't last forever."

She frowned. "Yes, they can. And they might. Good doesn't always win." Her eyes began to well up. "Why is it that good always has to fight an uphill battle?"

I thought for a moment, then said, "I don't know. Maybe that's the point. Good things are higher up."

She began to cry. "I'm tired of fighting uphill. We almost died on the *Ampere*. And for what? To slow them down?"

I put my arms around her as she started to sob. When she could speak, she said, "I'm just tired of being afraid."

I slowly rubbed her back. "Me too," I said softly. "Me too."

Just then we heard the ringing of the dinner bell.

I glanced down at my watch. "I wonder what that is. It's not time to eat."

Taylor wiped her eyes with the backs of her hands. "Something must be going on. We better go back."

We hiked back down to the dirt road and had been walking for about ten minutes when Jack drove up on an ATV. "Hey, everyone's waiting for you two."

"What's going on?" I asked.

"The chairman called a meeting in the main house. They sent me to get you. Hop on."

Jack drove us back to the house. When we got there, the main

room was crowded. Not surprisingly, the three of us were the last to arrive. The feeling in the room was tense and uncomfortable. The chairman walked to the front of the room.

"Thank you for coming on such short notice," he said. "I called this meeting because we've been contacted by the voice." He paused, looking at us. "Things are in motion. Big things."

I wondered what he was talking about.

"I suppose it's a good time to be an Elgen, if there is such a thing. The Elgen have overthrown the island nation of Tuvalu and established a base. In the last year their force has tripled in size to more than six thousand soldier-guards, and they have doubled their planned Starxource plants.

"But that is not why I called this meeting. An opportunity has presented itself that could allow us to destroy Dr. Hatch and the Elgen once and for all."

We all sat up at attention.

"Their electric youths have rebelled. Hatch has sentenced their leader, Quentin, to lifetime incarceration in a monkey cage."

"Where he belongs," Jack whispered to me.

"Tara and Torstyn have been sentenced to death. Kylee has also been imprisoned. Only Bryan remains free. They believe that he is the last loyal electric youth."

"That's only because he's too dumb to rebel," Nichelle mumbled.

The chairman looked at us for a moment, then said, "They could be invaluable allies. Not only because of their gifts, but because of their knowledge of Hatch's plans and how he thinks."

He was quiet again as he looked over at me. I suddenly had the sinking feeling that he was going to say something I wasn't going to like.

"The entire Elgen fleet is docked at Tuvalu. One of those boats is the *Joule*. For those not familiar with the Elgen fleet, the *Joule* is their most unusual and secretive boat. In fact, it's not only the fastest in the fleet, but it's part submarine. It can submerge to nearly a thousand feet. It is also the most valuable boat in the fleet. It is a floating Fort Knox. It holds billions of dollars of gold bullion, foreign currencies, and diamonds."

"Why don't they just put their money in banks?" I asked.

"They do, but only five percent. The rest they physically cache. Hatch is paranoid by nature, but especially of banks. And for good reason. If you're declaring war on the world, someone is eventually going to freeze your assets. He's not going to allow that. The voice tells us that right now there is currently more than nine billion dollars on board the *Joule*.

"We've also learned that the treasure won't be there for long. One of the reasons the Elgen overthrew Tuvalu was to build a secure facility for their treasure. Their own Fort Knox." He took a deep breath. "Wars aren't won with guns; they're won with checkbooks. Without that money, the Elgen can't support their growth in troops. At least for now. Nine billion dollars is enough money for us to turn it on the Elgen and shut them down. That is, if we can find the *Joule* and hijack it."

"How are we going to do that?" I asked.

"We have some help in locating it. But boarding it is going to be . . . challenging. If the *Joule*'s captain suspects danger, he simply submerges the vessel. The *Joule* can stay underwater for up to six months."

"That's bad news," Jack said.

"That's bad news and good news," the chairman said. "Because once we get on board, the other boats in the fleet won't be able to touch us. So getting onto the boat is the challenge. The only non-crew allowed on the *Joule* is Hatch. And even he has to use a secret code."

"Hatch isn't going to escort us on board," Zeus said.

"And he's not going to give us the secret code," Tessa said. "Even if we ask nicely."

"No. But Taylor can get it out of his mind."

"If I touch him," she said, looking as disgusted as fearful.

"And one of his youths, Tara, can make someone look like Hatch. With their help, we could steal the boat."

"How is Tara going to help us?" Ostin asked. "She's going to be executed."

"We'll have to save her."

"You're saying that you want us to rescue our enemy?" I asked.

The chairman nodded. "Remember, they are now Hatch's enemy."

"The enemy of my enemy is my friend," Ostin said.

"Exactly," the chairman said.

"Let me get this straight," Zeus said. "You want us to get onto the island undetected and rescue the Glows—who tried to kill us—from the most secure Starxource facility the Elgen have. Then hijack their most protected boat?"

The chairman nodded. "Basically, yes."

"That's basically insane," Zeus replied.

The chairman frowned. "Yes, it is. Which is why they won't be expecting it. And, God willing, if it works, the war is turned."

The room went silent. I looked around at the Electroclan, only to find that they were all looking at me, most with fear in their eyes. I put my head in my hands to think. This was likely a suicide mission. The odds of some, or all, of us being killed were high. But that was true too if we did nothing to stop the Elgen. This was what our resistance was all about. Up until this point, we had been chopping at the leaves of the Elgen tree, trying to bring it down. This might be our only chance to pull it up by the roots. *And who else was there to do it? Who was more qualified than the Electroclan?*

I looked at my mother. She was looking at me, her eyes fearful. Joel was holding her. Ostin's mother was dabbing her eyes with a tissue.

I looked back up at the chairman. "Zeus was right. What you're asking of us is insane. It's more than all of our other missions combined. But, all things considered, what choice do we have?" I looked around again at my friends. Taylor took my hand. I took a deep breath, then slowly exhaled. "When do we go?"

PART FOURTEEN

37

The Fugitive

June 27 (about six weeks earlier)
Geneva, Switzerland

Giacomo Schema very nearly knocked a half dozen people over as he frantically ran out the front door of the Bank of Geneva. Once outside he froze in the middle of the crowded sidewalk while other people, people who didn't have a price on their heads, passed him from both directions. He had no idea where he was running to. The direction he chose could mean the difference between life and death, but since he had no way of knowing which was which, his survival was no more than a toss of a coin.

At the moment, there were no Elgen in sight, which Schema knew didn't mean anything. He knew better than anyone that just because you didn't see the Elgen guards, it didn't mean they weren't there. Or, at least, watching. This he had learned the hard way.

He had only a few hundred euro in his coat pocket, and his credit cards were now worthless. They were worse than worthless; they were dangerous. Using them would lead the Elgen right to him.

He'd started running in the direction of the traffic, when a car honked. A black Mercedes pulled up to the curb, and the passenger-side window lowered, revealing the driver. It was the same driver who had picked him up from the airport and brought him to the meeting.

"Mr. Schema!" the driver shouted through the window. "Do you need a ride?"

"Yes!" Schema shouted back. He jumped into the front seat of the car, then shouted, "Go, go, go!"

"Yes, sir." The driver pulled out into the heavy traffic.

Schema took his phone from his coat pocket and threw it out the window.

The driver watched curiously. "Is something wrong?"

"Something is *very* wrong."

"Shall I take you back to the Geneva hotel?"

"No, they'll be waiting for me. I need to get out of the country." Schema turned and looked out the window. "Take Route de Malagnou south to E712 to E25."

"And where are we going, sir?"

"Turin."

"Italy, sir?"

"Yes. It's about two hundred fifty kilometers from here. How fast can you get there?"

"If I drive fast, we can be there in three hours."

"Then drive fast. Don't stop for anything."

"Yes, sir."

The driver's cell phone rang. As he reached for it, Schema said, "Don't answer it."

"But it's my boss."

"We can't take chances. I'll see that you are well rewarded for your service."

"As you wish," the driver said.

Once they were out of the city, Schema started to relax. As far as he could tell, no one was following them. For the moment, at least, he was safe.

"Do you have children?" he asked the driver.

"Children? No, sir. Do you?"

"Three. And a grandson. I was married a long time ago. I haven't seen any of them for many years."

"I'm sorry to hear that, sir. They must miss you."

Schema looked out the window. "I don't think they miss me."

The driver glanced over. "I'm sorry to hear that, too."

A half hour later, as the car sped along the autobahn into the country-side, the vehicle started to lurch.

"What's happening?" Schema asked.

"I don't know," the driver said. "A malfunction."

"Are you out of petrol?"

"No, sir. I'm sure it's nothing. I just need to get off the autobahn. I'll only be a minute." The driver took the next exit into the small town of Cluses, France. He pulled the car off the road onto a gravel strip and stopped. He got out and lifted the hood, then got back inside. "It might be a while."

"We can't wait here," Schema said. "They might be following. We need to get another car. We need to get out of here."

The driver suddenly pulled out a gun, leveling it at Schema's chest. "No, Schema. This is as far as you go."

"Are you mad? What are you doing?"

"This is where I'm meeting my associates to pick you up. As you know, Admiral-General Hatch offered a reward for you, dead or alive. It's more if you're alive, but if you're trouble, I'm not greedy. A million dollars is still plenty to share. Now put your hands behind your head."

Schema shuddered. "Whatever Hatch is offering, I'll double it."

"You have nothing to double it with," he said. "I know what has happened. You're penniless."

"That will change."

"Perhaps," the driver said. "Perhaps. The Americans have a saying—a bird in the hand is worth two in the bush. You're in hand."

"I'm offering you more money than you can comprehend. I'll give you ten million euro if you help me escape."

The driver just smiled. "Admiral-General Hatch has signed your death warrant. Your life isn't worth fifty cents. But your body's worth at least a million dollars. And should I betray him, there will be a bounty on my head. Then we'll both be dead."

"There's got to be something we can negotiate."

"No, sir. I have completed my negotiations. Now put your forehead against the dashboard and keep your hands where I can see them."

Just then a dark blue van pulled off the exit and stopped beside them.

Schema panicked. "Please," he said. "I'll give you whatever you want. Tell your friends I'll make you all wealthy beyond your wildest dreams. I just need time."

"These aren't my people," the driver said, looking suddenly anxious.

A teenage girl got out of the car and walked toward the driver. She was pretty, with cropped blond hair.

He lowered his gun. "If you say anything, I'll shoot you."

"*Excusez-moi, monsieur. Parlez-vous anglais?*"

"Yes, miss," the driver said. "I speak English."

"Thank goodness," she said, smiling. "My French sucks." She looked at them curiously. "Are you having car troubles?"

"We are fine, thank you. The auto club is on its way. What do you need?"

"Unfortunately, we seem to be a little lost. Is this the right road for Milan?"

"For a little way more. You need to get back on the highway; then you must go east at Ivrea."

"Ivrea?"

"Yes. It is about one hundred sixty kilometers."

"Thank you very much. *Merci.*" She started to turn away, then turned back. "I'm sorry, just one more question."

"Yes, miss," the driver said, trying to hide his annoyance.

"What were you planning to do with Chairman Schema?"

Suddenly the driver felt his muscles tense up and freeze. He was completely paralyzed. He looked at the young woman fearfully. "What are you doing to me?"

She smiled. "It's just a little something I do." She turned back to the van and shouted, "Come on, boys. Let's get this done."

Two large men climbed out of the vehicle and walked toward the Mercedes. Both men were muscular; the driver was tall and the other stout. The shorter of the two took the gun from the driver, then took his phone, opened it, removed the battery, and tossed it into the bushes.

"Take Schema," the girl said.

The other man opened the passenger-side door. Schema, who was also paralyzed, watched in fear. "Who are you?" he asked the young woman.

"My name is Cassy," she said.

"How much do you want?"

Her delicate brow fell. "How much of what do I want?"

"Money."

Cassy laughed. "Seriously, you're trying to bribe me? You're confused."

"Are you Elgen?"

"No. Are you?"

Schema hesitated. "I used to be."

"So I've heard."

The two men lifted Schema and carried him over to their van, then dropped him in the back. Cassy reached out and took Schema's wallet.

"What are you doing with that?" Schema asked.

"You won't need it anymore. You no longer exist."

Cassy, followed by the shorter man, walked back over to the car and tossed the wallet inside the car next to the driver. Then the man lay a stainless-steel metal canister in the backseat of the Mercedes.

"What is that?" the driver asked. "What did you put back there?"

"Don't worry yourself with that," Cassy said. "In fact, all of your worries will soon be over. *Au revoir.*" She looked at him. "No, wait, it's *adieu*. We won't be seeing you again. I told you my French sucks." She walked back to the van. "Let's get out of here."

The driver of the Mercedes cursed as the van drove away. Fortunately, his paralysis was slowly wearing off, and he could start to move his fingers, then his hands. "Finally," he said, lifting himself up. He looked out to make sure the van was really gone; then he heard a sharp click.

"*Qu'est-ce* . . ."

The metal canister exploded, blowing the car to oblivion.

38

Our Leader

"**Y**ou said your name was Cassy, but who are you really?" Schema asked again.

"I told you," Cassy said, slipping a dark sack over his head.

"Who are you with?"

"I'm with you." She laughed. "Sorry, just messing with you. We're with the resistance."

"The resistance," Schema said slowly. "You mean Michael Vey?"

"You know Michael Vey?"

"We've met."

"Then you have one on me. I haven't met him yet. But I'm looking forward to it someday. In the electric human world, he's a rock star. I hear he can deflect bullets."

"You're part of the same organization."

"Not really. Michael's not really a company man, if you know what I mean."

"I don't," Schema said bluntly. "Could you please free me? I have an itch."

"For a minute. But don't touch your hood. And if you try anything to get away, I'll not only paralyze your body, I'll paralyze your lungs and let you suffocate."

"I won't try anything," Schema said.

"Good decision," she said.

Schema groaned out as she released her power. Cassy watched him carefully, then said, "So, like I was saying, Michael's like a free agent, you know? We don't control him or his friends. They're helping us, I assume, because it's the right thing to do. Or maybe because he doesn't like you. Either way he's on our side. And that's a good thing."

Schema was quiet a moment. "He doesn't like me, or he doesn't like the Elgen?"

Cassy shrugged. "Is there a difference?"

"There's a big difference."

"Anyway, he freed you from the *Ampere*, so it must not be you."

"Is this hood really necessary?"

"Yes, it is," Cassy said. "So, you got me thinking. You're kind of like Dr. Frankenstein, aren't you? You created a monster, and it turned on you."

"It wasn't my creation that turned on me. It was Hatch."

"Weren't you Hatch's boss?"

"Yes," he said reluctantly.

"My point."

Just then a phone rang, and the man in the passenger seat answered. "Yes, we have him. Yes, sir. We'll be there." He put the phone back into his pocket and turned to Cassy. "He wants us to bring Schema directly to him."

Cassy turned back to Schema. "This is your lucky day," she said. "He rarely, rarely sees anyone. And you're about to meet him."

Schema swallowed with fear. "Who are you talking about?"

"Our leader," Cassy said. "We just call him the voice."

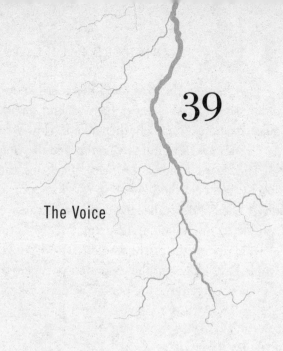

39

The Voice

The van arrived in the Italian town of Turin in less than ninety minutes. They drove to a small, private airstrip, boarded a private jet, and flew for two hours. Schema wore the hood the entire way.

"Why can't I take this off?" he asked.

"Quit whining," Cassy said. "You're a smart guy. You look out the window, you might recognize where we are going. You don't get it off until we reach our final destination, so get comfortable."

The plane landed on a small, seaside airstrip, where they were met by a new driver and vehicle. Then again they drove, this time for nearly two hours, through remote countryside until the car stopped at a mountain gate, where they were met by two guards dressed in camouflage. Both guards were carrying UZIs that were pointed at the driver as they pulled up.

"ID," the guard said tersely.

Even though the driver and the guard knew each other well, they didn't show it. The driver handed him an identification card. The guard examined it closely, then asked, "How were the roads in today?"

"It's always beautiful driving through the vineyards," the driver said.

The guard handed the driver back his card. The question was strictly protocol, and there were seven possible answers. Had the driver been under some kind of duress, his answer would have changed specific to his situation, including, "We got stuck behind an oxcart," at which point the guard would have triggered a remote switch that would have blown up the car and its occupants.

"Can you remove the hood?" Schema asked.

"Still no," Cassy replied.

"Where are we?"

"Our destination," Cassy said.

"Could you be a little more specific?"

"I could, but then I'd have to kill you."

The car pulled forward through the gate and up a long, tree-lined road. The trees were close together, and their branches reached across the passage, creating a long, arched tunnel. Finally the car drove up to another entrance, where a guard had already opened a gate and now waved them on through.

The road changed to cobblestone for the last fifty meters as they drove up to a beautiful French-style château. The mansion was large and had once been beautiful but was not well-kept, as weeds grew up between the black cobblestone drive and around the property. The surrounding forest seemed to be growing toward the structure, like a slow wave of foliage crashing over the architecture.

The driver pulled the car into an open garage, then closed the door behind them, leaving them in complete darkness. Then a light came on. Cassy turned back toward Schema.

"All right, we can take it off now." She pulled off Schema's hood. Schema now looked confused and somewhat subdued.

"Are you going to kill me?" he asked.

"That depends," Cassy said.

"On what?"

"On whether or not you do anything to get yourself killed. We didn't go to all this trouble to bring you here just to execute you. If we wanted you dead, I could have done that in France without even getting out of the car. I went to rescue you."

"Thank you," he said.

"I was wondering when you were going to get around to thanking me for saving your life," Cassy said. "But we didn't do it for you. We did it because the voice wants to speak with you face-to-face." She shook her head. "I still can't believe he is going to let you see him. And before you ask, you are at the headquarters of the resistance. That is all you will ever be told and is all you need to know. Not even our leaders in America know where we are. We intend to keep it that way. If you try to escape, you will be killed. We have no choice. There are just too many lives at risk."

"I understand," Schema said.

"Good. Now follow me."

She got out of the car, then opened the vehicle's door so Schema could get out. As he stepped out onto the cement floor, he suddenly froze, unable to breathe. For nearly a minute he grasped at his throat; then he fell to his knees, then to his side, unable to even make a sound, his panicked, questioning eyes locked on Cassy's. When he was just about to pass out, Cassy released him. Schema loudly gasped for breath, coughing and wheezing. After a moment he got back onto his hands and knees, then looked up at her. "Why did you do that?"

"In case you were feeling bold, I wanted you to know just how easy it is for me to kill you. I don't even need to be with you. I can smell your electrical makeup, which means I not only can feel you a mile away, I can reach you a mile away. This time I paralyzed your lungs. If you disappear from my sight, even for a minute, I will stop your heart. Those are my orders, and make no mistake, I will do as I've been ordered. Do you understand?"

"Yes, ma'am."

"Good." She smiled at the driver, who stood at attention next to the car. "He called me 'ma'am.'"

* * *

Cassy and Schema, followed by the three guards, walked briskly into the mansion. They entered into a foyer, climbed a circular staircase, and then walked down a long, dark corridor with polished parquet floors. Surveillance cameras watched them from every corner. The hallway was adorned on both sides with dozens of antlers from deer, elk, and moose.

For most visitors allowed this far into the house, the guards' guns would have been drawn, but since Cassy was with them, there was no need. Her power was instantaneous and much more potent than all of them combined. In a fight, she had never lost. Never.

Near the end of the hallway was a single solid mahogany door with an armed guard standing in front of it.

"Hiya, Cal," Cassy said as she approached. "How's your day?"

"Same old, same old," he replied. "He's been waiting for you."

"I hope he's been patient."

"Yeah, right," Cal said with a half smile. He opened the door, then stepped aside for them to enter.

"This way, please," Cassy said to Schema. She led him into a large, classically decorated reception area. The walls were wood-paneled, and where there weren't bookshelves, the walls were covered with beautiful still-life oil paintings. The floor was also wood, though mostly concealed beneath an aged Persian rug. The ceiling was coffered and had two brass chandeliers hanging down, lighting the room in a gold-yellow hue.

Sitting at a burled walnut desk in the center of the room was a fortysomething woman with bright red hair, wearing cat-eye glasses. She looked up at them as they entered.

"Howdy, Samantha," Cassy said.

"Welcome back, my dear," Samantha said in a formal British accent. "I see you brought us a guest."

"As commanded," she said.

"And how was your day?"

Cassy adopted a British accent. "I suppose I'm a bit *knackered*."

Samantha laughed. "You're so *cheeky*."

"Better cheeky than dodgy," Cassy said.

Samantha smiled. "He knows you're here. Please take a seat, he'll be right with you."

"Thank you," Cassy said. She led Schema to a leather couch, and they both sat down. Schema just looked around in anxious wonder. He might as well have had the hood on, as there was nothing to do as he waited. There were no magazines, no music playing.

The chime of a longcase clock sounded off in the corner of the room. He glanced again at the guards but quickly turned away since they just looked like they wanted to kill him.

After a moment, Schema asked the secretary, "Are you British?"

Samantha looked at him as if he'd just muttered some obscenity. Two of the guards stood, stepping before him.

"You will not speak," one of them said fiercely.

Schema quickly lowered his eyes. "I'm sorry," he said. "Very sorry. I'll keep quiet."

Cassy relaxed back in her seat. About five minutes later there was a soft buzz from Samantha's phone. "He's ready for you," she said.

"Great," Cassy said, standing. "C'mon," she said to Schema. "We don't keep him waiting."

She crossed the room past Samantha's desk and opened the office door. She stepped inside ahead of Schema. The office looked and smelled old, with the musty scent of antique leather books and wooden bookshelves, the intricate woodwork interspersed with technology. On the back wall there were five monitors playing the world news. The voice was turned away from Cassy and Schema, watching one of the channels.

"Please sit," he said.

Cassy and Schema each sat in one of the leather chairs facing his desk. Then the voice turned around and looked at them. Schema audibly gasped when he saw the voice's face.

"Giacomo Schema," the voice said. "It's good to see you again. Not a pleasure, mind you, but good. We have much work to do."

Schema stared, speechless. When he could speak, he said, "Impossible. This is impossible. How could it be you?"

Join the Veyniac Nation!

For Michael Vey trivia, sneak peeks, and events in your area,

follow Michael and the rest of the Electroclan at:

MICHAELVEY.COM

Instagram.com/MichaelVeyOfficial

Facebook.com/MichaelVeyOfficialFanPage

Twitter.com/MichaelVey

Look for

MICHAEL VEY

Book 6
Coming in Fall 2016

MERCURY
INK

SIMON
PULSE

W9-BYF-922